Unseemly Pursuits:

A Concordia Wells Mystery

K.B. OWEN

Unseemly Pursuits
A Concordia Wells Mystery

Cover design by Melinda VanLone, BookCoverCorner.com

Formatting by Debora Lewis
arenapublishing.org

To Nina Mangano,
and literature teachers everywhere.
Thank you.

Acknowledgments

Although fiction-writing is considered a solitary activity, no such project comes into being at the hands of only one person. I had tremendous support in this enterprise, both personally and professionally, and I'd like to thank them here.

To Janice Hamrick, Jenny Hansen, Natalie Hartford, and Marcia Richards, the best beta readers a gal could ask for: thank you for your thoughtful feedback. Your suggestions helped immensely.

To Nathalie Coeller, MD, for her generous help with medical questions. Any errors are solely mine.

To fellow Misterio Press authors Kassandra Lamb and JoAnn Haberer, who provided invaluable editing in the novel's final stages, and Kirsten Weiss, for her meticulous formatting. For the latest mysteries by these and other authors at Misterio Press, please visit **MisterioPress.com**.

Speaking of formatting, I'd like to thank Debora Lewis for her formatting of the print version. You truly make these words a thing of beauty.

To artist Melinda VanLone: you took my hazy ideas and produced a cover that I absolutely love. Thank you!

To Kristen Lamb, Piper Bayard, and the generous community of fellow writers known as WANAs, who contribute endless advice and support. We are truly not alone.

To my parents-in-law, Steve and Lyn, and the extended Owen clan of terrific sisters-and brothers-in-law, nieces and nephews. You continue to read my books and cheer on my milestones, and I am so grateful.

To my parents, Ag and Steve, who listen, sympathize and encourage during all the bumps along the way, just as they have done with all of my endeavors.

To my sons, Patrick, Liam, and Corey, who support my writing efforts, and can always make me laugh.

But most of all, I want to thank my husband Paul for his unfailing encouragement and love. This would not be possible without you.

K.B. Owen
November 2013

Chapter 1

Hartford Women's College, Sept 1896
Week 2, Instructor Calendar

Literature professor Concordia Wells could not understand why such a fuss was being made over old objects that smelled like musty curtains. They weren't even *books*, which at least would have been understandable. And yet, assembled in this lecture hall-turned-exhibit room were faculty, staff, assorted city dignitaries, and even a newspaper reporter, gathered around display cases of supposed treasures in the newly opened College Gallery of Antiquities.

It was a congenial space for such a purpose; plenty of natural light was provided by flanking rows of tall, pointed Gothic windows that reached nearly to the ceiling. The well-polished oak wainscoting, original to the building from its construction in 1822—when the college was a ladies' seminary—lent a collegiate dignity to the hall, a promise of permanence for those who might consider future gifts.

"Colonel, may I ask what prompted your donation of Egyptian artifacts to the college?" The question came from the reporter at *The Courant*, scribbling rapid notes as he spoke. He was an older man, with a tall and muscular build, and large hands that swallowed up the tiny pencil in his grip. A well-worn bowler was pushed back and out of the way on his head as he bent over his notes.

Concordia pictured reporters as rabbit-like and underfed, their thin quivering noses always poking into the next story. This man looked more like the robust expressmen along Main Street, who hefted bulky packages as easily as feather pillows.

Colonel Adams, the collection's principal benefactor, seemed annoyed at being interrupted in the midst of his dry lecture on Ancient Egypt. "I have long taken an interest in our local women's college," he said gruffly. "Now, recently retired from my military career, I have had more time to sort through the items."

Concordia wriggled her toes in cramped boots and let her mind drift. *What prompted this donation,* the newspaperman had asked. She suppressed a sigh.

Actually, it had all begun with a knife.

A seventeenth century European bodice dagger, to be precise. She'd found it last year, while rummaging for props to use in the senior class production of *Macbeth.* Later, it had turned up in the chest of a college staff member. Last spring's murder caused a local sensation from which the school was still trying to recover.

The discovery that the rhinestones at the base of the knife handle were in fact *diamonds,* and that the weapon was a rare historical artifact, sparked the idea of starting an exhibit at the college through further donations of antiquary. The college expanded the history department in order to catalogue and maintain the collection.

So Concordia blamed the knife, which she'd had the misfortune to find in the first place, for her presence here, when she could be grading student themes instead.

She turned her attention back to the newspaperman, who was asking more questions.

"Then your collection is an extensive one, sir? This is not the entirety of it?"

Concordia frowned. It seemed a strange line of enquiry, as the reporter was here to gather facts about the pieces in front of him, not the things that *weren't* there.

"Oh, no, indeed. The colonel's collection of antiquities is considerable," a woman chimed in, moving closer to Colonel Adams and putting a proprietary hand on his arm. She was a comely, golden-haired lady in her thirties, her slim-waisted walking dress of hunter green setting off her curvaceous figure. Next to the white-haired-and-mustached colonel, she looked to be his daughter, but Concordia knew she was Lydia Adams,

Colonel Adams' recent second wife. And, therefore, the stepmother to Concordia's closest friend Sophia.

Was Sophia here? Surely her friend would attend the event
that featured her father so prominently, despite the settlement
work which kept her so busy. Concordia and Sophia, both in
their late twenties, had been friends since childhood. Neither of
them was married: Concordia was busy with teaching at the
college, and Sophia spent the majority of her time working with
the poor at Hartford Settlement House, to the ongoing
disapproval of her family. Especially Colonel Adams.

Concordia glanced from side to side, but people were too
closely bunched together for her to see the entire room.

The reporter wasn't finished with his questions. "Will you
be making additional donations to the museum?"

Colonel Adams shook his head. "I've not yet decided. My
cataloguer still has to establish the extent of my acquisitions."

With that, the colonel resumed expounding upon items of
interest. He was shortly interrupted *again*, this time by the new
history professor, Dorothy Phillips. She carefully picked up a
smooth oval made of black stone, which nestled easily in her
hand. Colonel Adams flushed a dusky red and stared as if he'd
never seen it before.

"This heart scarab is a particularly exciting find," Miss
Phillips said. "The hieroglyphs on the back recount a typical
spell of the time, asking the heart not to testify against the
deceased in the weighing ceremony, and so be spared from
Ammut the Devourer. But the material is quite unique: rather
than glass or clay, it is lodestone, which has magnetic properties.
Experts believe the ancient Egyptians used such stones for
healing various ailments. Usually, though, they were used in
pairs, but only one of these was found. Isn't that right,
Colonel?"

Adams nodded mutely, still staring at the object.

Faculty members at the periphery of the group craned their
necks to see, while others surreptitiously checked watches or
carried on whispered conversations with a neighbor. *The
Courant*'s photographer repositioned his tripod for a picture of

the president and lady principal with the colonel in front of a display case. Soon the bright flash and odor of magnesium filled the room.

Concordia sidled to her left to look for Sophia. Ever-cursed by a short stature, she had to stand on tiptoe to see over people's heads. Ah, there she was. She recognized Sophia's slim, angular form, her erect carriage and the elegant tilt of her head. Sophia stood beside the wall near the front of the room, no doubt where she would have a clearer view of her father. Next to her was a young girl whom Concordia recognized as Sophia's sister Amelia. She had the same soft pale hair and brown eyes, although her face still held the chubby-cheeked remnants of babyhood. Concordia started to make her way over to them, slowed by the press of people.

"My dear, you *must* consult Madame Durand," someone murmured nearby. Concordia turned. Mrs. Adams, who had wandered away from the limelight, was speaking to a portly woman she didn't recognize.

"She is the best in her field at getting results," Mrs. Adams continued. "We have already communicated with one person from *the other side,* and we are very close to making contact with another."

As this seemed a more interesting discussion than the one they were all supposed to be listening to, Concordia paused and shamelessly eavesdropped. What *other side* did she mean? The Atlantic Ocean? China? And who was Madame Durand? The name seemed familiar.

"But how does she do it?" the portly woman asked.

"Oh, my dear, it is not for us to ask *how*," Mrs. Adams answered. Her voice, though barely above a whisper, dripped with the condescension of one with exclusive knowledge. "Mediums inhabit another world, where our rules and reality do not apply. But Madame Durand is a most *benevolent* woman. She only wants to do good in the world, to help the bereaved who wish to talk with their departed loved ones once more."

The heavy-set woman harrumphed. "I've heard about some of those tricks they use. A pack of charlatans, if you ask me."

Concordia felt a chill settle in her spine. So it was *that* "other side": the boundary between life and death. She didn't think of herself as the superstitious sort, but felt certain that one should not meddle in such matters. She now remembered the name of Madame Durand, the spiritualist medium who had recently taken up residence in Hartford. The students were buzzing about the celebrity, especially since Madame had approached President Langdon about establishing a "spiritualist club" at Hartford Women's College. The previous college president would have chased her out of the office; the mild-mannered Langdon, by contrast, had agreed to the proposal. Concordia didn't care, so long as Madame Durand restricted her spirit-summoning activities to areas off-campus. The college did not need more tomfoolery than it already had.

A round of polite applause roused Concordia. The presentation was over.

Thank goodness. She could say hello to Sophia, then extricate herself and return to the Chaucer essays that required her attention. The group was thinning, with the newspaper reporter, photographer, and city dignitaries making a quick exit.

"Concordia!" Sophia cried when she saw her. She gave her a hug.

"It's good to see you," Concordia said. She looked down at the little girl, who gave a pretty little bob and smiled.

"My, how you have grown, Amelia!" Concordia exclaimed. "I haven't seen you in ages. How old are you now? Eight years? Why, you're practically a lady."

Amelia flushed with pleasure. "Thank you, Miss Wells. I'm going to school now, too."

"Wonderful! Be sure to study hard, if you want to be as accomplished as your sister."

Now it was Sophia's turn to smile.

"It was very generous of your father to donate so much of his collection," Concordia added, looking down at the little girl.

Amelia plucked at a blond ringlet and started to play with it, looking up uncertainly at Sophia, who pulled her close and patted her head affectionately. "I'm afraid Amelia doesn't quite know what to make of all these doings, but Father insisted we both come. I'll be taking her back home…"

"*Here* are my favorite two young ladies!" a gravelly voice interrupted. Colonel Adams, accompanied by Miss Phillips, drew closer. The colonel stooped down to pick up the little girl. Sophia tightened an arm around her sister. Adams must have thought better in light of the occasion, and straightened up.

"We were just about to leave, Father. You remember my friend, Concordia?" Sophia said. Colonel Adams turned a sharp eye in her direction.

Concordia hadn't been in the company of the colonel since she was a little girl. Strangely, even though the daughters were close and lived in the same neighborhood, their parents had never socialized; no doubt because the colonel was often away from his family during his military career. Sophia rarely spoke of him while growing up, but Concordia knew the relationship between the two had always been fractious.

In looking at him up close, she could see that he had aged well in the past two decades. Despite his thinning gray hair and heavily creased features, his eyes were bright and his figure still trim.

Colonel Adams was looking Concordia up and down in an appreciative manner. "I haven't seen *you* since you were in a pinafore. You turned out well, my dear."

Concordia blushed and changed the subject. "Thank you again, Colonel, for your generous gift to the college—"

Miss Phillips, a silent observer up to this point, broke in. "Oh, yes, most generous indeed. I look forward to cataloguing more of your collection, should you see fit to make a future donation. I participated in several digs myself. Is that how you came by your pieces?"

This new professor was certainly enthusiastic, Concordia thought. It was easy to believe that the woman standing before her had trekked through Egypt. Though of middle age, Dorothy Phillips was vigorous and sturdily built, without a hint of gray in her smooth brown hair, which was cut sensibly—though unfashionably—short. Her skin was also darker than fashion called for, doubtless from repeated sun exposure. The lady squinted through her spectacles a great deal, either because she needed stronger lenses or, as Concordia preferred to imagine, as a result of peering across sun-bleached desert expanses and into dark tombs.

Sophia gave Concordia's hand a quick squeeze in good-bye as she saw her opportunity to leave with Amelia. The colonel watched them go, frowning, before he turned his attention back to the history professor.

"I acquired these artifacts through other collectors," he answered stiffly. "I visited Egypt only once, and it was not an occasion I would care to repeat. I wonder at *you* making the trip, Miss Phillips. Rather an unseemly pursuit for a woman." He looked around the room, as if searching for someone. "If you will both excuse me."

He walked briskly down the hall, toward the Gallery's lavatories, leaving Miss Phillips flushed and Concordia open-mouthed in a retort she'd had no time to voice.

"How utterly rude," Concordia said.

Miss Phillips shrugged. "I've dealt with far worse over the years, Miss Wells. At least it isn't the prevailing opinion these days."

Concordia checked her watch. "I should be getting back."

A high-pitched female shriek stopped the conversations. All turned as one toward the lounge.

"I b-b-beg your *pardon*, miss!" It was the voice of Colonel Adams. He backed out of the door marked "Gentlemen," looking flushed and confused. President Langdon rushed down the hall toward him.

"Oh, dear," Dorothy Phillips murmured, with a glance at the side-by-side lavatory doors. "It looks as if someone has switched the signs."

"Those students *are* a mischievous group of girls," said a grinning Hannah Jenkins, who had joined them. "At least that reporter is gone. We won't be reading about it in the papers."

Miss Jenkins was in charge of the college's infirmary. Her experience as infirmarian served her well in her roles as basketball and tennis coach, too. Hannah Jenkins' snow-white hair and age-spot-mottled skin belied her ageless energy, and a twinkle of humor was never far from her eyes.

"That scream sounded like... Miss Pomeroy." Concordia could barely speak in her effort not to laugh. Gertrude Pomeroy, one of the college's classical language professors, was notoriously absent-minded. She *would* walk into a water-closet marked "Gentlemen," if that was the door she was used to walking through. There seemed to be little room in her head for anything other than medieval French literature.

"I'd better go and check on her," said Miss Jenkins. "Miss Wells, could you switch the signs back to where they belong? We must get the custodian to nail them down properly."

Just before Concordia reached the restrooms, the door marked "Ladies" was flung open, barely missing her, and a grumbling Colonel Adams stalked down the stairwell without a backward glance.

"The old codger needs taking down a peg or two, anyway. Too big for his britches," muttered Miss Jenkins, now returned with a trembling Miss Pomeroy. "Here, Gertrude, sit down and compose yourself. He's gone," Miss Jenkins said, guiding her to a chair.

Miss Pomeroy gave a sniffle. "I never noticed, oh dear. How embarrassing. I would have switched the signs back if I'd realized. How long do you think they've been that way?"

"There's no telling. No one has used this wing since Miss Phillips began cataloguing the collection. And it's kept locked otherwise," Miss Jenkins said.

Concordia rolled her eyes. "The students have gone sign-crazy, and we've only just begun the semester. When they're not *switching* the signs, they're stealing them altogether."

Hannah Jenkins smiled. "Whoever took the 'Caution: Wet Paint' sign is going to be in particular trouble with Lady Principal Grant if she's caught. I wonder if the Ogre ever got the paint out of her skirt."

Concordia glanced at her in surprise. It was the first time she'd heard a faculty member using the student nickname for

Miss Grant, the new lady principal. She looked around to see if Miss Grant was still here, but there was no sign of her. Thank goodness. The woman had the ears of a bat.

Some clever student had made apt use of Olivia Grant's initials, and the name had stuck. Not that anyone could really blame the girls; the lady principal *was* rather ogre-ish: short, squat, sour-faced and sharp-tongued, all combined with a strict disciplinary style. Rather like a grumpy toad. Apparently, she was not beloved among the faculty, either. Concordia hoped to stay on the lady principal's good side. If she had one.

By this point, Miss Pomeroy had calmed sufficiently for them all to leave. Everyone else had already gone, except for Dorothy Phillips, who was tidying the room, putting relics back in their cases, adjusting labels.

Good. Now she could go back to the cottage and get some work done. She followed Miss Pomeroy and Miss Jenkins to the door.

"Oh, Miss Wells?" Miss Phillips called out, before she could escape.

Drat. Concordia watched the others leave.

"I've been meaning to ask you if you share your father's interest in Egyptology," Miss Phillips continued.

"My father's interest?" Concordia echoed blankly.

"Yes. In *Egyptology*," Miss Phillips repeated carefully, as one would to a slow-witted child.

"Regretfully, he passed away more than a decade ago," Concordia said. "He was never interested in Egypt, to my knowledge."

"But wasn't your father Dr. Randolph Wells?" Miss Phillips persisted.

"That's right," Concordia said, "he was an ancient Greek and Latin scholar, not an expert in Egypt."

"*Hmm.* Dr. Wells *did* suspend his work in the field more than twenty years ago. No one knows why. Perhaps you were too young to remember. But growing up, you saw no displays of the artifacts he acquired? None of his writings? He never spoke of his early work?"

Concordia shrugged. Miss Phillips must have him confused with another Randolph Wells, surely? She remembered how enthusiastic her father had been about his study of early Greece and Rome. He certainly would not have been mute about a subject he loved. He never talked about pyramids, tombs, mummies, or anything of the sort.

"If you're interested, I have a few articles of his among my books that I can show you. Just give me a few minutes to finish cleaning up first."

"No, no—don't trouble yourself, Miss Phillips. I really must go," Concordia protested.

But Miss Phillips paid her no attention.

"Oh, *no*. Where is it?" Miss Phillips dropped to her hands and knees and crawled under the table, heedless of the dust collecting on her skirts. Concordia realized the professor was looking for something other than a scholarly article.

"What's wrong?" Concordia asked.

"Perhaps he set it down…? Oh, this is awful. My first day as curator."

Dorothy Phillips looked up in despair. "The heart amulet—it's *gone*."

Chapter 2

While Concordia wasn't yet familiar with the habits of the new history professor, she suspected that clambering around furniture while mumbling to oneself in a panic were not typical behaviors of a well-respected department head. Especially one who had trekked through the far-flung, inhospitable terrain of foreign lands.

So Concordia dropped to the floor to help her look.

"It's no use," Miss Phillips sighed after they had combed the room. She dusted off her skirts and tucked a stray lock of hair behind her ear. "It's gone."

"But how?" Concordia asked, brushing off her own skirts. If the back of her dress looked anything like Miss Phillips', she was going to have to change her clothes entirely. "It obviously hasn't been mislaid. It isn't anywhere *here*. Was it stolen? Is it a valuable item?"

The history professor shook her head. "While it's an interesting piece in terms of its magnetic properties, it isn't terribly rare or sought-after. At least, not singly." Miss Phillips fiddled with a pencil as she thought. "There's one possibility," she said at last. "During the assembly, I had the distinct impression that Colonel Adams was surprised to see the amulet among the displays."

"So you believe the amulet was *accidentally* included in the donation, and the colonel has stolen it back?" Concordia raised a skeptical eyebrow. "Wouldn't it have been simpler for him to point out the error and reclaim the item?"

Miss Phillips grimaced. "I know it sounds far-fetched, but is the alternative any more agreeable?"

Concordia could see her point. If the colonel wasn't responsible for the relic's disappearance, then it was someone else in attendance. But she had difficulty imagining anyone who had been here—the college board, the faculty, the administrators, the mayor?—committing such a deed.

"What will you do now?" Concordia asked.

Dorothy Phillips squared her shoulders. "I suppose I shall have to pay a call upon the colonel, heaven help me." She looked at Concordia. "Can you keep this confidential in the meantime? I'd like to settle this quietly."

"Of course," Concordia promised.

Chapter 3

This bodes some strange disruption to our state.

Hamlet, I.i

Week 2, Instructor Calendar
September 1896

Concordia had been both expecting and dreading this meeting.

She took a deep breath and knocked on the door.

"Enter!"

Lady Principal Grant's office was much different in style than that of her predecessor. Gone was the light, airy, elegant feel of the room, the stacks of well-thumbed books, the open window. Instead, Olivia Grant's office was dark and formidable: heavy draperies made the room stuffy and confining; dark wood frames held dour-looking historical figures, painted in stiff poses; matched leather-bound book sets lined the walls like well-trained soldiers. Knick-knacks occupied every ledge not already spoken for.

The lady principal herself filled the chair with her bulk. Without getting up, she gestured toward a chair.

"Sit down, Miss Wells." Her tone was chilly.

Concordia had just smoothed her skirts in her chair when there was a knock at the door.

"Enter!" Miss Grant called.

Charles Harrison, the new mathematics professor, stepped in. He was a short, dapper man, his black hair parted precisely down the middle. Everything about him, in fact, appeared precise and perfect: the sharp trouser creases, the polished shoes and watch chain, the deliberation as he shut the door and seated himself at Miss Grant's bidding.

"Thank you for coming, Mr. Harrison," Miss Grant said, a broad smile crinkling the fat folds of her face.

Concordia couldn't help but notice that the atmosphere of the room had thawed since his arrival.

Miss Grant settled her attention again on Concordia. "I understand, Miss Wells, that you directed the senior play last year."

Concordia had expected this, and had her speech ready. "That's true, Miss Grant, and I was happy to be of assistance. However, this year, I would ask that you not—"

"Young lady, do you think that I would assign *you* to direct the play?" Miss Grant interrupted. "While it is my understanding that you had a modicum of success with the endeavor last year, it isn't a prudent course to have someone so young in such a position of authority. These seniors need a firm hand."

Concordia was confused, and relieved. She would *not* be directing the senior play this year. Good! Yet a small part of her was perversely a little disappointed and insulted. Of course she could control the seniors. What nonsense.

However, she avoided saying any of this aloud.

The lady principal continued. "Mr. Harrison has volunteered to direct the play this year." Mr. Harrison sat up even straighter, if that were possible.

"With all due respect, Mr. Harrison is a mathematics professor," Concordia protested. Why was she objecting? Stop talking, she thought. Just stop.

But she couldn't.

"The seniors have chosen *Hamlet* this year," Concordia continued, turning to Charles Harrison. "Are you familiar with the play?"

"I had read it in my youth, of course," Mr. Harrison said in his thin-voiced, meticulous diction, "and I am reviewing it now. I see no problem."

"That is why I'm assigning you to *assist* Mr. Harrison," Miss Grant said, fixing Concordia with her dark eyes, like currants pressed into pale dough. "You can give him the benefit of your experience from last year, along with your knowledge of Shakespeare—if that is necessary—and carry out whatever tasks he sees fit to assign you."

Harrison's face took on a nostalgic look. "I have fond memories of my own time among the footlights, back in my college days. I'm looking forward to it." He turned to Concordia. "I would be grateful for your help, Miss Wells. I have some wonderful ideas to bring to the production."

Concordia didn't like the sound of that. *Wonderful ideas* often translated into *dreadful headache*.

"Miss Grant, I'm honored, but I don't see how I have the time," Concordia said. Was she recklessly consigning the fate of the senior play to a... *mathematician?* So be it. "I already have charge of the Literature Club and the Bicycle Club. And there are my cottage responsibilities, too." Which Mr. Harrison, as a man, did *not* have, she added silently. Except for the most senior faculty, female professors at Hartford Women's College were required to reside in the cottages with their students, acting as live-in chaperones, seeing to their day-to-day needs, making sure the girls did not get up to mischief.

Miss Grant's lips thinned into a hard, narrow line. Concordia was to quickly learn that when this happened, woe betide the offender.

"I care not about your schedule, Miss Wells," came the cold response. "Should you feel you are not up to the task, given your responsibilities, I am perfectly happy to dissolve the Bicycle Club to afford you more time."

Concordia knew when she had been bested. She gritted her teeth. "That will not be necessary. I will manage."

The lady principal smiled sweetly. "I thought as much. Oh, and one more thing, the play will be performed in December, rather than May. There are far too many distractions at the end of the spring term, so I have decided to change the date."

Charles Harrison looked as startled as Concordia. "Surely we need more *time*? Could it not be in February or March, at least?"

While Concordia privately agreed with Miss Grant about the plenitude of distractions in the spring, the senior play was a time-consuming production. No doubt they would have to scale back some of Mr. Harrison's *wonderful ideas*.

Miss Grant shook her head. "We'll present it along with the other Christmas-time festivities, before the students leave for winter recess. The matter is closed."

With that, she heaved herself out of the chair and shooed them out.

Chapter 4

I might not this believe
Without the sensible and true avouch
Of mine own eyes.

I.i

Week 2, Instructor Calendar
September 1896

C oncordia was about to meet her first spirit medium.
Had someone told her last week she would be
meeting a two-headed llama, she would not have been any more
amazed. It was true that mediums had grown in popularity over
the last decade, with some making their livelihood through stage
performances in packed concert halls. Others, like Madame
Durand, conducted private séances for the wealthy, and acted as
"consultants" to grieving families who set store in such things.

So perhaps mediums *were* more plentiful than two-headed
llamas, but Concordia had always expected her chances of
willingly seeing either one were the same. Yet here she was,
seated next to Miss Pomeroy in the quickly-filling dining hall of
Sycamore House, where Madame Durand would address her
first meeting of prospective members of the Spiritualist Club.

Sycamore House was the college residence for the president
and other male administrators. It had been built, too, with social
functions in mind: balls, recitals, and teas were often held in the
capacious dining hall, or the smaller drawing room. A few years
ago, the building had been updated with the most modern of
conveniences: a telephone, electric wall lamps, steam heating,
and a new coal-burning cook stove—which had produced no

end of dismay among the kitchen staff as they tried to figure out the contraption.

Concordia wished she were here for any other occasion but this. It was Miss Pomeroy who had coaxed her to come.

"I'm worried," Gertrude Pomeroy had said, pulling Concordia aside after the morning's faculty meeting. She took off her spectacles and polished them distractedly on her sleeve, returning them to her face slightly askew.

Concordia resisted the impulse to straighten them upon the language professor's nose. "Is something wrong?"

"It's about Madame Durand," Miss Pomeroy said. "I understand that she's of some European background. At least, she's *supposed* to be, but—"

"You mean she isn't?" Concordia interrupted.

Miss Pomeroy grimaced in dismay. "I don't want to say *that,* but her accented English is not consistent with a non-native speaker. Yesterday—she had just come out of Dean Pierce's office, you see, probably finalizing arrangements for tonight's meeting—and she was speaking to him through the open doorway. Her accent was nonsensical: sometimes Slavic-toned, sometimes the inverted noun-adjective order of a Romance language speaker... to my ear, at least."

If anyone would recognize an inconsistent accent, Concordia thought, it would be expert linguist Gertrude Pomeroy, who was fluent in six languages.

So, who was Madame Durand really, and what was she up to? If she was a charlatan, which certainly wasn't a shocking thought, why focus her energies on the school? She wasn't getting paid for her involvement with the college. On the other hand, should her deceits be exposed, the college's reputation could be blemished, and all of them appear to be simpletons. They were playing with fire.

"Did you say anything to the dean?" Concordia asked.

Miss Pomeroy shook her head and pushed back a lock of frizzy brown hair. "I'm not sure I *should* say something. She could have her own harmless reasons for the pretense. These clairvoyants are quirky, I hear."

Now *that* was the pot calling the kettle black, Concordia thought. She wondered if Miss Pomeroy had wandered through any mis-marked doors today.

"I was hoping you would attend the spiritualist meeting with me this evening," Miss Pomeroy continued. "You could see for yourself, and give me your opinion."

So here they were, sitting in the front row (Miss Pomeroy had said nothing about *that*), staring at a dimly-lit platform. A curtain had been drawn across the deep end of the space. In the foyer, they had walked by a basket with a sign: *Please leave a personal item here. It will be returned this evening.* There was an assortment of keys, gloves and handkerchiefs in the basket already when they passed it by. Both Concordia and Miss Pomeroy declined to donate an item, but Concordia wondered at the reason for such a request.

More than prospective student members were in attendance tonight; the curious, the wary, and those seeking entertainment on a Thursday evening also filled the room. Concordia noticed that many of the faculty were here. The newspaper reporter from the exhibit opening was here, standing in the corner, scribbling notes as he spoke with students. Was the event really so newsworthy?

Concordia turned toward the soft sound of creaking wood and rattan. Dean Pierce had wheeled himself into the aisle space beside her. He smiled.

"Good evening, Miss Wells."

Augustus Pierce was another new member of the college staff, having replaced Dean Langdon when that gentleman took over as the college's President. There were several new faces this year, but Pierce was their first staff member in a wheelchair. Over the summer, ramps had been installed and doorways widened to accommodate his chair. The school was happy to have him, as he was considered quite a catch. Dean Pierce's last two schools had increased their enrollments by at least twenty percent during his tenure; in addition, he possessed glowing references from his time as a museum curator for a prestigious collection in London.

It must have taken something quite devastating to put Pierce into a wheelchair, Concordia thought; he had a powerful upper body and a restless energy that she wouldn't normally associate with a chronic invalid.

"You are interested in the occult, Dean?" Miss Pomeroy said, leaning across Concordia.

Pierce threw back his head and laughed, which drew startled looks from those nearby. "Hardly, Miss Pomeroy. Madame Durand seems to be a charming young lady." He looked over at Concordia. "Not much older than yourself, Miss Wells. I was curious."

The lights were dimmed and the students whispered excitedly. All waited for the medium to appear.

Very quietly and without fanfare, a slightly-built woman of average height walked through the curtain and faced the audience. Despite her delicate physique, she walked with a confidence that made clear her possession of the stage. She was attired in a dress with long, flowing sleeves which partially fell over her hands. A flash of jewels in the light revealed rings on several fingers. Jewels also bedecked her neck and hair, which was dark and lustrous.

Undoubtedly, the lady's profession was a profitable one, Concordia thought.

But Madame Durand's eyes were her most striking feature: the sort of pale blue that made others feel as if she could see right into their souls. Concordia, for one, wished she could sit farther back.

"Welcome, students and friends, to the first meeting of the Spiritualist Club," Madame Durand began. Her voice was soothing, hypnotic, and heavily accented. To Concordia's ear, it merely sounded exotic; she couldn't distinguish the inconsistencies that Miss Pomeroy had noted. "For those interested in the world beyond, prepare for a journey of wonder this year. What you know, or think you know, about this mortal world will be challenged. Tonight I will give a small demonstration of what mediums can do."

Madame Durand gestured toward a man standing in the shadows beside the back corner of the platform. Concordia started; she hadn't even noticed him. He was tall and thin to the point of gauntness, with flat black eyes and graying dark hair. His face and hands looked extraordinarily pale, as if he hardly stepped into the sunlight.

The man brought forward a small table and a chair, and helped seat the woman.

"We require two volunteers from the assembly, to act as witnesses."

A number of hands were raised. Madame's assistant walked through the audience, and touched two people on the shoulder: President Langdon and... *Concordia's mother.* Concordia blinked in surprise. What was her *mother* doing here?

Although she lived nearby, Mother rarely attended any college functions. In fact, until the death of Concordia's sister Mary last spring, the rift between Concordia and her mother seemed irreparable. Mary had always been Mother's favorite, while her relationship with Concordia had been tense at best. Concordia had been most at ease in her father's company; he was the one who had encouraged her love of books. In fact, it was her father who had given her the name *Concordia,* after the Roman goddess of harmony.

Unfortunately, only Concordia's relationship with her father had been harmonious. The tension between mother and daughter had finally come to the breaking point when Concordia left home to go to college and build a life for herself—an appallingly unladylike life, in her mother's eyes. By that time, her father had been dead several years. Papa would have championed her dream.

She looked up at her mother, who was now being led onto the stage. She was saddened to see how much Mother had aged since they had spent time together this summer. Concordia knew that her mother's grief over Mary, dead six months ago, had dealt a hard blow.

Mrs. Wells and Mary had both been beauties in their time, sharing the same heart-shaped face, fine pale hair, plump mouth, and china blue eyes. But time and grief had not been kind to Mrs. Wells—graying her hair, thinning and paling her lips, and tugging at the loose flesh of her once-piquant face.

She wore a simple navy skirt, cut flatteringly to emphasize her still-slim waist, and a blouse of soft ombre plaid, in the latest three-quarter sleeve fashion. Concordia was glad that Mother was no longer wearing mourning for Mary. Perhaps she was starting to heal.

Since the events of last spring, when Concordia had successfully resolved the mystery of her sister's death, she and her mother had put aside a great deal of the animosity and hurt between them. Most of their interchanges these days were cordial, but a close relationship eluded them.

Mrs. Wells, now facing the audience, caught her daughter's eye. She gave a little nod in greeting and a shrug of her shoulders to acknowledge the strangeness of it all.

Concordia turned her attention back to Madame Durand as the lady spoke. "All mediums have a spirit guide. One who first sought us out. Spirit guides act as go-betweens; they help to bring forth other souls from the far world so that we can communicate with them. They also counsel us, with the wisdom gained from their time in the other realm. My spirit guide is a young Egyptian boy. Meti. He was a humble servant in the household of the high priest, Imhotep."

A murmur of disbelief rippled through the faculty, although no one interrupted. The students in the audience leaned forward in their excitement. Concordia rolled her eyes, wondering what wisdom could be gleaned from a boy who had never spoken English and had been dead for thousands of years.

"Meti has been able to guide many spirits to speak to their grieving loved ones, at my request. His heritage makes him one of the better guides. Out of all the ancient civilizations, the Egyptians had the closest relationship with the world of the dead; the boundary was almost as nothing to them."

The medium looked around the room, noting both the enthusiastic students and the skeptical teachers. Her chill-blue eyes settled on Concordia, and when she spoke again, Madame Durand seemed to address her directly.

"So you do not believe? Perhaps we can put my Meti to the test, and then with your own eyes will you see. Because Meti dwells in the world of the dead, he sees and knows things that we would not." Concordia shuddered, and was relieved when Madame finally turned to glance around the rest of the room.

"I do not presume to account for *how* these things happen," the medium went on. "Some say it is supernatural, others say it is the power of the mind, or some sort of electrical aura. Whatever the explanation, I can assure you: it is *real.* " She gestured to the man, who placed upon the table the basket of items Concordia had seen earlier.

"Give me an object, please," Madame. Durand asked the man. He plucked a woman's handkerchief, dainty and deeply-edged with lace, from the depths of the basket.

He let it dangle between his long, thin fingers for a brief moment, giving the audience a good look at the object, then passed it to Madame.

Holding the handkerchief, Madame Durand closed her eyes. After a few minutes of silence, she began to hum what sounded like a chant, and tipped her head back.

"Is she going into a trance?" an excited whisper asked from the row behind.

Someone else made a *shushing* sound as Madame Durand grew quiet and opened her eyes.

"The owner is a strong-minded woman, of high ideals. She seeks after knowledge. She is in a position of great responsibility."

That narrows the field, Concordia thought.

"I sense from my spirit guide that this woman has recently lost something of great value." There was a sharp intake of breath behind her; Concordia couldn't tell from where. Madame Durand closed her eyes again.

Dean Pierce shifted restlessly beside her, echoing Concordia's impatience with the theatrics. *Just get on with it. Give us a name.*

Madame opened her eyes abruptly, stood, and pointed to the third row. "It is... Miss Phillips."

Amid the collective gasp, Madame's helper brought the handkerchief over to a flushed Miss Phillips, who accepted it without a word. The audience burst into applause.

"That was a trick," someone behind them murmured. Concordia turned around to see the newspaper reporter seated in the next row, behind Miss Pomeroy. He bowed his head in mute greeting, and went back to scribbling in his notebook.

"I saw no initials on the kerchief. How could she have done it?" Miss Pomeroy said, leaning over to whisper in Concordia's ear.

"I don't know," Concordia whispered back. And how could Madame Durand have known about the stolen amulet? Perhaps Miss Phillips had confided in someone else who had gossiped about it? She must have a talk with the history professor.

The session continued in the same vein for the next two objects, to the utter amazement of the audience, revealing secrets of pilfered food and unrequited love, before the objects' owners were identified. Concordia was thankful that she hadn't contributed anything to the collection of parlor props. Heaven only knew what the lady would have said about *her*. It had to be a ploy of some sort, as the newspaper reporter had said. She would try to speak with him about it afterward. Still, all this talk of spirits was unnerving, and Concordia would be glad when the evening was over.

She was about to get her wish.

While cradling the next object in her hands, Madame Durand slumped back in her chair.

The man stepped onto the stage and spoke for the first— and last—time that evening. "The spirits will do no more. Madame must rest now. It is very tiring." With a bow, he gestured for the witnesses to leave the stage. Amid the spectator applause, he turned and helped Madame Durand out of her seat.

Just as she reached the front of the stage, Madame shook off the man's arm, and stiffened in a rigid pose.

"*Beware!*"

The booming voice coming from the petite woman bore little resemblance to Madame Durand's. The audience, in the midst of getting out of chairs, stopped and stared.

"*I see Death's bony hand, reaching out to someone in this company.*"

Amid the stunned silence of the room, she collapsed.

Chapter 5

Her companion caught her and eased her on to the platform. Several men nearby, including the newspaper reporter, hopped up on the stage to help.

Soon Madame was revived, although neither she nor her companion gave any explanation of her strange behavior. She leaned heavily on his arm as they left by way of the back curtain of the temporary stage. The room burst into a flurry of chatter.

"Well, that was certainly dramatic," Dean Pierce observed wryly. He stifled a yawn. "If you will excuse me, ladies, I must say goodnight." He wheeled himself out.

As it was close to bedtime curfew, also known as the "ten o'clock rule," the faculty began shooing students back to their cottages and the crowd dispersed. Concordia looked around the room for her mother, but didn't see her. What on earth had brought her here, Concordia wondered.

Miss Phillips, clutching her handkerchief with a trembling hand, made for the door, hesitated, locked eyes with Concordia, and approached.

"How did she know?" she demanded, eyes snapping in accusation.

"I did not tell anyone," Concordia said quietly.

Gertrude Pomeroy, standing at her elbow, looked confused. Dorothy Phillips gave her a quick glance. "Does *she* know?"

"Of course not," Concordia retorted, "but I think she should. Miss Pomeroy was the first to notice that all is not as it seems with Madame Durand."

Comprehension dawned on Miss Pomeroy's face. "Ah. You *did* lose something, Miss Phillips."

Dorothy Phillips looked around the nearly empty room and drew them over to a quiet corner beside the stage. "It is the heart amulet relic, Miss Pomeroy. It disappeared a few days ago, just after the ceremony to officially open the Gallery. Miss Wells and I searched the exhibit hall. It looks as if it was stolen."

Miss Pomeroy's mouth gaped open. "But who would steal it?"

"It may have not been stolen in the conventional sense." Miss Phillips quickly explained her theory that Colonel Adams may have surreptitiously taken it back, not intending to donate the piece in the first place.

"Have you asked him about it yet?" Concordia asked.

Miss Phillips sighed. "How does one ask a man if he took back something he had given away? And asking him would make the absence public; if he doesn't have it, I could be in trouble. I must confess I have avoided going to see him."

"You won't be able to put it off much longer," Concordia pointed out. "Someone will be bound to notice."

Miss Phillips nodded in dejection. She looked at Miss Pomeroy. "You won't say anything to anyone about it, will you?"

Miss Pomeroy nodded in sympathy. "Certainly not, unless you give me leave to do so. But how did Madame Durand know?"

"Perhaps it's just a coincidence," Concordia said. "After all, nearly everyone loses something at one time or other. The medium could have simply been guessing something quite common, hoping to get lucky."

"There's more to it than that," a voice chimed in.

They turned around to see the newspaper reporter nearly at her elbow. Concordia wondered how much of the conversation he had overheard.

The man gave a little bow. "Benjamin Rosen, at your service, ladies."

Miss Pomeroy, as senior faculty, completed the introductions of their group. "What did you mean, 'There's more to it'?" she asked.

The burly man ran a thumb along his mustache as he weighed his answer. "I'll tell you, if you can keep a secret for me."

Miss Phillips stiffened. "I suppose that depends upon the secret. We don't want to be involved in anything illegal."

"Not at all," he assured them. "I'm trying to scoop another reporter who's also investigating spirit mediums and their tricks. I've already learned a lot, but Madame Durand is the most skilled one I've seen. I haven't been able to catch her out—yet. If she knows what I have in mind, though, I'm out of luck. That's why I've been covering several of the college events; to get a chance to see Madame at work. She certainly won't let a reporter attend one of her 'private' séances."

"So you don't believe in the spirit world?" Concordia asked.

Rosen gave a snort of derision. "Hardly."

"We'll keep your secret, Mr. Rosen. We're curious about Madame as well," Miss Pomeroy said. "Do you know how she did the trick tonight?"

Rosen nodded, stowed his pencil in the brim of his bowler hat, and plunked the hat atop his wavy gray hair. "I know how this sort of trick *generally* works. The medium and her partner work out a set of signals ahead of time, to indicate the person or item in question. A scratch of the chin, a tugging of the ear, and so on."

"I didn't notice anything," Concordia protested.

"Madame is *very* good at what she does. I noticed a throat-clearing early on—that could be one of the signals. The cues can be subtly verbal, with the partner starting a sentence with a certain word or phrase. If her confederate was spying on the ladies who contributed to the basket in the foyer, they could have worked out between them ahead of time whom to select."

"What about the pronouncements she made?" Miss Phillips asked.

"Some of that, as Miss Wells surmised, is guessing at generalities," Rosen said, "or she could have heard rumors of crushes, pranks, little incidents on campus. I don't doubt she did her homework before tonight."

"Amazing. Thank you, Mr. Rosen," Miss Pomeroy said. "This has been most instructive."

The man tipped his hat, and then put a finger to his lips. "But remember, not a word."

When the reporter had left, Concordia returned to the earlier issue of the missing amulet.

"What are you going to do?" she asked Dorothy Phillips.

The history professor squared her shoulders. "I suppose I *must* contact the Colonel now, and then, if that doesn't work, the administration—which means the lady principal."

With that, she said good night, and left.

"I hope Colonel Adams has it," Concordia murmured. She wouldn't wish the Ogre's wrath on anyone. She shivered, and not just from the draft that quivered the curtain nearby. Students were always careless about the doors.

Miss Pomeroy looked around the nearly-empty room. "Oh, dear, I've missed Dean Pierce. Perhaps that's just as well." She sighed. "What do you think, Miss Wells? Should I talk to the dean or President Langdon about Madame Durand? Based upon Mr. Rosen's information, they should be warned. Although we *did* promise Mr. Rosen we wouldn't say anything about him."

Concordia hesitated. Most of the administration considered Miss Pomeroy "flighty." Those new to the school regarded her with condescension, while the ones familiar with Miss Pomeroy's ways looked upon her with tolerance and good humor. Only a few of the teachers, really, understood how brilliant the lady actually was. Concordia doubted that Gertrude Pomeroy would be taken seriously by those in charge. Especially if they couldn't bring the newspaper reporter into it to verify their assertions.

"Let us wait a while," she said. "But she bears watching, nonetheless."

Chapter 6

By the mass, I was about to say something.

II.i

Week 2, Instructor Calendar
September 1896

"I tell you, Miriam, I did *not* borrow your wretched shirtwaist, and I'm tired of you going on about it!"

A chorus of high-pitched complaining followed.

In her first floor faculty quarters beneath the hubbub, Concordia looked up from her reading, wondering if she was going to have to intervene. Again.

Except for cliques and occasional pranks, the students generally got along amicably in their cottages. Of course, rivalries between freshmen and sophomore classes or between the cottage residences were to be expected, but it was good-natured and friction was relatively low. She wondered if the new lady principal had cast a pall over the mood of the campus this year, with her single instigator / collective punishment policy. Concordia believed in discipline, but she felt uneasy about the lack of fairness behind such an approach. It hadn't put a stop to the more minor pranks, or the petty "borrowings" that had been going on in the past few weeks: a teapot swiped, then making a reappearance; personal articles mislaid, only to be later found in odd places where the owner had not been.

With the din overhead subsiding, Concordia returned to reading her Keats and sipping her tea. They had just returned from morning chapel. She had no classes to teach today. A little peace and quiet would be a welcome change.

But she was destined to be interrupted. Soon Ruby, the resident matron of Willow Cottage, knocked on her door.

"A messenger boy, miss. He won' let me pass the message along. Says it's just for your ears." Ruby shook her head. "Stubborn, that one is."

"It's all right. You can show him in," Concordia said.

Ruby raised a skeptical eyebrow. "Are you *sure?*"

"Of course."

With more head-shaking, Ruby opened the door wider and called down the hall. "All right, then, deliver your message, and be quick!" She shut the door behind her as the boy walked in.

Concordia understood Ruby's reluctance now. He was one of the grubbiest children she had ever laid eyes upon: patched knee pants several sizes too big for him, deeply stained with grime and other unidentifiable substances, with clumps of cat hair clinging to them. His face was smeared where he'd rubbed his nose, and the tips of his ears were almost black with dirt. And then there was the smell. *Oh, my.*

He looked to be about ten years old, but he was slightly built, so she wasn't sure. He had large, intelligent gray eyes, which carefully appraised both her and the room. His eyes brightened when he noticed the tea tray. He was not at his ease, however, awkwardly shifting from one foot to another.

"Won't you sit down?" Concordia asked kindly. *They could fumigate the furniture later.* "Would you like some tea and a biscuit?" She wished it could be something more, like a sandwich; the child could use some nourishment, but that was all she had at the moment.

The boy sat, gingerly, on the edge of a red upholstered chair. Concordia tried not to notice the marks—was that *soot?*—he was leaving on it. She produced another cup, and loaded the plate with cookies.

Although it was obvious the child was hungry, he tried not to eat the food too fast or slurp from the cup.

"What's your name, young man?" Concordia asked.

"Eli, miss," came the soft answer.

"And, Eli, what message do you have for me?"

Apparently recalling his errand, Eli stood and plucked at Concordia's sleeve. "Miss Sophia sent me. She said please come. A turrible thing has happ'nd, she says."

Concordia stood. "What terrible thing? What's wrong?" Had there been an illness? An accident? Her friend Sophia was enormously self-sufficient; she wouldn't send someone unless she absolutely couldn't come herself.

Eli shook his head. "Doa'n know, miss. She wan' me to bring yer back. That's all."

Concordia left a quick note for Ruby, then followed Eli to the trolley stop outside the campus gate.

Chapter 7

Murder most foul.

I, v.

The Adams house was an impressive structure, situated among equally impressive homes along the illustrious block of residences dubbed "Governor's Row." Built in the once-popular Italianate style, it sported wide, elaborately-corniced eaves overhanging curved windows. A heavily-ornamented second-story gable crowned the whole. While it wasn't the largest house on the block, it certainly spoke of the family's wealth and privilege.

Concordia hadn't been here to visit since Sophia had gone to live at Hartford Settlement House. However, the settlement house was currently undergoing extensive renovations and expansion, so available space was tight. Sophia had volunteered to move back to her childhood home to ease crowding.

Concordia knew it was a sacrifice for her friend to live at home. The colonel had never approved of his daughter's work with the poor, and father and daughter shared the same stubborn temperament. The situation had not been helped by the death of Sophia's mother two years ago nor the recent addition of a wife who was close to the age of her new step-daughter. The only bright spot was that Sophia could spend more time with Amelia.

The parlor maid who answered the door gave the grimy Eli a skeptical look as she let them in.

"You know better," the maid chided the boy. "Next time, go around the back entrance or the housekeeper will have my hide." Her look softened. "Since you're here, scoot back to the kitchen. Cook just took some bread out of the oven. If you wash your hands, I reckon she'll give you a slice. But stay out of the way; there's policemen here."

Eli was gone in a flash.

Concordia started. "Police? What has happened?"

The girl shook her head. "It's the colonel, miss. He's dead." She paused and dropped her voice for dramatic emphasis. "*Murdered.*"

Concordia sucked in a breath. It had only been a week since she'd seen Colonel Adams at the opening of the antiquities exhibit. How could this have happened?

"Was anyone else hurt?" Concordia asked anxiously.

The maid shook her head. "Must have happened in the night. We were all asleep. Didn't find him 'til this morning, in a heap on the floor, shot. Blood everywhere. It's a wonder we weren't all murdered in our beds, *I* say." She shivered. "But lemme take you to Miss Sophia; she's real anxious to see you."

Sophia was pacing in the sitting room. She was still clad in her dressing gown, hair down past her elbows.

"Concordia!" she cried. The maid discreetly closed the door as Sophia hugged Concordia and sniffled into her shoulder. "Thank heaven you came," she said in a muffled voice.

Concordia sat her friend down on a well-worn ottoman near the fire, and pulled up a chair to sit beside her. Although the mid-September day was only a little chilly, Sophia was shivering. Concordia chafed her hands gently. They felt so cold.

"What happened? What are the police saying?"

Just then, the door opened and Amelia ran across the room and flung herself into Sophia's arms, hair a tangled mess of golden curls, tears streaming down her cheeks. Although the girl's sides convulsed in sobs, she didn't make a sound.

"Amelia, don't cry. I'm here, dear heart. I won't let anyone hurt you," Sophia murmured into her sister's hair.

She looked past Concordia, eyes blazing. "Don't you have some deranged individual to chase down, Lieutenant?" she demanded coldly. "Why traumatize a little girl who has been through too much already, and can't even tell you anything?"

Concordia turned to see that a man had followed Amelia into the room. A policeman. In fact, it was a policeman she knew.

Lieutenant Capshaw was unmistakable, with his flame-red hair and perpetually gloomy expression. He walked with his tall, spare frame slightly stooped over, as if he were continually looking for something he might have missed.

Until a few months ago, Concordia had never thought she'd be on speaking terms with a policeman; the two didn't exactly occupy the same social sphere. However, events at the college last spring had changed that, and the lieutenant had had several occasions in which to shake his head over Concordia's "impulsive ways" and declare that he never understood young ladies nowadays. Or "college people."

While Capshaw looked equally surprised to see Concordia, he ignored her for the moment and addressed Sophia.

"I regret it's necessary, miss. From what I've seen so far, I doubt we are dealing with a madman in this case. We have to interview everyone in the household. Someone may possess an important detail without realizing it."

He gestured towards Amelia. "Why can't she talk? She makes no sound at all. But I know she can hear."

Sophia tightened her arms protectively around her sister. "Wouldn't finding your father dead be traumatic enough to render *you* mute, if you were such a tender age as she? We have called for the doctor to see what can be done for her; he'll be here shortly."

Capshaw stifled a sigh and turned his mournful eyes to Concordia. "It's a surprise to see you again, Miss Wells." The question *What are you doing here?* was implicit in his tone.

"Miss Adams requested I come, Lieutenant," Concordia said.

"Indeed? I would imagine that a young lady's mother would be of more comfort than a friend in such a trying time. Wouldn't you, miss?" he asked Sophia.

Sophia gritted her teeth. "The current Mrs. Adams is *not* my mother," she hissed.

Concordia listened to the exchange in silence. As Mrs. Adams was barely five years older than Sophia, and obviously *not* her mother, Capshaw's disingenuous question had just provoked Sophia into revealing the animosity she harbored toward Lydia Adams. For the sake of propriety, Sophia had tried to keep these feelings hidden, Concordia knew. The gossips had had enough to flap their tongues over when the Colonel married a woman young enough to be his daughter, only ten months after the death of his first wife.

There was a tap on the door, and the maid ushered in an elderly man carrying a medical bag. Ignoring everyone else, he knelt beside the child, while Sophia murmured comfortingly to Amelia and reluctantly disentangled herself from the little girl's grasp.

"How long has she been like this?" he asked, pulling out a stethoscope.

"For a few hours, since she found our father early this morning," Sophia said.

"Yes, I was informed of that. Most unfortunate," the doctor answered, glancing over at Sophia. "I am terribly sorry for your loss, Miss Adams. I can leave a sedative for your later use, if you wish."

"That won't be necessary, doctor." Sophia answered. "But what about Amelia?"

The doctor was feeling the girl's scalp. The child winced.

"What's this?" He pulled aside her hair. Just behind her left ear was a bruised, swollen lump, the matted hair behind her neck stiff with blood. "Did you hit your head?" he asked the child, who just stared back at him, blankly.

"I didn't see that," Sophia said, startled. "Perhaps she fainted when she first saw Father, and hit her head on something?"

"Possibly," the doctor answered over his shoulder as he checked the rest of her head, "but this complicates her condition."

He looked up at Concordia, Capshaw, and the maid, who was hovering uncertainly, not sure if she was still needed. "Let me complete my examination. All of you... out, please. Except for Miss Adams." He glared at Capshaw. "Don't you have a murderer to apprehend, lieutenant?" Without waiting for a reply, he turned back to his patient.

Concordia felt a bit sorry for the policeman, trying to get information from people caught in the vise of family turmoil and emotions. Rather like trying to capture one particular straw in a whirlwind.

The maid went back to her duties while Concordia and Capshaw lingered in the hallway, waiting for Sophia and the doctor.

Capshaw seemed content with the silence, spending the time looking at the paintings along the paneled walls, running an absent finger along the dust-free frames. Concordia couldn't stand it any longer.

"What happened, Lieutenant? Whom do you suspect? What have you learned?"

Capshaw hesitated. "Miss Wells, I know you are concerned for your friend's welfare. However, even though your meddling was successful in the past, I would advise you to stay out of this. You will not like the outcome."

"I don't like it already. Can't you at least share the basic information with me, so that Sophia is spared the distress of telling me about it? She did send for me, so obviously she *wants* me to know what is going on." *Hmph. Meddling.*

"Very well," Capshaw said, reluctantly. "The colonel was found in his study by Miss Amelia this morning. Apparently the child often wakes early. However, since she can't answer our questions at the moment, we don't know why she would have gone into her father's study at that hour. According to Miss Adams' account, the child woke her around six o'clock and dragged her back to the study to show her the colonel's body."

"The maid said he was shot," Concordia said.

Capshaw nodded. "We haven't found the weapon yet, but the colonel's own pistol is missing. One of the French doors has a broken window and the outer door of the safe was ajar. That suggests three possibilities: either Adams was about to open the safe when the intruder came in, the intruder tried to coerce the colonel to open the safe and shot him when the man did not comply, or the intruder himself made an unsuccessful attempt to get into the safe. The study is the only room in disarray, but the family is doing an inventory now, to see if there are any missing items. So far, nothing appears to have been taken." He gestured to the artwork in front of him. "These paintings are quite valuable, and yet, here they remain."

"But it *was* a burglary, surely? Perhaps aborted when the colonel was shot and the intruder fled in a panic?" Concordia asked.

"If so, it's the first in *this* neighborhood. There *have* been recent burglaries in the Charter Oak area. In those instances no one was harmed, the windows were broken more cleanly, and the items stolen were mostly silver plate. This one looks nothing like those."

The door to the morning room opened, and Sophia and the doctor stepped out. As the doctor left, Sophia murmured to Concordia, "Will you sit with her? I'll be back in a minute." She motioned toward the room, where Concordia could see Amelia on the sofa, asleep.

Concordia, Sophia, and Capshaw were gathered in the parlor. It was a space decked out in the latest style to receive callers. Delicate cherry side-tables clustered about the seat groupings, ready for tea trays. Embroidered pillows flanked a divan, which looked to be newly-upholstered in a warm gold fabric of geometric patterns. Fragrant burgundy roses filled crystal vases scattered throughout the room. A large Japanese silk fan, perched atop the cottage piano, looked to be tickling the ear of the other policeman standing by the door. The man, obviously younger than Capshaw and his junior in rank, batted at it in annoyance.

"How is the child?" Capshaw asked.

"The doctor has given her a sedative," Sophia explained, "but he wants someone beside her at all times. The housekeeper is with her now."

"What's wrong with her? Why doesn't she speak?" Concordia asked.

"He called it 'hysterical mutism.' It's unusual but not unheard of, apparently, especially in young children who have had a shock they cannot grasp. Then there's her head injury, which doesn't look severe, but the doctor thinks it could be inhibiting her speech as well."

"Will she recover?" Lieutenant Capshaw asked.

Sophia nodded. "The doctor says he has not heard of a case going beyond a few days, perhaps a week. Right now the hysteria is suppressed. She could have quite a violent reaction when it surfaces. That's why he wants someone always with her, so she doesn't harm herself. And we're applying compresses to the lump on her head, until the swelling subsides."

"Poor little thing," Concordia murmured.

Capshaw clucked his tongue. "It is inopportune that the child cannot tell us what she knows." He made a motion to the policeman by the door who turned and walked out.

"These things seldom work to one's convenience," Sophia responded tartly. "She could not tell you much more than I can. She came to get me as soon as she found our father. I saw everything she saw."

"Perhaps," Capshaw said, "but you cannot tell us why she was there in the first place. Surely Colonel Adams had strict rules about the presence of children in his study. And in the early hours of the morning. Did she hear the shot? The murderer might have been making his escape, even as she was opening the door. The doctor believes that your father had been dead for only a short time. The pool of blood was quite fresh, if you will pardon me saying so."

Concordia shivered.

"That is a most *indelicate* observation, lieutenant," an imperious voice said.

Lydia Adams stepped into the parlor. She moved with the languid ease of one accustomed to admiring looks from others. Her china-doll daintiness gave her the appearance of fragility. This morning, she wore a simple wrap dress of midnight blue, which was nonetheless cut in the latest fashion: a full skirt that nipped-in at the tiny waist, and balloon sleeves large enough to look at risk of collapsing, but ending in snug-fitting lower sleeves to emphasize delicate wrists. She was obviously making do until her widow's mourning wardrobe was prepared.

Capshaw stood, flushing a dark red that reached his hairline. "I beg your pardon, Mrs. Adams," he said stiffly. "Please sit down."

Mrs. Adams held out a slip of paper before seating herself. "Here is the list you requested."

"Ah." Capshaw looked it over carefully, frowning. "Only two items? 'A necklace and a statuette from the colonel's collection.' Can you be more detailed?"

Lydia Adams sighed. "Several weeks ago, when my husband was going through his collection to finalize what he would be donating to that... ladies' school, he showed me several pieces that he said he was holding back and wanted to give to *me*."

Concordia bristled at *that ladies' school*, but stayed silent. She looked over at Sophia, who shrugged.

Mrs. Adams fixed her eyes upon Concordia, as if noticing her for the first time. "You are from that place, aren't you? I remember you at the opening. I wished he'd given you *those* things, too."

"What did this necklace and statuette look like, Mrs. Adams?" Capshaw asked, keeping his impatience in check.

"The figure was about so tall," Mrs. Adams said, holding her hands ten inches apart. "It was a rather horrid little thing—a nude woman." She shuddered. "He told me it was an Egyptian fertility symbol. Sometimes the colonel could be rather... indelicate."

"And the necklace?" the lieutenant prompted, scribbling upon his wad of paper.

"Very large, with rows of multi-colored beads—it looked like a heavy collar. With a hideous *beetle* in the middle. I ask you, who gives his wife such things?" She rolled her eyes.

"Where did you see the stolen items last?" Capshaw asked.

"On my husband's desk in his study. But, mind you, I'm not saying they were *stolen*. I certainly did not want them, and I made that very clear to Roger at the time. I encouraged him to sell them or give them away. But you asked me what was missing, and I don't know what he did with them."

"No household valuables were taken? Paintings, silverplate, jewelry?"

Mrs. Adams shook her head. "Nothing."

Capshaw folded the paper and tucked it away in his tunic. "When did you last see your husband alive, Mrs. Adams?"

"Shortly after dinner. He was working in his study when I told him good-night. I decided to retire early—it had been a *most* trying day. I was being fitted for a new gown—heaven only knows *now* when I'll get to wear it—and Mrs. Pemberton's tea was interminable, with her going on and on about how precocious her dear little moppets are, when everyone knows they are as dimwitted as stumps—"

"And none of you heard the gunshot?" Capshaw interrupted. "I find that strange, madam."

"I customarily take a sleeping draught, so I heard nothing," Lydia Adams said, "and the servants sleep in the back of the house. You no doubt noticed the heavy wood door of his study. The more proper question would be, why didn't the watchman making his nightly rounds hear anything? Whatever is he being paid for?"

Capshaw didn't respond to the jibe, but turned to Sophia. "What about you, Miss Adams? You heard nothing?"

Sophia shook her head. "I slept heavily last night, lieutenant. I, too, had had a trying day. Although mine had more to do with settlement business than listening to…gossip over crumpets," she added. She gave her stepmother a sharp look.

Mrs. Adams either didn't hear the last remark, or chose to ignore it as she plucked a speck of lint from her sleeve.

"What can you tell me about Colonel Adams' visitors yesterday, Mr. Rosen and Miss—er—Phillips?" Capshaw said, looking down at his notes.

Concordia gave a start of recognition, which earned her an inquisitive glance from Capshaw.

So, Dorothy Phillips had finally worked up the courage to talk to Colonel Adams about the missing amulet. An inopportune day to do so, Concordia thought, as it had now landed her on the lieutenant's list. And what about the newspaper reporter—why had *he* been calling upon the colonel?

Mrs. Adams gave an elegant shrug. "I wasn't aware my husband had visitors, but I stay out of his business affairs. As I mentioned before, I was out most of the day."

"Would anyone have harbored ill-will toward him, ma'am? Business partnerships that had ended badly? Problems with servants?" Capshaw persisted.

"There are always problems with servants, lieutenant, although I'm sure you wouldn't have any experience with that," Mrs. Adams answered. "I can't say we've had anything unusual or alarming. Just the occasional lazy, slipshod, or nosy domestic. Of course, the people across the square have a butler who— well, let us just say it's a wonder they haven't been robbed blind. That man is as shifty as the day is long, and I suspect–"

"Yes, yes," Capshaw said hastily, "that should be all I need from you for the moment, Mrs. Adams. Except I'll want the name of your husband's attorney for additional questions about the colonel's will."

"Sophia knows it; I don't remember." Mrs. Adams stood and raised a dramatic hand to her brow. "If you will excuse me, I have a headache and must lie down."

After the policeman by the door had escorted her out, Sophia went over to the desk and wrote down the attorney's name and address. "Here, lieutenant. We'll need him to come open the safe anyway."

"Indeed? No one else but the colonel and his lawyer knew the combination? Your father was a cautious man," Capshaw said.

Sophia shrugged as she re-seated herself. "I never understood why, but I haven't been living at home until recently. It never made any difference to me."

Capshaw turned his attention to Concordia. "Tell me about Miss Phillips. I understand that she, too, teaches at the college."

Drat. There wasn't much that got by the man. "She's our new history instructor, replacing Miss Banning, who retired last year," Concordia said. "She's also the curator for the college's new antiquities collection."

Capshaw made a quick note, tapped his nub of a pencil against his wadded notepad, and asked: "What was her business here?"

This was dangerous territory, and Concordia was not about to venture off the path. "I didn't know that Miss Phillips intended to visit the colonel yesterday. She doesn't make a habit of consulting with me beforehand," she said carefully. Which was strictly true, of course. "Why would the colonel's day-time visitors be pertinent, anyway, lieutenant? Miss Phillips was in her bed at the college when the man was killed." At least she hoped so.

"It is standard procedure, Miss Wells," Capshaw said patiently. "In cases like these, we retrace recent events and people in the victim's life."

"What about his other visitor, Mr. Rosen?" Concordia asked, trying to re-direct the conversation away from Miss Phillips. Let the newspaperman fend for himself.

Sophia jumped in to the conversation. "He's the *Courant* reporter, isn't he? The man who attended the college's exhibit opening, and wrote the article about it?"

Capshaw scribbled some notes on his oft-folded wad of paper. "Do you know why Mr. Rosen would visit your father?" he asked.

Sophia looked at the policeman. "I don't know. He was quite interested in my father's collection."

"That's right. I remember him asking about the colonel's future donations," Concordia said. Could that be it? Had Rosen been after the colonel's collection all along? Perhaps he was even the person who had stolen the amulet from the exhibit?

Capshaw looked up from his note-taking. "Hmm. I'll have to make further inquiries in that direction. In the meantime,

Miss Adams, I want you to recount again the events of this morning. Please tell me exactly what you did, and what you and Amelia might have touched or disturbed."

Sophia was quiet for a long moment.

"I woke up to Amelia tugging on me. She was in near hysterics. Tears were streaming down her face, and her nose was a runny mess. She was still in her nightgown. She was barefoot. She had obviously just gotten out of bed. She wasn't speaking, but just kept pulling. I didn't know what to think, so I threw my dressing gown on over my nightgown, stepped into slippers, and followed her." Sophia looked down ruefully at her sleeping attire. "I haven't thought to change yet." She hesitated.

"Go on," Capshaw prompted, his voice softer.

"He was on the floor, on his side, with—with blood. Under his back." She shuddered. "His eyes were open—just—staring."

"Did you or the child go near the body?" Capshaw asked.

Sophia shrugged. "Of course, I don't know about Amelia's actions before she brought me to the study, and... well, I really don't remember where exactly I was. The sight of him was quite disturbing."

"The little girl's nightgown is free of any bloodstains, suggesting that she kept her distance." Capshaw said, giving her a long look. Sophia fidgeted, but said nothing.

The lieutenant tried a different tack. "Has anything unusual happened lately? Any new business associates or friends of your father? Or enemies that you know of?"

"My father had retired from military service two years ago, after my mother died. The only friend I've ever known him to have was Concordia's father, who has been dead nearly a decade now. I know nothing of any current acquaintances, business or otherwise. I doubt if he has any. He was a difficult man to get along with."

Capshaw gave her a sharp look. "Am I correct in assuming you and your father were not close, Miss Adams?"

Sophia gave the barest of nods.

Concordia decided it was time to intervene. "Lieutenant, how is that relevant? Surely you are not implying that Sophia had anything to do with her father's untimely end?"

"I am merely exploring all possibilities, Miss Wells. Now, if you will excuse me." He stood to leave, gesturing to the policeman by the door. "The sergeant will remain to question the staff. After I have spoken to your father's lawyer, I'll have additional questions for the family." He looked at Sophia intently. "Especially you, Miss Adams. Considering the smear of blood on the hem of your nightdress"—he pointed—"I'd say you got a lot closer to the body than your sister."

Chapter 8

He seemed to find his way without his eyes.

II. i

By the next day, the house was quiet. The policemen were gone for the time being. Servants were dispatched to clean the study and put out the customary mourning adornments for the front door, pulled out of storage from Sophia's mother's death.

What a strange household, Concordia thought; not a single person red-eyed from crying, or grieved at the loss of the Colonel? Yes, there was agitation here, apprehension about a murderer at large who had struck as they slept. But nothing more. What sort of man had Colonel Adams been, to have left this world, without a single soul to mourn him?

Concordia had not been in the company of the colonel since her own father was alive, when the two men spent time together more than two decades ago. Sophia spoke little of her father over the years. Concordia had the impression of a hard man, with a quick temper. But surely there was more to his character than that? He remarriage last year spoke of a softer side to his nature. But why was his widow not affected?

Then there was the problem of Sophia. Capshaw had pointed out the blood on her hem. Surely that could be explained?

Even so, Concordia knew her friend well enough to see that she was holding back something. Given Sophia's stubbornness, Concordia decided to bide her time before asking her any pointed questions.

At Sophia's request, Concordia had made arrangements to stay several nights. She'd found someone to cover her classes. So far, the lady principal hadn't raised an objection.

Concordia hoped she could learn what Sophia was concealing. But Capshaw's warning troubled her: *you will not like the outcome*. What did he suspect?

She glanced over at Sophia, pushing her food around with her fork. They'd had breakfast trays sent up to the sitting room, even though neither felt much like eating. "When will you be going back to your settlement work?" Concordia asked.

"As soon as Amelia is better," Sophia answered. "I can't leave her like this. You may have noticed Lydia is not the most attentive, nurturing soul. She has little experience with children."

"She's not much older than we are," Concordia observed, "so I suppose that isn't surprising."

"Perhaps," Sophia sighed. "Can I ask a favor?"

"Anything," Concordia said.

"Do you remember Eli, the boy I sent to get you? He'd been staying at the settlement house, but then they had no room for him with the renovations taking place. I've been letting him stay here, in the servants' quarters, but in light of what's going on, it would be better if he stays elsewhere temporarily."

"But, Sophia, I can't take care of him," Concordia objected. Heaven only knew what the lady principal would say to *that*. Women professors couldn't even be married, much less have a child living with them.

"No, no, I meant can you find a job for him at the college, perhaps as a messenger boy or something of the sort? He's very reliable, and quite intelligent. Of course, he has an aversion to bathing on a regular basis…"

"I'll ask around and see what I can find for him," Concordia said, "but the more difficult problem would be finding a place for him to stay." It was a *women's* college, after all.

"It would only be until the Settlement House's renovations are finished," Sophia said, "then there will be plenty of room for him."

"He has no family? Where does he come from?"

"We haven't been able to find any. He claims he doesn't even know his own last name. We're not sure of his age, but he's probably about ten. Based on what he remembers, we've concluded that he must be the child of a prostitute. She either abandoned him or died. All he knows is that she disappeared. He stayed with friends of hers whom they'd been living with— probably a brothel—but something happened there that caused him to run away. He won't tell us what happened. He hid aboard a rail car and got off here. He cannot read or write, and claims not to know the name of the town he came from."

Concordia felt a twinge of pity for the boy. "How did he come to be here?"

"One of our workers rescued him after he was caught stealing a loaf of bread from the baker's shop. If she hadn't paid the man for it, Eli would have been locked up. We've had him for a few weeks, but he comes when he wants food and then leaves again. We can't seem to keep him clean and presentable-looking for very long. But he really is a bright child, obliging and quick to learn." Sophia looked at her expectantly.

Concordia thought for a minute. "The college's gatekeeper, Mr. Clyde, lives in a small cottage on the grounds. Maybe I can persuade him to share the quarters and keep an eye on the boy for a while. I'll ask when I return." Which had better be soon, she thought. Although a fellow teacher was covering her classes, Ruby had been handling the girls back at the cottage by herself. Lady Principal Grant wouldn't tolerate an extended absence.

Sophia let out a breath and squeezed Concordia's hand. "Thank you."

Concordia was reading to a listless Amelia in the girl's bedroom when there was a knock on the door.

"Come in!" she called.

Concordia was well acquainted with the gentleman who walked in. He looked much the same as when they had said good-bye a few months ago. The same twinkling brown eyes, dimpled cheek, and black wavy hair that curled against the nape of his neck in just the way Concordia remembered. As always, he moved with the energy of a youthful man, though he was in his thirties."

"David!" Concordia cried. "What are *you* doing here?"

He sat down on the edge of the bed next to Amelia.

"I came to see my little goddaughter," he said, as Amelia's eyes brightened. She silently threw her arms around his neck, clinging tightly. He looked at Concordia over the child's head.

"That's right, I'd forgotten Amelia is your goddaughter," Concordia said. She moved to seat herself in a proper chair. It would not do to sit on the bed with a man, no matter how many children were between them. Especially Mr. Bradley.

When Concordia had first met David Bradley last year, he had divided his time between teaching chemistry classes at Trinity College and at the women's college. Her time with David had been a welcome solace from a difficult spring semester, when the mysterious death of Concordia's sister and the murder of two college officials had thrown her life into chaos. She had wondered if their friendship had begun to border on something more.

However, neither had seemed willing to venture across that boundary, and David, dealing with a family crisis of his own, had decided upon a change of scene. Concordia was both hurt and relieved when he'd left. All this time, she had convinced herself that she was fine with his absence. Now he was back, and her cold fingers, warm cheeks, and the strange lightness in her chest proclaimed that a lie.

"Are you here for long?" she asked in an even voice.

"I *am* still living in Boston," he explained, "but when Sophia sent for me, I came right away. I have a colleague taking over my classes this week." He looked down fondly at the child in his arms. Amelia had fallen asleep.

Concordia suppressed a pang of jealousy over how easily David would drop whatever he was doing and take the train down from Boston for Sophia.

Stop being petty, she told herself. The Adams' house was dealing with a murder, after all, and a traumatized child.

"How are *you*, Concordia?" David asked softly. "I was hoping that you –"

He broke off as they heard angry voices in the hall. Amelia woke up abruptly, eyes widening. She dove under her bedcovers.

Concordia flung open the door to find Sophia and Lydia Adams in heated debate. She motioned toward the cowering girl. "You're frightening her," she hissed.

Sophia lowered her voice. "She"—pointing to her stepmother—"wants to have a *séance* here tonight. It's outrageous."

Concordia frowned. A séance?

"Madame Durand is a dear friend of mine," Lydia Adams reprovingly. "She has offered her services to help identify your father's killer, Sophia. I would think that you, of all people, would want the person brought to justice."

Concordia gave a start of surprise. Madame Durand? It seemed she could never get away from the woman. But she remembered the side conversation Lydia Adams had engaged in during the exhibit opening. She had consulted Madame Durand before.

"I doubt if the supernatural world can be of help to us in this situation," Sophia said dryly, "the killer is of *this* world."

"Nevertheless, we *will* be having a séance tonight. I am now in charge of the goings-on in this household. I require you to be there. You must come, too, Miss Wells. I understand that Madame Durand has been involved with your school lately so I am sure she will not mind." She looked into the room, at Amelia. "We should have her attend as well."

Sophia stiffened. "That child has been through too much already, Lydia. Do you have a heart of stone? How could you ask that of her? Concordia and I will attend so long as you leave Amelia out of it."

"I'm afraid I must agree, Mrs. Adams," David said, joining them in the hallway. He had just settled Amelia in her bed again. "The girl is frightened of her own shadow. She would be more of a disruption than a help. But I would be happy to come to your...séance." He smiled charmingly.

Mrs. Adams hesitated. "I suppose you are right," she said, grudgingly. "Be ready at nine o'clock."

When she walked away, Sophia turned to David and Concordia. "I hope you don't mind. I would do anything to keep Amelia from experiencing additional distress."

"Of course," Concordia said, wondering what tomfoolery she'd just been volunteered for.

"Could be fun," David answered.

Chapter 9

It harrows me with fear and wonder.

I.i

They had just finished their meal when the doorbell sounded. Concordia checked her lapel watch: eight-thirty. Madame Durand was a bit early; she must be eager to get the séance underway.

Well, *she* wasn't eager to do this, but at least it would be over with sooner.

To her surprise, the maid ushered in Lieutenant Capshaw and a small, ferrety-looking man she didn't recognize.

"Excuse us for disturbing you, ma'am, but Mr. Kaufmann and I are here to open the colonel's safe."

"This is a most inconvenient time, Lieutenant," Mrs. Adams chided. "We are expecting company."

Both the policeman and the family attorney raised an eyebrow over that. One did not typically entertain company with a member of the family lying dead in a police morgue.

"No, no, you don't understand," Mrs. Adams said hastily, no doubt aware of how that must sound, "we are trying to get to the bottom of this murder ourselves, since *you* appear out of your depth. Madame Durand isn't paying a social call. It is more an errand of mercy."

"Who is Madame Durand?" Capshaw asked.

Mrs. Adams looked appalled. "You have never heard of Madame Durand, the famous spirit medium? I would think someone of even your... *social circle* would know of her. She was the toast of New York, and has recently moved to Hartford.

She is rapidly becoming a sensation here, too. Most talented. Why, I remember during one séance where the table shook—"

Capshaw cut across what promised to be a lengthy recounting of the delights of the spirit medium. "You mean that you are having a *séance* here, tonight?"

"Of course."

He stole a quick glance at Concordia and Sophia. "Are these ladies participating as well?"

"Yes, yes, naturally," Mrs. Adams said impatiently.

"Indeed?" Capshaw looked over at Concordia, his lips quivering in his attempt to suppress a grin.

Concordia could almost hear the unspoken thought running through the policeman's mind. *I didn't know* college people *believed in such things.*

"And you are Mr. Bradley, are you not?" Capshaw said. "I remember you from last year. What are you doing here, sir?"

"I'm a family friend, lieutenant," David answered.

"I see. Well, this family can use all of the friends it can muster," Capshaw said.

Mrs. Adams looked thoughtfully at the policeman and Mr. Kaufmann, who had been silent during the introductions. "You know, it might be a good idea for the two of you to join us. After all, you—" she pointed at Capshaw—"are trying to catch my husband's murderer, and you—" she pointed at Kaufmann—"were my husband's lawyer, and had known him for years. I am sure Madame will agree that your energies will aid our chances of success this evening."

Mr. Kaufmann leaned forward excitedly. "You want *me* to participate? I have never been to a séance before. What do I do?"

Mrs. Adams patted his hand. "Don't worry; Madame will guide you. It's the spirits who do all the work, really."

Concordia smothered an unladylike snort, which came out as a cough. Sophia patted her back.

"What spirits are you trying to call forth?" Capshaw asked, straight-faced.

"Why, my dear husband's, of course," Lydia Adams said tartly. "Only *he* knows the truth."

The bell rang again after this pronouncement, and Concordia nearly jumped out of her chair. All this talk of ghosts was making her skittish. She squelched the fanciful thought of the colonel's spirit ringing the front doorbell.

"Oh! That must be Madame." Lydia Adams hustled down the hall with all the eagerness of a schoolgirl about to be introduced to royalty. The rest of them followed, with varying degrees of reluctance—save for the lawyer, who looked rather entertained by the entire proceeding.

Madame Durand presented a more flamboyant appearance than Concordia remembered from the demonstration at Hartford Women's College. She wore a deep-sleeved gown of dark burgundy velvet trimmed in silver braid, cinched to a small waist on her almost girlish form. It gave her pale skin a translucent quality, already in sharp contrast to the glossy black hair piled high atop her head. Jewels gleamed and clinked softly around her wrists, and she moved with her usual grace. But her most striking feature, as Concordia had noticed before, was her piercing pale-blue eyes, fringed with thick black lashes, and tonight heavily lined in kohl. The effect was exotic and mesmerizing.

The medium was accompanied by the pale-faced man Concordia recognized as Madame's assistant at the college demonstration. He was introduced to the group as her husband, Jacques Durand. The man was dressed plainly as before, in sharp contrast to his wife, as if he would fade into the background so as not to rival the lady for attention.

As Lydia made the introductions, explaining that there would be more participants at the séance, Jacques Durand bowed silently and looked especially long at Lieutenant Capshaw, his dark eyes without expression.

Madame Durand reached for Mrs. Adams' hands. "Ah, *ma petite*, I am sorry. It is most difficult. So little time you were together. But he is here, watching over you, still. I feel it."

Lydia Adams sniffed delicately. "You are most kind, Madame. Did you sense anything strange the other day, when you came to call? A psychic disturbance of our impending calamity? The parlor maid just told me that you came to the house."

This drew a look from both Concordia and Lieutenant Capshaw. There seemed to be a lot of traffic around the Adams' home in the hours before the colonel's death.

"When was this, Madame? Was there a particular reason for your visit?" Capshaw asked.

Madame Durand paled at the sight of the policeman pulling out his pad and pencil, waiting expectantly.

"Oh, no, no, it was nothing. I was on my way to see another client, and wanted to thank Madame Adams for her kind words." Madame turned to Concordia. "She recommended me to your mother, *mademoiselle*. I am humbled by her confidence in my abilities."

Concordia closed her mouth, once she realized it was hanging open. Her *mother*, consulting a spirit medium? So that was why she had attended the college demonstration. She had wanted to see Madame's abilities for herself. And the medium had certainly put on an impressive show. It was all very upsetting, the thought that this woman preyed upon those in grief, for her own profit. Concordia dreaded the talk she would be obliged to have with her mother later.

"The room must be prepared," Madame said, her voice lilting with anticipation. She gestured to the satchel her husband carried.

Lydia tugged on the bell pull. "I have set aside the drawing room for you, and a table has been placed there, according to your specifications. We will be a bit more crowded around it now, of course."

Madame shrugged. "It is of no matter."

As the Durands were escorted to the drawing room, Concordia asked, "What does 'prepare the room' mean?"

Lydia waved a vague hand in the direction of the room in question. "Madame must get the space ready to welcome her guide from the spirit world, and eliminate any negative auras. She burns incense and places certain objects around the room. I'm not sure exactly what's involved," she admitted. "She must conduct the work in solitude."

"Interesting," David murmured.

Soon, Madame Durand was ready, and the group was brought into the room.

Lydia Adams was right, Concordia thought, about them being crowded in the small space. At first, all eight of them were crammed at the table, until Madame objected.

"Such cramped quarters, it does not bode well for the session."

"I will sit out," her husband offered. He took his chair to the far corner of the room by the window, but first dimmed the lamps.

Even with seven, their knees were touching. Concordia held herself rigidly, so as not to end up in the lap of David, seated to her left, or Lieutenant Capshaw, seated to her right. She could feel each breath they took. She was especially mindful of the warmth of David's firm, muscled leg against her hip. It was very distracting.

The entire arrangement was ridiculous, she thought peevishly. What possible good could come about from seven adults sitting cheek-by-jowl at a table in the dark?

"Please to put your hands on the table, fingers touching the hands of your neighbor. We make a circle, unbroken," Madame said. "Now close the eyes. Yes. Good. Breathe deeply, slowly."

Concordia was aware of the lingering incense in the air, a sharp spicy scent. As she inhaled and exhaled, the smell intensified. The smallest of sounds reached her ear: a creaking floorboard in the hallway, the rustle of a skirt, the breathing of her companions.

When the room had quieted and people had stopped fidgeting, the medium spoke again, in a hushed, hypnotic voice. "Please to keep the eyes closed. I will be calling upon my spirit guide, Meti, who died as a boy in the service of one of the great houses of ancient Egypt. But be advised that I cannot always control the spirits, once they begin to speak through me. Sometimes they are mischievous, and do or say improper things. Sometimes they will not cooperate, or are not able to do as we ask."

Someone in the room sighed. Concordia couldn't tell who.

Madame began a throaty, tuneless humming. Concordia opened her eyes a tiny bit to see the lady's head thrown back, eyes closed, swaying as much as the cramped space around her would allow.

A slight breeze stirred the curtains and prickled Concordia's neck. It felt more like an exhalation than fresh air. Or maybe it was the primeval sounds coming from the diminutive woman at the table that had this effect upon her? She shifted in her seat. How long was this going to go on?

Cautiously, Concordia turned her head to see if anyone else was disobeying Madame's "eyes shut" dictum. Mr. Kaufmann's lids fluttered, as if he had just closed them hastily, but immediately to her right, Lieutenant Capshaw made no pretense to be following the medium's instructions. He was quietly taking in the whole with open eyes, although he couldn't twist his body around to see behind him without disturbing the others.

"He is coming!" Madame Durand opened her eyes, as did the rest of the group. "Meti, you are here?" She cocked her head, as if listening.

"Ah, Meti. Can you bring Colonel Adams to us? Ye-es, if I must—" she seemed hesitant while answering her unseen companion.

Abruptly, she threw her head back again. Someone gave a little squeak of fright—Lydia Adams, Concordia guessed—as the medium's mouth dropped open and a white vapor emerged, lingered for a moment, then dissipated. David's eyes went wide in surprise.

"C-C-Con-n-n-cor-di-a-a—" The sound was coming from Madame Durand, but it was not her voice, at all.

Concordia gave a little shriek and nearly fell out of her chair. The large, steady hands of Lieutenant Capshaw caught her before she toppled over.

"Easy there, miss," he whispered encouragingly. Uncharacteristically, he gave her a wink, which for some reason made her feel much better.

"Concordia... it is *Papa.* I must... say something to you." The voice was getting stronger, although still husky and low. It sounded nothing like her father.

"Answer him!" Lydia Adams hissed from across the table.

Feeling equal parts apprehensive and silly, Concordia cleared her throat. "Yes? I am listening."

"You must help me... atone for the wrong... I have done... long ago."

"What do you mean?" Concordia asked.

"My sin... will come down on you, Concordia. You... are in *danger.*"

"What sin? What sort of danger?" Concordia's hands shook.

"It should have stayed buried... in the sands of Egypt, but it is *here*, now," the voice continued, becoming weaker. "You must put my secret... to rest."

"Does this have anything to do with Colonel Adams death?" Capshaw interrupted.

Suddenly, the table rocked violently, causing everyone but Madame Durand to jump away. Instead, the medium slumped against Mrs. Adams, who supported her as Monsieur Durand rushed over to help. Lieutenant Capshaw calmly stood and went around the room, turning up the lamps. The séance was over.

"Are you trying to tell me that my *father* has come back from the dead to warn me of danger?" Concordia demanded.

"Your father's *spirit*," Madame corrected.

Concordia tried not to roll her eyes.

They were in the parlor with David, Sophia, and Mrs. Adams. Jacques Durand was busying himself with packing up the various incense trays and other spirit paraphernalia. Lieutenant Capshaw and the family attorney had gone to the study to open the safe.

"Why didn't my *husband's* spirit come to us? We weren't even *trying* to summon Miss Wells' father," Lydia Adams complained.

Madame put a soothing hand on Mrs. Adams' arm. "The spirits, sometimes they do not behave as we wish. Perhaps it is too soon, and your husband has not crossed to the other side? Do not worry. We can try another time."

"But why Concordia's father? And what did it mean?" Sophia asked.

The medium fixed her pale blue eyes upon Concordia. "I worry for you, *mademoiselle*. The urgency of that troubled spirit, I felt it. You are in danger."

Concordia suppressed a shiver, but spoke firmly. "I'm sorry, Madame, but I do not believe in spirits. Besides, it didn't sound at all like my father." Her father had been a sensible man in his lifetime; he certainly wouldn't have participated in such mumbo-jumbo, even in the afterlife.

Madame shrugged her elegant shoulders. She was obviously accustomed to skepticism.

Still, Concordia was more disturbed than she appeared. It was the second time this week that the subject of Egypt had been associated with her father; first, when Miss Phillips asserted that he was a famed Egyptologist in his early years, and now the other-worldly voice of Madame in a trance, claiming to be her father, asking her to atone for his "sin"—or was she being asked to find something that hadn't "stayed buried" in Egypt? Even if Concordia was so inclined (which she most certainly was not), how was she supposed to do that? It was all a confused muddle.

Lieutenant Capshaw and Mr. Kaufmann walked in, just as the Durands were preparing to leave.

Kaufmann gave a little bow to Madame Durand. "Thank you for allowing me to participate. It was... fascinating."

Turning to Lydia Adams, he said, "I have made a cursory inventory of the papers and other materials in the colonel's safe. With your permission, I'll take them back to my office to go over them more thoroughly tomorrow."

"Of course," Mrs. Adams answered.

"Pay particular attention to any receipts the colonel may have kept," Capshaw instructed the lawyer. "We need to establish if those two missing artifacts were sold before his death, or were taken by his killer."

Kaufmann inclined his head in acknowledgment. "Naturally, lieutenant. I will look over the whole quite carefully, I assure you. In my examination so far, I have not run across any such receipts. But I did find something rather unusual." He pulled a small package from his pocket and, much to Concordia's surprise, handed it to her. "It's addressed to you."

"Me?" Concordia repeated blankly. She looked down at the writing, familiar though faded: "*For my dear Concordia. To be given to her upon the death of Colonel Adams.*" It appeared to be a small trinket box, wrapped in layers of paper, affixed with intact wax seals. The hand was unmistakable. Her father's writing.

The group looked on with interest as Concordia broke the seals and unwrapped the box. She pulled out the object.

It was a bracelet, clasp-style, with decorative colored beads threaded along rigid wire strands. From what Concordia had already seen of the college's Antiquities exhibit, she knew it was very old. And Egyptian.

"It is an omen," Madame Durand intoned. Concordia wanted to smack the woman.

Finally, the house was quiet and bedded down for the night. All of the séance guests had left, including David Bradley, who was staying with his family in town, and who promised to return the next day to keep Amelia company.

After Concordia prepared for bed, she paced restlessly around the room. She felt not at all sleepy. The package from her father was foremost in her mind. What did the bracelet mean? What lay in Randolph Wells' past that she didn't know? Was she really in danger, or was this just a melodramatic trick? But to what end? And why was this all coming back *now*?

Then there were the questions about Colonel Adams' death, and what Sophia knew. Concordia was convinced her friend was hiding something. Could Sophia be responsible for her own father's death? The relationship between father and daughter had always been tumultuous, but Concordia had difficulty believing Sophia capable of such an act.

Finally, she came to a couple of decisions. When she returned to the college tomorrow, she would ask Dorothy Phillips for more information about her father's Egyptology background. The history professor had been the first to mention the connection; perhaps she could solve the puzzle. Concordia also wanted to know the outcome of Miss Phillips' visit to Colonel Adams on the day of his death, and warn her that Capshaw would come calling. If he had not already done so. The lieutenant was remarkably efficient.

Until then, Concordia had one more thing to do. Picking up her candle, she quietly opened the door and peeked down the hallway. No one in sight. Good.

She slipped down the hall in her nightgown, barefoot so as to make no sound. She reached Sophia's door. Here was the hard part. What if Sophia was awake and saw her march right into her room?

Setting her candle aside, Concordia crouched down and put her eye to the gap under the door. No light. That was promising.

She would have to take a chance.

As quietly as she could, she turned the handle and eased the door open. Thank heaven the staff kept the hinges well-oiled.

Sophia was indeed asleep, and Concordia let out a sigh of relief as she closed the door behind her. She wanted a closer look at the blood-stained hem of Sophia's nightdress.

She finally found the garment, tossed in a crumpled heap in a corner of the room. Concordia shook it out and looked it over.

It was a challenge to see in the dim light of the single candle, but she found the telltale hem stain that Capshaw had pointed out. Upon close examination, it was more like a smear, really. Not wicking up from the edge of the fabric, as one would expect from a hem having been dragged through a puddle of the stuff.

Concordia found other dark smudges at one shoulder, an area hidden by the dressing gown, and therefore from Capshaw's sharp eye. But what did they mean? None of the stains seemed particularly large, but she was woefully ignorant of such things.

Concordia put the night dress back and cast her light around the room. It was orderly, as usual, and devoid of knick knacks, according to Sophia's simplicity of style. Only two framed photographs, of Amelia and the girls' dead mother, graced the top of the dressing table.

What now? Concordia went over to the bed. Sophia slept on her side, one arm flung over the edge. She was breathing deeply, evenly.

On impulse, Concordia crouched beside the bed, and felt around underneath. She didn't know quite why she was searching here or what she was searching for. She set the candle on the floor, careful to keep it away from the bedskirts. The last thing she needed was to set the bed ablaze. But this also meant that she couldn't really see what she was doing.

Drat. She couldn't reach far enough under. With a sigh, she lay flat on her stomach and reached in. Her hand brushed another heap of fabric, and she felt around to grab a better hold of it. It was wrapped around something hard and heavy. The material itself felt stiff with something dried upon it. Her heart lurched. She hoped it wasn't what she thought it was.

Concordia heard Sophia's breathing change, becoming lighter, more rapid. She'd better get out of here. But first she just needed to pull out the bundle a little bit more…

"What're yer doin' down there, miss?" came a whispered voice.

Smothering a yelp, Concordia twisted around and nearly knocked over the candle on the floor beside her. She looked up to see the boy, Eli, staring at her in confusion.

He was surprisingly strong for a child his age, and helped her to her feet.

"Yer hair's a-fire," he said.

"Oh!" Concordia swatted at the smoldering tip of her braid. She thought she'd smelled something odd. She looked over at Sophia, still sleeping, strangely undisturbed by the ruckus.

"I heard the maid say Miss Sophia took somethin' to help her sleep," Eli murmured.

So that explained it. All the same, Concordia picked up her candle. Fortunately, she hadn't set fire to anything *else*. She steered Eli out of the room before continuing the conversation.

"You gave me quite a fright, young man," she scolded. "What were you doing in Miss Sophia's room?"

The boy cocked his head at her as if to ask what *she* had been doing in Sophia's room, but seemed to think better of it.

"I couldn' sleep, miss. I was worried the murderer 'ud come back to get the rest of us. I got up fer a cup of milk and saw Miss Sophia's light on. I thought mebbe she'd want some, too. But it was you."

"Ah, yes, I see," Concordia said. "I was checking on her, too, and then I dropped something that rolled under the bed and bent down to retrieve it." She felt guilty about lying to the child.

"Uh huh." Eli looked doubtful.

"You don't have to worry about the intruder coming back. I'm sure he's as far from here as he can get. I'm going back to bed, and you should, too," Concordia said, her hand on the door.

"Yes, miss. G'Night."

As Concordia got into bed, she wondered what Eli had really been up to. Most likely, he was wondering the same thing about her.

Chapter 10

The cat will mew, and the dog will have his day.

V.i

Week 3, Instructor Calendar
September 1896

Concordia welcomed the return to her normal routine of classes, chapel, clubs, and cottage living. The girls new to the school were starting to settle in, finding their own place in the multi-threaded tapestry of college life. Everyone was getting ready for the Founder's Day celebration tomorrow. In addition to the usual recitation of this year's winning student poem, the weaving of the flower chain, and a reception, there would be a dedication ceremony to officially open the newly-remodeled student dining hall.

In her first free period, she decided to find Miss Phillips. She pocketed the bracelet her father had left her and headed for the college's exhibit room, where the history professor spent most of her time these days.

Instead of Miss Phillips, however, she found a stooped old lady who was all too familiar. Concordia stopped dead in her tracks.

"Miss Banning? Whatever are *you* doing here?" she exclaimed. Didn't that woman *ever* retire?

The lady turned around in her seat beside the Egyptian artifacts table. It was Miss Banning, all right. Her form and startling manner of dress were unmistakable. The long-time professor of history was wearing her customary layers of shawls and petticoats, making it impossible to determine her figure, stout or thin; she looked as if she had cleared the ladies' dry goods table at Sage Allen and wore the entirety of it upon her back.

"I was an instructor here when *you* were playing with dolls, my good miss," Margaret Banning snapped. She adjusted her large bottle-glass spectacles as she looked Concordia up and down in a frank, if rude, appraisal. "Hmph. You're more freckled than ever, if that is possible. You should wear a bonnet in the summer, young lady."

Concordia bit off a retort about preferring freckles to the antiquated Swiss muslin breakfast caps that Miss Banning habitually wore—one of which was currently sitting askew on the old lady's head. "Where is Miss Phillips?"

Miss Banning waved her into an adjoining chair before answering. "Our *dear* lady principal decided to relieve her of her curator duties, and called upon me to take over."

"What! Why?" Concordia asked. She had only been away from campus for two days; what prompted such an abrupt decision?

"With the murder of the colonel, that nosy policeman came around asking questions. Lieutenant—what's his name? Capuchin? Capybara? ...well, you know who I mean: the one from last year. Well, the Ogre got wind of it, so Miss Phillips had no choice but to report the missing amulet. That Grant woman's a mean old toad, if you ask me. *'He that hisses in malice or sport, is an oppressor and a robber.'* Samuel Johnson."

Concordia couldn't agree more, and it was obvious that Miss Banning found the situation upsetting, too. After all, the woman had used only one quotation so far, well below her average in a conversation. She'd also picked up on the *Ogre* nickname quickly. Concordia wondered why Miss Banning would do the lady principal a favor by assuming Miss Phillips' duties.

"Why did you return? Aren't you already retired?" Concordia asked. Miss Banning seemed to dither as to whether she was really retired or not.

Miss Banning ignored her and continued with her tirade against Miss Grant, thumping her cane on the floor emphatically.

"We don't seem to have good luck with lady principals lately, do we? That Hamilton woman last year had a shady past and left after one year. And no wonder, with all the trouble we had during *her* tenure. *This* one worries about the reputation of the college, but can't see past her own nose and use some common sense. Punishes students and faculty without getting to the bottom of matters, getting everyone in a uproar."

Concordia was certainly no fan of Miss Grant, but she felt obligated to stem the tirade. "The lady principal is new, and has had many pranks to deal with. The loss of a rare artifact has no doubt been stressful."

"The amulet was obviously stolen, not lost," Miss Banning retorted. "How is that Miss Phillips' fault? *Incompetence*, Miss Grant called it. Bosh. *'How difficult it is to save the bark of reputation from the rocks of ignorance.'* Petrarch. The woman should be calling the police, not me. What am I supposed to do, I ask you: *run* after the next thief who steals one of these musty old bits of clay?"

Concordia stifled a snort over the mental image of Miss Banning hobbling after a robber, trailing shawls and wraps in her wake.

"Where's Miss Phillips now?"

"*Hmph.* Moping in her office, most likely."

Concordia left Miss Banning to her cataloging.

Miss Phillips' office looked more like a crammed closet, created from an awkward corner of the third floor of Founder's Hall. There was room for a tiny desk, two chairs, and an even tinier window. Sagging shelves lined the walls, crammed willy-nilly with books, papers, pottery, and other objects Concordia couldn't identify, but took to be artifacts of some sort. Unpacked boxes spilling over with more items had been stacked in a corner.

"Welcome to Miss Grant's version of the woodshed," Dorothy Phillips said in mock cheerfulness. Her face, tanned and crinkled at the corners of her eyes, was paler today. The usual twinkle was gone.

Concordia wedged herself into the second chair, knees against the desk. She hoped she could extricate herself later with some modicum of grace.

"Miss Banning told me what happened," Concordia said, "although not all of it. I'm sorry. So Colonel Adams could not help you, when you talked with him about the amulet?"

"I didn't get the chance to speak with him," Miss Phillips said. "He was too busy to see me, so I left my card. But of course, the policeman came to question me because of my visit. Then I knew I had no choice but to tell everything to the lady principal." She made a face. "It wasn't a pleasant scene. Now that I'm no longer curator, I had to move out of that office—" she looked around ruefully—"to here."

"Miss Banning said that Miss Grant hasn't called the police about the loss. Is that true?" Concordia asked.

"Yes, indeed. She wants to leave the police out of it. She has even convinced President Langdon to go along with the idea. I know she's concerned for the reputation of the college, but isn't that taking discretion a bit far? Besides, it's now common knowledge that the amulet is missing. There are no secrets on a college campus." Miss Phillips made a face.

Concordia nodded. How true that was. The rumor mill turned briskly at Hartford Women's College and was a favorite activity of both students *and* staff.

"I heard that Madame Durand made a pronouncement about it at her Spirit Club meeting yesterday," Miss Phillips added. "She called the amulet 'cursed.' It certainly has been for me."

"Well, if it *is* cursed, we're better off without it," Concordia said. "Still, it's unfortunate you couldn't speak with the colonel before his death. Do you really think he took it back?"

Dorothy Phillips shrugged. "It's the only explanation that makes sense. But if the colonel *did* take it back, it isn't there anymore. I described it to the policeman, and he hasn't seen it. I understand they made a thorough inventory."

"I was at the Colonel's house, and I didn't see it there, either." Concordia proceeded to explain that her friend Sophia was the colonel's daughter and she had stayed there to lend her support. "Perhaps the amulet was stolen by the intruder who killed him."

Miss Phillips sat back dejectedly. "If that's the case, then we have little chance of seeing it again. Oh, why didn't Colonel Adams simply come to me and ask for it back? Then we wouldn't have the embarrassment of the amulet being featured in the newspaper, and now no artifact in our possession! We were hoping for future loans from other collections, but now…" she trailed off.

"When things settle down in the Adams' house, I'll ask Sophia to look for it," Concordia said. "If Colonel Adams took it, perhaps he hid it somewhere."

Miss Phillips brightened. "Oh, would you?"

"Of course. But there's another reason I stopped by," Concordia added. "I was hoping you could tell me more about my father's studies in Egyptology. …And this." Concordia pulled out the bracelet left for her in Colonel Adams' safe.

The history professor reached for it. She laid it gently upon the table and plucked out a magnifying glass. Her eyes narrowed along their etched folds, as if she were squinting at something far away. "Interesting," she murmured, turning it over with deft fingers.

"Is it valuable?" Concordia asked.

"Probably not," Miss Phillips said, "especially since a few of the beads have symbols on them that aren't Egyptian, even though the rest of it unquestionably is. Those beads are crudely etched, too, in comparison with the other carved designs."

"Not Egyptian?" Concordia asked, confused.

Dorothy Phillips shook her head. "It was probably hard for you to tell without a magnifying glass, but here's a bead—it is definitely a "W" on a background of loops. It was undoubtedly added to the bracelet later."

She passed bracelet and glass. "Here, take a look. See how the metal has been bent to slip them on, and the tarnish marks are darker underneath?" She looked at Concordia with open curiosity. "Was this from your father's collection?"

"Yes," Concordia admitted, "but it only just came into my possession." She told Miss Phillips about the opening of the colonel's safe, and the discovery of her father's package and letter. She also related the story of the strange séance that preceded her receiving the package.

Miss Phillips frowned as she listened. "Madame Durand again. I remember that unnerving demonstration, where she announced I had lost something. That was only a day or so after the amulet went missing. Could she have anything to do with its disappearance?"

"I don't see how; she and her husband weren't even in attendance at the opening that day."

"'*It should have stayed buried in the sands of Egypt, but it is here, now*,'" Miss Phillips quoted. "Could that mean the amulet?"

Concordia felt a prickle along her neck. "I don't know."

They were both quiet for a moment.

"What can you tell me about my father's work in Egyptology?" Concordia asked.

Miss Phillips went over to a shelf and pulled out a sheaf of papers. She leafed through the stack as she talked.

"Randolph Wells was a prominent scholar in the field of Egyptology, particularly the subjects of language and ciphers. A brilliant man. Even though he only worked in the field for roughly fifteen years, his interpretations of stelae—those are boundary markers," she added, noting Concordia's puzzled expression, "along with other engravings, helped unlock information critical to several major tomb expeditions. Including—ah, well, they wouldn't mean anything to you, of course, but rest assured your father was highly respected in his field."

She thrust a bundle at Concordia. "Here is perhaps his most brilliant work, 'The Immortal Language of Ancient Pharaohs'. You can borrow my copy. Dozens of scholars, including me, have built upon what he accomplished."

Concordia took the article Miss Phillips had given her and headed for her own office, located in the opposite wing of Founder's Hall. It was a good deal more spacious than the one Miss Phillips occupied, with a sunny window and plentiful shelf space. Which was filling up rapidly, she noted, as she let herself in and propped the door open for more air. She would have to do something about that soon.

The only unpleasant aspect of her office was its proximity to Lady Principal Grant's. Lately, Miss Grant had taken to sticking her nose in Concordia's office and either giving her a task, or asking her about a task she'd already been given, such as the senior play. Concordia wouldn't have an answer for her on this occasion; there had been no time since she'd returned to see Professor Harrison and determine their progress.

Concordia didn't understand why the lady principal kept asking *her* about the play; after all, Mr. Harrison was in charge of it (a *mathematician*—she still couldn't get over that), and his office was within sight of hers, down the same hall. Olivia Grant, it seemed, took special delight in vexing *her.*

As Concordia waited for students, she pulled out her father's article. *Let's see if a literature teacher can make heads or tails of ancient Egyptian scholarship.*

She was already feeling a bit lost by the third page, but she knew right away it was her father's composition. The tone and idioms sounded just like him, during those times when he would expound upon a point of history or an area of philosophical contention. She set down the pamphlet as childhood memories drifted into her consciousness: the smell of pipe tobacco on his jacket, the timbre of his voice, the lopsided grin when he had a new puzzle or cipher for her to work out. Although it had been eleven years since his death, she still missed him, and would like to think he would have been proud of what she had accomplished, in earning a college degree and becoming a professor.

A hesitant tapping interrupted her thoughts. She straightened. "Enter!" she called.

But instead of the student she was expecting, it was Eli.

"What's wrong? What are you doing here?" Concordia asked anxiously.

"Miss Sophia told me to come, miss," he answered, shifting from one foot to the other.

The child looked tidier today. His neck and hands were washed, his clothes were clean, and his hair had been slicked down neatly on his head, although a couple of cowlicks insisted upon springing up. Something moved in his arms, and Concordia realized it was... a cat.

Concordia did not exactly *detest* cats, but she wasn't fond of them either. And this one was a particularly bedraggled specimen of his tribe. His hair was longish in some places and shortish in others; his coat was a patchwork of so many colors that it was impossible to tell what the base color would be; an ear looked as if a chunk had been taken out in a fight, and one eye was swollen shut, probably from a more recent fight. The other eye was yellow, and looked at her calmly.

"*That* goes out," Concordia announced, walking to the door. She hastily changed her mind when she stuck her head out into the hallway and saw Miss Grant chugging toward her door. The last thing Concordia wanted was to explain the boy's presence—or the cat's, for that matter—to the lady principal.

"Quick! Over there, and *be quiet!*" Concordia hissed over her shoulder. Quick as a flash, the boy melted into the shadows of the room, still holding the animal. Concordia stepped out into the hallway to intercept the lady principal before she came in.

"Miss Grant, hello!" Concordia said, realizing too late that she sounded suspiciously cheery, a response the lady principal did not usually generate in others.

Miss Grant's eyes narrowed. "Did you wish to see me?" she answered icily.

Concordia said the first thing that popped into her head. "I was wondering if you have seen Mr. Harrison. I wanted to ask him a casting question."

The lady principal's lip curled as she gestured to the open door of Mr. Harrison's office in the far corner of the corridor. "Have you tried *knocking* upon his door, Miss Wells? Perhaps you should try exercising your powers of observation, young lady." She turned away, plodding with her characteristically heavy step down the hall to her own office.

Drat. The woman must think she was demented. Concordia had always been horrible at lying, and was even worse at thinking up one on the spot.

Miss Grant threw her one last look of derision before stepping into her office and closing the door.

Detestable woman. With a sigh of relief, Concordia slipped back into her office and closed the door. Eli was crouched in a corner, the cat dozing in his arms.

Concordia waved him into a chair as she sat down in her own. "What's going on?"

At the sound of her voice, the cat stirred and jumped out of Eli's lap.

"Miss Sophia sent me to talk to you, miss, 'bout staying here fer a while an' working as a messenger boy, or something like. She woulda come wi' me, but she's been ill with fever."

Concordia didn't know what to address first—Sophia being ill, or saddling her with Eli. She decided on the former. "It's not serious, I hope? Did she send for me?"

"Oh, no, miss," Eli said quickly, "she's better now, just a bit too poorly fer travel. She couldn' go to the colonel's funeral— not that anyone seemed to want to—and that policeman couldn' talk to her, either."

Well, that was a blessing at least, Concordia thought. But she knew Lieutenant Capshaw wouldn't be thwarted for long.

"What about Miss Amelia? Is she better?"

Eli shook his head. "I ain't seen her, but I hear them say she still don't talk to anybody. It's a sorr-ful house, for sure. That's why Miss Sophia sent me here."

"So we need to find you a place to stay," Concordia said.

Eli nodded eagerly. "Just fer a little while, Miss Sophia says. An' I'm real quick, an' remember long messages, an' I don't mind where I sleep." His eyes were pleading, and his lip trembled, just a little.

The cat chose this moment to twine itself around Concordia's skirts, kneading the folds with its paws and purring loudly. *Ugh. It probably has fleas.* Concordia twitched her skirts out of the way and brushed at them.

Eli came over and scooped up the cat. "He likes you, miss."

"Yes, well, we won't be seeing much of each other," Concordia said. She went to the door and looked out cautiously. The coast was clear. "All right, let's go."

The best course, Concordia decided, was to bring him back to Willow Cottage for the time being, and put him in Ruby's care. The cottage matron would undoubtedly fuss and complain about it, but Concordia knew the woman really had a heart of gold. Ruby could at least feed the boy while Concordia went to talk to Clyde, the gatekeeper, and make arrangements for Eli. And the cat.

Ruby Hitchcock was none too pleased to see the grubby messenger boy again. She stood, hands on ample hips, looking him over.

"Well, at least you're cleaner today, young man. But you missed a spot behind that ear—" she proceeded to give it a gentle tug "—and we expect the gentlemen around here to keep the'selves neat."

She looked down and shook her head at the mangy cat, currently winding itself around her ankles and purring with great energy. "I know yer ways, puss. Don't think I'm going to let you stay. I run a clean cottage." The cat, as if understanding, proceeded to switch allegiances to Concordia, scooting under her skirts as she tried to step away.

"Ugh. By all means let's put the cat out, but can you give Eli something to eat while I talk to Clyde?" Concordia asked.

Ruby looked Eli over, her expression softening. "I expect you *are* hungry. Boys your age always are. Put the animal out the back door and go wash your hands. I'll make you something."

Concordia hurried over to Clyde's gatehouse post, the disreputable cat trailing after her.

Chapter 11

Something is rotten in the state of Denmark.

I.iv

Week 4, Instructor Calendar
September/October 1896

Founder's Day started out in the full glory of a warm, sunny day in late September. First, there was the longer-than-usual chapel service, during which the school anthem "Forward, Woman, to Thy Calling" was sung. Then this year's winning student poem was read aloud by President Langdon.

After chapel and a special Founder's Day breakfast feast, the student body gathered at the quadrangle to weave the customary chrysanthemum chain. It would be presented to the freshman class as a token of welcome and official acceptance, a mark of respect after the first grueling weeks of pranks and other mischief that had been played upon the new girls. This year, the chain would then adorn the balusters of the dining hall's new upper balcony, where the dedication was taking place.

The faculty attended all of the Founder's Day ceremonies, naturally, but were not an active part of making the chain, so Concordia found herself in a spectator role at the moment. She watched the girls cavorting around each other, their white dresses gleaming in the sunshine, weaving the stems and twine. She breathed in the cool air, sharp with the scent of bruised chrysanthemum blossoms. It had come to symbolize fall in her mind, as much as the sweep of burnt oranges, yellows and reds in the wooded distance.

She felt a calm settle over her. Eli had been taken care of; Clyde had fixed up an extra bunk for him in the gatehouse cottage, and had even found some serviceable clothing for him. He'd drawn the line, however, at taking in the beast, who had no name other than Cat, it seemed. Concordia had no choice but to bring the animal back to Willow Cottage. Ruby was less than enthused by the idea—until last evening, when the Cat came out of the kitchen with a dead mouse in its mouth. It promptly placed the prize at Concordia's feet.

Ruby chuckled as she brought out the dustpan and Concordia grimaced. "Maybe he's worth keeping, after all. We won't have no more mice problem, at this rate. Looks like you're a favorite of his."

Concordia could do without that sort of devotion.

Her thoughts turned to Sophia, and how she was dealing with her distraught little sister and their father's death. She hadn't heard from her friend in nearly a week, but with her being ill, that was understandable. After the building dedication, when Concordia had some free time, she would send a letter. She hoped Amelia's condition was improving. She wondered if David was still there. The little girl was obviously devoted to him, and perhaps he could help the child get over her condition.

A smile tugged at the corners of her mouth at the thought of David Bradley. It had been good to see him again, even if their first meeting after so long had been a bit awkward. If he hadn't returned to Boston yet, perhaps she should talk with him about what she'd found under Sophia's bed. But then, she'd have to admit to snooping in her friend's room. Maybe not just yet. Lieutenant Capshaw was bound to have made progress by this point, without her interference.

"Miss Wells," a voice murmured behind her. Startled, she turned to see Lieutenant Capshaw at her elbow, almost as if her thoughts had conjured him. She shook her head. Wonderful. Now she was thinking like one of those *spiritualists*.

"I need to speak with you, miss, if I may," Capshaw said in a low voice.

Several faculty members, recognizing the lieutenant from his recent visit, looked over at them with undisguised curiosity.

Concordia led the policeman over to the arbor at the near end of the common area. "You've made progress?"

"That depends on what you'd call progress. We've made an arrest, but—"

"Oh, what a relief! But you don't look happy about it," Concordia added, noting his troubled expression. "Is something wrong?"

Capshaw shifted from one foot to another and hesitated. "That's why I came to see you, Miss Wells. It's your friend, Sophia. I had no choice but to arrest her for the murder of her father. She has confessed, you see."

Concordia's neck tingled and her head felt light as she tried to absorb this news.

Capshaw gently eased her onto the arbor bench and waited for her to collect herself, glancing down at her with his customary gloomy expression.

Her mind was a flurry of conflicting thoughts and emotions. The outrageousness of Sophia as a cold-blooded killer warred with the very doubts that had prompted Concordia to search her friend's room in the middle of the night.

No. A world where Sophia was a murderer would never make sense to her.

Concordia drew a shuddering breath and finally looked up at Capshaw. "You know there has to be some mistake, lieutenant. Sophia could not have murdered her father."

Capshaw shook his head. "She confessed after we found the colonel's gun hidden in her room. There was also evidence of her having destroyed something in her bedroom fireplace, probably a garment, but she won't tell us about that. Even if her confession is a lie—although why she would do so makes no sense—she *is* involved in some way."

Concordia knew the policeman was right about that part. She'd noticed it at the time. Sophia was holding back something. Concordia remembered the fabric she'd felt under Sophia's bed, stiff with a dried substance on it. She'd never had the chance to look at it before Eli had interrupted her, but what else could it be but blood? She felt a little sick.

"What happens now? Can I see her?"

"She's on her way to the station. There will be paperwork, which may take a little time, but I can take you over there whenever you are ready."

Concordia looked at the gathering, which was already moving to the dining hall for the building dedication. The lady principal was among them, and caught Concordia's eye, frowning at the sight of one of her teachers sitting in the arbor with a policeman.

She sighed. She knew there was no getting out of attending the dedication ceremony. She turned to Capshaw.

"Have you ever been to a building dedication, lieutenant? No? Well, here's your chance. It should only take thirty minutes. Then we can go."

The new wing, with its spacious upper balcony that wrapped around one corner, was swathed with the freshly-made chrysanthemum chain, along with bows and more flowers. The effect was quite festive. Chairs were arranged for the faculty to sit out upon the balcony, with the students below. A wide, white ribbon had been tied to opposite balustrades for the official cutting ceremony.

As the faculty found the seats tagged with their names, Concordia heard the strident voice of Miss Grant.

"This chair placement is unacceptable. Why have I been put in a cramped corner? I don't want to be hanging over the railing, young man," Lady Principal Grant said, chiding the custodian's helper who was still arranging chairs. The man blushed and made a futile attempt to move the seats again.

Concordia could see Miss Grant's point; with that lady's bulk, such a position would be tight in the extreme.

She touched the man's sleeve. "I'd be happy to switch seats with Miss Grant," she offered, pointing to her own chair at the end of the middle section, which was more congenially placed for a woman of the lady principal's size.

The young man looked relieved and directed Miss Grant to the other chair. Concordia stepped around other teachers to reach her seat. They really were wedged in here, she thought: the railing was just at her shoulder. The iron work looked to have a fresh coat of paint on it, and there were faint marks of adhesive—from a "Wet Paint" sign, perhaps?—still on the nearby surface. She leaned away as best she could. If another sign had been stolen, she certainly wasn't going to be the butt of the joke.

Looking down at the crowd, she saw a cluster of girls centered around a petite woman with black hair. Concordia craned her neck for a better look. It was Madame Durand, talking animatedly with the group of students. The woman seemed to be more and more involved in the doings of the college with each day. Standing nearby was Lieutenant Capshaw, patiently waiting to escort Concordia to the police station to talk to Sophia.

Sophia. Why? Why confess to your father's murder?

As she dabbed at her eyes with her kerchief and tried to regain her composure, she glimpsed a bundle of fur, scurrying along the ground below and being chased by a boy. *Oh, no.* She couldn't see where they went, but she had a sinking feeling they were now in the building. Please heaven they wouldn't come up *here.*

Concordia, Ruby, and Clyde were trying to keep Eli's residence at the college as little noticed as possible. To the rest of the faculty and administration, he was just a messenger lad. No one else knew he was actually staying at the school. She suspected the lady principal would strongly disapprove if she knew.

President Langdon stood, and was handed the scissors by the dean. Let's hope he doesn't give one of his long, meandering speeches, Concordia thought, trying to adjust herself more comfortably in the hard chair. Just cut the ribbon, and let's go.

As the president spoke, Concordia was aware of movement. Glancing down, she saw the Cat, slinking under her seat. *Uh-oh.* Wherever the Cat was, Eli was sure to follow.

Sure enough, Concordia turned and saw Eli squeezing behind the back row, trying to be as unobtrusive as possible. So far, only those seated in the very back were paying him any attention. The rest of the faculty focused on President Langdon, who kept waving the scissors tantalizingly near the ribbon, and then stopping and saying something more.

Eli made it to her chair, whispered a quick "Excuse me, miss," and, with his back to the railing, reached under to extricate the animal.

Then it happened.

With a great *creak* and a sickening scrape of metal, the railing gave way, pitching Eli nearly into oblivion, save for Concordia's quick grab of his suspenders. She heard a yowl from the Cat, as Eli's hands were around its middle when he lost his balance. She felt the buttons start to give way and dove out of her chair for a better grip on the boy.

The crowd gasped, and—as crowds usually do—ineffectually gave advice from below, or, in the case of the faculty immediately surrounding Concordia, extended hands to pull at whatever they could. To Concordia's dismay, this included her skirts, her *hair*, and her ankles. *She* wasn't the one in danger of going over the side, Eli was, but she was blocking anyone else's reach, so people were just grabbing at what was at hand.

"Let... go... of the... Cat," Concordia hissed between clenched teeth, for Eli still instinctively clutched the animal, rather than her arm. Her shoulders ached, and she didn't know how long she could hang onto him.

But Eli was paralyzed in fear, whimpering and holding the cat even more tightly. From her vantage point, Concordia saw the people below looking up anxiously, except for Madame Durand, who appeared to be mumbling to herself, her expression trance-like. She kept mouthing one word over and over. Concordia finally caught what it was: *doom... doom...*

A tall shadow loomed over them, as Lieutenant Capshaw shouldered people out of the way, reached over her, and with his long, strong arms, hauled them both to their feet in one fluid motion. The Cat, released at last, ran for its life. The one silver lining, Concordia thought later, was the fact that the beast stayed out of her way for two entire days afterward.

The balcony was cleared and everyone was sent back to their residences. Concordia walked to the gatekeeper's cottage with a very shaky Eli so that the boy could recover from his experience.

And clean up, too. As Concordia had suspected, the railing paint had still been wet, and Eli's clothing had black smudges in a number of places. Concordia's shirtwaist hadn't come away unscathed, either, so she hurried back to change.

Once she was presentable, she went back to the dining hall to find Capshaw. He was still at the gap in the balcony railing, along with President Langdon, examining the posts.

"What did you find?" Concordia asked, crouching down for a closer look. The metal post had twisted as it bent, and was nearly coming out of the crumbling concrete around it.

Langdon frowned. "Looks like shoddy workmanship. Perhaps the cement for these posts wasn't mixed correctly, or not allowed to harden properly. What do you think, Lieutenant?"

Capshaw sighed. "A re-inspection of the entire structure would be a wise precaution, Mr. Langdon, but I can't say for certain that there wasn't tampering here." He pointed to the base of the iron post, where the metal was irregular along a small seam. "This looks to be cut, then poorly soldered, which would create a stress point. The concrete footings may not be to blame."

"So someone deliberately cut the railing? But why?" Concordia asked. Her stomach clenched. Had someone targeted the lady principal, the chair's intended occupant? They had enough trouble on campus lately, without adding fuel to that fire.

Capshaw stood and dusted off his trousers. "It's difficult to say for sure. The workers might have made an error when they were constructing the railing, and started to cut in the wrong place. Then, rather than waste a good piece of iron, they soldered the cut. It doesn't go clean through, so perhaps they thought it would hold. It's just a theory, of course." He turned to President Langdon. "We'll need the contact information for the contractor you used, so we can make inquiries. Meanwhile, keep everyone away from the area." He frowned at Concordia. "Especially young boys and their cats."

Chapter 12

One woe doth tread upon another's heel,
So fast they follow.

IV.vii

Week 4, Instructor Calendar

"Notebooks out," Concordia said, with a gesture to the blackboard. "You have twenty minutes to write on today's theme." She swiveled the board to tilt it more towards the light, amid the sighs of girls who struggled to undo buckles on satchel flaps and twitch skirts out of the way of each other's feet. It was a rainy, gloomy day, and the turned-up lamps did little to brighten the far corners. The weather matched the overall mood of the campus. The happiness of Founder's Day seemed a distant memory.

Concordia suppressed a sigh herself. She didn't like to begin the period with a writing exercise. Although this was only her second year at Hartford Women's College and her fourth year of teaching overall, she knew that writing, when performed as a chore rather than as a result of intellectual engagement, lent itself to poor results. She preferred to first involve the class in a lively exchange of questions and ideas before turning to a writing assignment. One must prime the pump before something potable comes out.

But this assignment was intended to penalize, not stimulate, and Concordia had no say in the matter. Lady Principal Grant had instructed that all rhetoric teachers issue this assignment to their classes as punishment for the students' role in the events of the day before. Hence, the following writing topic:

"Reflect upon why practical jokes are a danger to one's fellows and not to be tolerated in the future."

While it was understandable that Miss Grant would be just as distressed as everyone else by the incident, to lay blame for yesterday's near-disaster at the door of the students' rampant sign-stealing was taking it a bit too far. In Miss Grant's twisted form of logic, she reasoned that no one would have leaned against the railing to begin with if the sign had still been there. It was futile to point out that the uneducated Eli wouldn't have been able to read the sign in the first place. Besides, the less attention paid to the boy, the better.

President Langdon's energies were directed more practically, toward getting the railing re-installed, this time employing different workers and overseeing the job himself.

Concordia didn't know if Lieutenant Capshaw had yet determined if shoddy workmanship was to blame, but given the tension among the administrators, she guessed he had not.

She shuddered. Her shoulders and back still ached from the abrupt pull of muscles, as she'd clung to the boy in an awkward, crouched contortion.

A stirring of students in their seats called Concordia's attention back to the task at hand. "If you are finished, pass up your papers, and turn to the 'Wife of Bath's Tale' on page forty-one. Read quietly while the rest of the students finish."

She hoped she could keep her class on topic today. The students were distractible enough in the normal routine of things.

Normal? We have an exhibit theft and a near-disastrous railing collapse. We also have a Lady Principal on the warpath, and an exotic séance medium making grand prognostications of doom, just to make it more interesting. What is normal?

Concordia knew her own attention was flagging, too. Between her worry about Sophia's murder confession, the mystery of Papa's connection to Egypt and why he'd kept it from her all those years, and keeping Eli and his abominable Cat out of further trouble, she was ready to hide under the bedcovers.

Somehow she got through the Chaucer class, but it was with relief that Concordia finally dismissed them. After going back to the cottage, changing out of her wrinkled shirtwaist into a fresh one and re-pinning straggling locks of hair, she hurried to the gate to meet Lieutenant Capshaw. The events of yesterday had kept the lieutenant on campus beyond prison visiting hours, so he had arranged to take her today to see Sophia.

Capshaw was not waiting alone at the gate, however. Concordia's hands went cold when she saw the grim-lipped lady principal standing with him. This could not be a good sign.

Miss Grant's small, dark eyes narrowed into the pudgy creases of her face as Concordia approached. "Where do you think you're going, Miss Wells?" she said coldly.

Concordia looked over to Capshaw, who stepped hesitantly toward the women. "I have explained our errand to Miss Grant, but there appears to be a problem."

"There certainly is, Mr. Policeman," Miss Grant snapped. "I'm restricting this young lady to the confines of the college grounds until further notice."

"Why?" Concordia asked warily.

"You are getting too big for your britches, Miss Wells. Taking it upon yourself to arrange for that little street arab, that harum-scarum boy who destroyed the balcony, a place to *live* here on campus? Without my permission, or my knowledge? You have exceeded your authority, and I cannot permit that to go unanswered."

"But—"

Capshaw stepped into the fray. "Miss Grant, of course you must deal with your staff as you see fit. However, Miss Wells is needed at the station. She has yet to dictate her statement about the balcony incident and sign it."

"I thought that was the result of shoddy workmanship, and not criminal sabotage," the lady principal said suspiciously.

"I haven't yet concluded my investigation. Even if it is worker error, the incident must still go on record, in case of future litigation," Capshaw said.

"What about seeing Miss Adams? Was that not your original purpose?" Miss Grant demanded.

"That is only part of our errand, but the paperwork is essential," Capshaw said.

Miss Grant looked at Capshaw for a long moment, then said grudgingly, "Very well. I will make an exception, *this time*. But do not be long," she added, wagging a finger under Concordia's nose. "I will be keeping my eye on you."

Concordia suppressed a shudder.

As they walked through the gate, Concordia's knees wobbled, and Capshaw put a steadying hand under her elbow.

"Thank you for helping out back there," Concordia said.

Capshaw gave her his usual melancholy look. "I don't envy your return. I'd rather meet an angry drunk in a dark alley than tangle with that... lady."

"At least now I'll be able to talk with Sophia," Concordia said.

"I didn't have the chance to say so before, miss," Capshaw said, "but Miss Adams' fever returned last night. She's been moved to the prison infirmary, at least until she's well enough to return to the women's ward. The doctor has allowed you a brief visit."

Poor Sophia. It wasn't surprising that she'd suffered a relapse under such circumstances. Concordia would have to make this visit count; heaven only knew when she would have another chance, with Lady Principal Grant confining her to campus and keeping predatory watch over her movements.

The Kinsley Street Station was undergoing expansion, which made it impossible to enter by the front door. Capshaw took Concordia around to the Temple Street entrance instead. At least it was quieter back here, although no less dusty. The hallway was cluttered with desks and chairs from emptied rooms. Capshaw gave a nod to the desk sergeant on duty as they maneuvered around the furniture.

The prison infirmary was tucked into a quieter corridor of the building.

Capshaw knocked, and they waited.

"I'll have to be nearby, miss—prison rules—but I'll give you as much privacy as I can. I hope you can get the real story out of her. I sure haven't been able to."

A sturdy-looking matron with a large ring of keys at her waist opened the door to the ward, and Concordia hesitantly stepped through. She'd never been in a prison infirmary before. It didn't look as prison-like as she imagined. Except for bars on the windows and the stout lock on the door, which was turned behind them once they were in the room, it looked like any hospital ward. It had the same double-row of white beds, bedpans and instruments, and the unmistakable carbolic acid smell. Then she noticed one sleeping woman with shackles around an ankle, secured to a bolt on the floor. There was a fabric restraint across her torso and arms.

"That's Hattie," the matron said, observing Concordia's glance. "She's one of the regulars, in and out of here. It's been years now. She gets quite violent while the liquor is wearing off. But then she's fine after that, just as nice as can be. She'll serve her sentence, leave, and be back in a couple months."

The matron sounded so matter-of-fact about it. Concordia shuddered. She hated to think of Sophia being in this place.

Sophia was lying white and still in her bed, deep shadows visible under her light lashes and in the hollows of her cheeks, her frame more gaunt than Concordia remembered. She opened her eyes when Concordia sat on the side of her bed and patted her hand. Capshaw and the matron moved to a discreet distance, conducting a murmured conversation, looking over from time to time.

"Concordia, why are you here?" Sophia turned her head away. "I don't want you to see me like this." She sniffled into her pillow.

"Nonsense," Concordia said briskly, "we are friends, and I want to help. Where else would I be?"

Sophia struggled to sit up. Concordia propped some pillows behind her.

"There's nothing you can do. I'm to blame for this. It's my fault."

"Since I know that you didn't kill your father," Concordia said bluntly, "then you must be talking about something else. But confessing to something you didn't do isn't going to fix whatever you are feeling guilty about."

Concordia could see from the sharp look Sophia gave her that her comment had hit home.

But Sophia was known for her stubbornness. It was the quality which had enabled her to spurn all attempts to marry her off, and dare to leave behind her comfortable place in society to work for the poor of Hartford. Stubbornness gave her the perseverance to successfully campaign for funds to expand the settlement house, to start a free health clinic for poor women, to establish a nursery education program for the children of working mothers.

Concordia admired her friend, but saw the prideful, arrogant side of Sophia's stubbornness, too. Her way was the right way, and she had to carry on alone if others did not follow. She could be quick to judge and impatient with those of her former social circles, including her own family. In some ways, she was the Colonel's daughter, although Concordia was sure the thought would appall her.

"It is my responsibility," Sophia answered, "and I am taking care of it."

Concordia tried a different approach. "Very well. Can you at least tell me what happened, so I can understand why?"

Sophia leaned back wearily against the pillows. An aide came by with a pitcher of water and filled a glass for her. Sophia took a few sips before speaking.

"I've told the policeman all of this, but I suppose you deserve to hear it from me." Tears welled in her eyes, and her voice grew husky. "I'm sorry, Concordia. I know you can never forgive me."

"Just tell me what happened." Concordia looked over at the wall clock. "They will make me leave soon."

☙❧

"Well? What did she tell you?" Lieutenant Capshaw asked.

They were sitting in his office. Capshaw had just set down weak tea in front of her, served in a mug with a chipped handle. It was hot, and sweetened with a tooth-numbing amount of sugar. Surprisingly, it was just what she needed. She was chilled and dazed from the experience, but as she drank the tea, she felt her composure return.

"She's sticking with her story. I don't believe it, though. She's hiding something. Perhaps she's protecting someone?"

"We'll get to that later," Capshaw said hesitantly. "Repeat for me what she related to you. We can compare it to her original confession. Perhaps some inconsistencies will emerge."

"It was very straightforward. Sophia said that she got up late that night to get a book to help her sleep. Her father's study door was open, so she went in to talk with him about a family matter. She wouldn't tell me what it was. She said the discussion got heated, he lost his temper and came at her with a poker. She grabbed the gun from his desk, and shot him."

"What did she do then?" Capshaw asked.

"She said that, in her distraction, she must have had the gun in her hand when she ran up to her room and then set it down somewhere, but she can't remember. She'd heard of the robberies in the Charter Oak neighborhood, and so decided to make it look like an aborted burglary. She broke the glass of the French door, messed up the desk, and went back to her room to wait until the morning, when a servant would find the body."

"But her sister found the body instead, a short while later," Capshaw said.

Concordia nodded. "Sophia said she felt badly about Amelia having the shock of finding him, especially since the trauma has rendered her mute." She looked over at Capshaw. "There's no change in Amelia's state?"

"Not as of yesterday, when I was there last," Capshaw answered. "This has gone on for weeks now, beyond the time frame the doctor predicted."

Concordia sighed. Poor Amelia. First her father murdered, now her sister in prison, self-accused of the deed.

"Then what happened? Did Miss Adams say anything about the missing artifacts? If she took those to make it look like a robbery, why didn't we find them when we found the gun? And what about the safe? Did she try to open it?"

Concordia thought back to Sophia's account. "She didn't mention either the safe or the relics when she told me what happened. She merely said she broke the glass on the French doors of the study, disarranged the desk, and went back to her room to wait. But we still don't know if those items were even stolen; they might have been disposed of by the colonel beforehand."

"True," Capshaw acknowledged. "Did she mention the gun, or the evidence she destroyed in the fireplace?"

"Oh, yes, I forgot. She did say that she changed her nightgown because there was blood on it, and burned it later. And that she found the gun in her bedroom after the police came. By then it was too late to put it back, so she hid it until she could dispose of it. But of course, she became ill before she could do anything about that. You can't burn a gun."

Capshaw ran his hands through his bright red hair, making it stand on end. He gave the appearance of a Pomeranian with its hackles up. "I *know* she's lying, Miss Wells. There are definite gaps and inconsistencies that her confession does not explain. First, she said she took nothing from the room except the gun, yet we cannot find any evidence that the colonel sold the missing artifacts before his death. So where are they? Second, the man was shot from *behind*. If you were in danger of your life from a man coming at you with a poker, wouldn't you shoot him from the *front*? And Miss Adams is nearly of a height with her father. Did she crouch down when she shot him? If so, why? And if she burned a bloody nightgown in the fireplace and put on a fresh one, why did we see bloodstains on that gown as well?"

Concordia shook her head. "I don't understand any of it. Even under duress, Sophia is too level-headed to do something as stupid as carry the murder weapon to her room, rather than simply leave it in the study. It was the colonel's pistol, after all, it would not have incriminated her."

"She is too clever for that," Capshaw agreed.

"But why did you arrest her, lieutenant, with doubts such as these?" Concordia asked.

Capshaw propped his elbows on the desk, and his head in his hands. He looked utterly weary.

"I had to arrest her when we found the gun in her room, and she confessed. My superiors are anxious to solve this case. It doesn't look good for the murder of a prominent citizen like Colonel Adams—unpleasant as most people considered him to be—to go for weeks without the killer being apprehended."

"Surely you wouldn't sacrifice Sophia for political expediency, and leave a murderer to go free?" Concordia exclaimed.

She had gone too far; it was the first time she had ever seen the usually mild-mannered Capshaw truly angry. His face flushed a dusky red. He slapped his hands on the desk, pushed away from the chair, and leaned over toward Concordia, who shrank back.

A moment passed. Whatever he was about to say, Concordia never knew. Instead, the redness receded from his face, he sat again, and calmly sharpened his pencil. "Is that what you really think, Miss Wells?" he said finally.

Concordia felt chastened. "No, lieutenant. I apologize." She looked down at her gloved hands. "This has been most trying."

"It's not going to get better, miss," Capshaw said. "We have to consider whom Miss Adams is shielding. There are more trying times ahead."

Concordia felt cold all at once, from the top of her head to her hands and feet. There weren't many people in the Adams household whom Sophia would sacrifice herself to protect. In fact, there was only one person.

Amelia.

Concordia couldn't sleep. She couldn't get the image of Sophia's drawn, haggard face out of her mind, and the events of the day weighed heavily upon her. Sophia had confessed to the murder of her father. She had faked the burglary attempt. But, if Sophia were lying to protect someone—Amelia—and had done all these things to confuse the police, that would make sense.

Capshaw had noticed that Amelia's nightgown had been absolutely clean, while Sophia's had smears of blood upon it. But what if that wasn't the *first* nightgown Amelia had worn that night? What if Amelia had come to Sophia, gun dangling between nerveless fingers, mute with shock, wearing a bloodied nightgown? Wouldn't Sophia have gotten rid of the evidence to protect her sister? Gone in to the study, broken the glass in the door, and disordered the room? Changed the child's gown, and hidden the bloody one, burning it later? Had Sophia discovered the gun when it was too late to put it back, and hidden it, too?

There was a problem with this line of thought, but Concordia couldn't quite get at what it was. Her exhaustion was clouding her thinking.

Then she realized what she was missing. *Why* would Amelia kill her father? If it was an accident, why not call the police immediately and tell all? Accidents with guns were sadly all too common. No one would blame an eight-year-old girl for such a tragedy.

But Sophia had not considered it an accident. She had acted swiftly and with great deliberation to protect her sister. Did Sophia know of a powerful motive Amelia might have had to kill their father? But could a girl so young be capable of such a horrible deed?

It was time to act. Lieutenant Capshaw was doing his best, Concordia knew, but as Sophia's friend she had the duty to sort this out, despite the impediments Sophia herself was putting up. And perhaps she had a better chance at getting at the truth than Capshaw. Servants and family members wouldn't be on their guard around her as they would the policeman.

But there was one big problem with that: her restriction to campus. Well, she wasn't going to let the Ogre stop her from going into town and finding answers. She would have to manage to sneak off campus somehow. But she was going to need help.

Having made her decision, Concordia finally slept.

Chapter 13

Though this be madness, yet there is a method in't.

II.ii

Week 5, Instructor Calendar
October 1896

Concordia sat down with Ruby and Eli in her sitting room, the door and windows closed, and shades drawn. She felt like a sneak thief planning her next "job."

Over the past few days, she'd seen enough to know that Miss Grant had a network of spies at her disposal: teachers, staff, and even students, those who liked to be in the lady principal's good graces and gain favor. Concordia had noticed an unusual number of glances through her windows when she was reading or grading papers, and felt the eyes follow her throughout her day, as she attended chapel, taught classes, and went from building to building. She knew enough to be careful in the company of the mathematics teacher, Mr. Harrison, whom everyone knew was a particular favorite of Miss Grant. Other than that, Concordia didn't know exactly who was reporting back to the Ogre, and it was making her nervous.

But she could trust Ruby and Eli.

"Feel free to say 'no'," Concordia began, "because it could get you in trouble."

Eli's eyes opened wide. Concordia knew he'd spent his young life avoiding trouble, and she hoped she wasn't making more for him.

"You know that Miss Grant has confined me to campus for an indefinite period. The problem is my best friend Sophia desperately needs my help. She's in prison. I *know* she's innocent. But the only way to find the truth is to go back to the Adams' home. I need a way to slip out of the grounds, without the lady principal finding out. I was hoping you two could help me." She expelled a breath, and waited.

Eli's lip trembled. "It's 'cause of me, in't it? But I'm not stayin' here anymore. Ma'dm Doo-rand's lettin' me stay with them, in exchange fer work. Won't Miss Grant change her mind, and let you go now?"

Concordia patted his arm. "It's... complicated. Maybe she will, in time. But I can't wait for that." She looked at Ruby. "Do you have any ideas?"

Ruby sniffed. "Ooh, I could just throttle that 'un! Not that you heard it from me," she added with a wink.

She grew quiet for a moment. "I think that bicycle machine of yours might help," she said finally.

Concordia listened as Ruby explained her idea.

It was a sparkling clear autumn day when Concordia set out for the far sheep tracks on her bicycle. She felt the eyes upon her again, as she cleared the quadrangle and made her way up the hill. It was a bit more cumbersome pedaling than usual, as she wasn't wearing her bicycle outfit of knickers and leggings. But she would soon be leaving the bicycle behind and slipping through a gap in the far gate, with Eli's help. She couldn't possibly visit the Adams household in her bicycle attire. It showed a shocking amount of leg.

Eli was waiting for her on the other side of the gate, and helped her slip through. He handed her a large basket. "Ruby says these scones, with her special honey butter, would unlock some tongues in the kitchen."

"That woman is a treasure." Concordia took a quick look under the gaily-checkered napkin. The house matron had also tucked in some of her rhubarb jelly and a flask of dandelion wine, for good measure. Leave it to Ruby to come up with a little gastronomic bribery.

"Can you manage the bicycle?" Concordia asked, watching Eli step through the bars and awkwardly straddle a machine too large for him.

"Yes'm. I'll tuck it behind the gatekeeper's house, and you can fetch it tonight when yer back, jus' like we planned." There was a hint of pride in his voice, as he was a key conspirator in a grand strategy to outwit the enemy.

"Make sure to keep to the wooded trail, so no one sees you," Concordia said.

Eli gave her a scornful look that only a boy his age, whose powers of guile were just called into question, could muster. "Of course." And off he went.

Concordia spent the trolley ride to the Adams' house planning out what she would ask—and, most importantly, *how* she would ask her questions. She didn't want to appear to be a scandal-monger, nor did she want the household in a panic that they were murder suspects. She was so lost in thought as she clutched the hand strap and unconsciously swayed with the lurch of the streetcar, that she almost missed her Asylum Avenue transfer point. She needed to keep her wits about her.

As Concordia got off the trolley and walked the rest of the way, she tried to push to the back of her mind the worry that even if she were successful in clearing Sophia, it might be at the expense of a little girl's future. What if Amelia really had killed her father—as improbable as that seemed—and Concordia's actions brought that to light? Sophia would never speak to her again.

She went around to the back door staff entrance, where the real business of the household took place. She wasn't prepared to deal with Mrs. Adams. Yet. Better to see first what she could learn from the staff.

The cook's assistant opened the door. "Miss Wells! Why, this is a surprise, miss. Come on in." She opened the door wider, and Concordia stepped into the Adams' kitchen, fragrant with the smells of roasting chicken, onions, carrots, and rosemary.

"I came to bring you this, with Ruby's love," Concordia said, pulling back the napkin to reveal Ruby's melt-in-your-mouth scones, a generous pot of butter, and the bright glass jar of rhubarb jelly, twinkling in the light. What really produced the most exclamations, though, was the bottle of wine.

"That woman is a gem, she is," Mrs. Lewis, the cook, said, stepping around a gawking kitchen maid to relieve Concordia of the heavy basket. "And thank you, kindly, miss, for bringin' it to us. Why don't you stay a while? I was jus' about to put on the kettle. You must be perishin' thirsty after that long trolley ride—them cars get so hot and crowded, even this time o' year, don't they?"

Concordia was familiar enough with Mrs. Lewis' style of hospitality to hope for that very invitation. "I'd love to, Mrs. Lewis. A cup of tea would be just the thing."

"An' we can have a few of them scones, I'd expect," Mrs. Lewis answered, eyeing them. "There look to be plenty."

While Mrs. Lewis made the tea and Concordia settled herself comfortably, word of the treat basket must have spread, for the butler, parlor maid, and even the butcher's boy on a delivery appeared in the kitchen just as everything was ready. Stools and tables were pulled 'round, and there was comfortable silence for a little while.

Now was the time.

"It must be difficult, a house in mourning, especially with Miss Sophia…gone," Concordia said tentatively.

Everyone turned and looked at Mrs. Lewis, expecting her to take the lead. Her kitchen, her rules.

The cook nodded vigorously, scattering crumbs across her ample bosom in the process. "Aye, it is. I dunna believe it of Miss Sophia. No'un here does, actually, but what possessed her to own up to such a thing, I have no idea."

"Mebbe she's gotten a little barmy, what with all that settlement work o' hers," the boy chimed in.

He got a quick cuff on the ear from Mrs. Lewis. "Yer nowt to talk like that about Miss Sophia. Yer know better'n that." The boy flushed and looked at the floor.

"What has Mrs. Adams decided to do about the staff? Will you all get to stay?" Concordia asked.

"I'm not staying," the parlor maid said. "You couldn't pay me to sleep in this house another night more than I have to."

"The police are requiring those who want to seek other employment to stay until the investigation is finished," the butler clarified.

"So, Mrs. Adams inherited everything from the colonel?" Concordia asked.

"Aye. An' she has grand plans fer when her mournin's up, you can be sure o' that," the cook said. "She's gonna hire *more* staff, I hear."

Perhaps that shouldn't be a surprise, Concordia thought. After all, the colonel and Mrs. Adams had been married little more than a year. Mrs. Adams moved in the very heart of blueblood society, and wouldn't want to be away from it long.

"How is Amelia?" Concordia asked.

The cook clucked her tongue in sympathy. "The poor little 'un. She's still a'feared, and won't talk. The missus sent her off to her great uncle's house in the country."

Drat. Concordia had been hoping to talk to her. Even if the girl couldn't speak, perhaps she could have communicated in some other way. Now that part of the plan would have to wait.

"I assume that Mr. Bradley has also left town?" she asked. She had to admit to dressing a bit more carefully than usual, in case he was still at the house. But now with Amelia gone, why would he stay?

The maid sighed, and the cook gave her a sharp look before answering.

"Aye, he did. Mr. Bradley is a favorite around here—with some in particular," she added with a wink at the maid. "But he had to go back to his coll'idge. He was right sorry to go, with all that's happ'ning here."

Concordia was experiencing a mixed reaction to David's departure herself. While she was spared the distraction of tumultuous feelings, she was hoping to talk with him about what was troubling her. He was of particular help last year, when the problems on campus reached their height.

"What was the colonel's funeral like?" she asked, in a change of subject. "Did any of you go?"

The butler suppressed a snort while the parlor maid giggled into her apron.

Mrs. Lewis looked as if she would have cuffed them both, if she could. But the parlor maid was too far away for her to reach, and one doesn't box a butler's ears, not even if you're the cook.

"We senior staff went—Mr. Chester an' me," Mrs. Lewis said, glaring at the butler instead of whacking him. "An' Mrs. Adams, o' course. Miss Sophia and Miss Amelia were feelin' too poorly to go."

"It *was* a grand spectacle, though," the butler added, reaching to spoon some jelly onto his scone. "Military pomp and circumstance and all that. The police chief and the mayor were both there."

"Was the colonel well-liked, then?" Concordia asked. "I didn't know him all that well, although he had been a friend of my father's a long time ago."

"Aye, that's right, miss, I forgot about that," Mrs. Lewis said. "I'd just started workin' fer the household back then. Your father—such a nice man, I remember—and Colonel Adams were in business together. Even went to fair-rren lands, and such-like."

Foreign lands. Concordia's heart beat a little faster. Quite casually, she asked, "Do you mean Egypt, Mrs. Lewis?"

The cook dabbed at a little butter dribbling down her chin before answering. "Aye. The colonel liked to collect dusty old bits of things from heathen places. I was a maid back then, and I sure was relieved when the colonel shut up his study and would'na let us dust in there."

"How long did my father and the colonel work together, do you know?"

Mrs. Lewis thought for a moment, then shook her head. "I'm sorry, lamb, but I don't remember much about the colonel's visitors after he got back fro' that trip. By then, I went to work in the kitchen an' didn't hear much after that." She looked around her kitchen with the pride of a queen in her domain. "This place is its own li'l world, it is."

Concordia had gotten side-tracked long enough. Time to get back to the issue at hand, before everyone returned to their work. "What *was* the colonel like? Had he made any enemies?"

The butler rocked back so hard in his chair that he nearly fell to the floor. Mrs. Lewis gave him a disdainful look.

"An easier question to ask, miss, is who *wasn't* an enemy of the colonel." She sighed. "He was a hard man, not to speak ill of the dead. Not even his own family liked him much, sad to say. But I should'na be telling tales out o' school." She stood and started clearing plates. Everyone took the cue; after thanking Concordia for the basket of goodies, they went back to their duties.

Mrs. Lewis handed back the now-empty basket. "Give Ruby my regards. Be sure to tell her them's the best scones she's ever made, and I'm much obliged."

"Thank you for the tea," Concordia said, standing.

"Yer welcome, dearie. Come back anytime. Let me know if we can do anything to help Miss Sophia." She shook her head. "That policeman is fishin' in the wrong pond." She gestured to the parlor maid. "Show Miss Wells out the *front* door, like a proper lady should leave."

Concordia followed the parlor maid down the hall to the door. "How is Eli?" the girl asked. "Funny, how I miss that grubby little urchin."

"He's fine, doing odd jobs at the school. He's staying with the Durands now."

"Well, tell him that Clara says hello," she said. She looked around and lowered her voice a bit. "And when you see him, can you ask him to bring back the spare house key? We've been missing it and I'll get in trouble if it doesn't turn up soon."

"You gave Eli a house key?" Concordia asked, confused.

Clara opened the door and pointed to the potted urn beside the door. The flowers in the pot were starting to fade as the autumn days grew cooler. She pulled aside some of the stems, and Concordia could see a clear space in the soil.

"It's the back door key, of course," Clara said, "but we started keeping it there in case someone got locked out. The colonel used to get terrible mad when that happened. Eli used it the most, 'cause he used to sell papers, you know, and sometimes it isn't until late before the boys sell them all. He must have forgotten to return it before he left. But Mrs. Lewis will give me a time of it if she finds out."

"I'll have him bring it back as soon as he can," Concordia promised.

It was close to the dinner hour when Concordia found the gap in the gate again. She would be expected to make an appearance in the dining hall, and still needed to change. She hurried along the wooded trail, and cleared the open grassy area to the gatekeeper's house without being seen. She left the basket in a shadowed corner, picked up her bicycle, and pedaled quickly down the path to Willow Cottage.

And nearly ran down the lady principal.

Concordia panic-braked and swerved, tumbling into the grass. Miss Grant, hands on hips, glared and did nothing to help her up.

"Miss *Wells.* Have you been riding that infernal machine *all day*? You seem to have more leisure time than the rest of us. I will have to reconsider your responsibilities. And perhaps a ban on riding these—" she waved a hand at Concordia's bicycle "—these *machines* is in order. Hardly decorous behavior in our lady instructors."

Concordia winced as she got up, brushed off her skirts, and righted her bicycle. "I'm s-s-sorry, Miss Grant." Hang the woman for getting her so rattled. If the lady principal knew what she had really been up to, she would be fired, for sure.

Then they both heard it: a *thump-bump, thump-bump,* along the sidewalk, and looked over to see Margaret Banning crossing the pavement from the quadrangle, coming along at more speed than Concordia would have given the elderly lady credit for.

"What's the problem here?" Miss Banning demanded, taking in the sight of the trembling Concordia gripping the handlebars of her bicycle, and the red-faced Miss Grant practically hopping in her fury.

"This is none of your concern," snapped the lady principal.

"*To sin by silence when they should protest makes cowards of men.*' President Lincoln," Miss Banning retorted, as she adjusted the muslin cap on her head, which had listed to one side in her haste. She fixed a glaring eye on Miss Grant, who faltered under the old lady's gaze.

"Well, if you must know, Miss Wells has been shirking her responsibilities, *again*," Miss Grant said. "Riding that blasted contraption, and gadding about. She has not been seen all day. I was weighing disciplinary action, when you *interrupted*."

"'Shirking'? 'Gadding about'? Oh, my," mocked Miss Banning. She thumped the ground emphatically with her cane. "And whatever do you mean, 'she has not been seen'? Was she reported missing from a class? Were you making active inquiries about her, in your singular *concern* for her welfare? Was a search party involved?"

Concordia, open-mouthed, turned her head from one lady to the other, as though watching a game of lawn-tennis, waiting to see who would score an advantage first.

But Margaret Banning had been at the game too long to lose to the likes of the Ogre, who flushed a dusky red. "Miss Wells has been restricted to campus; I was merely ascertaining her whereabouts," she muttered defensively.

"Oh, so you see fit to turn spies upon her, to make sure she doesn't *escape*. What would she do if you weren't watching her, *climb a fence?*"

As this was uncomfortably close to the truth, Concordia focused her attention upon digging the toe of her boot in the grass.

Miss Grant began to pout. "I will deal with my staff as I see fit."

"Ah, but you didn't 'see fit' to have your spies in *my* office today, now did you, Miss Grant?" Miss Banning asked, stabbing the ground with her cane again to emphasize her point. "If you had, perhaps you would have seen Miss Wells there, lending me a hand in cataloging that monstrous collection of ours."

Concordia's eyes widened at Miss Banning's outright falsehood, but the old lady flushed with unabashed triumph.

The match was won, and the lady principal knew it.

"Go change into proper supper attire before you're late," Miss Grant tossed over her shoulder at Concordia, stomping off toward the dining hall in a *swish* of taffeta.

Miss Banning gave a gleeful chuckle when the woman was barely out of earshot.

"Thank you for rescuing me," Concordia said.

"She would have given up soon, anyhow. I doubt the woman has ever been late for a meal in her life."

"You lied to her," Concordia said. "Aren't you worried she'll find you out?"

Miss Banning thwacked a tire rim of Concordia's bicycle with her cane. "I did *not* lie, my good miss. I said '*perhaps you would have seen Miss Wells there*'. She chose to interpret it incorrectly. A sloppy-minded woman. Still, you should do what she says and get changed for supper. It's getting late."

As Miss Banning turned toward the dining hall, she added, "I don't know what you were *really* up to, but be careful. You've made an enemy."

Chapter 14

Speak. I am bound to hear.

I.v

Week 5, Instructor Calendar
October 1896

The mood on campus was picking up a bit. Lieutenant Capshaw was able to determine that the collapsed railing was indeed the result of careless workers, a relief to everyone's mind.

In the meantime, preparations for the Halloween Masquerade Ball had begun in earnest. Perhaps that was why there had been no new pranks in the past few weeks. But Concordia knew that practical jokes were a time-honored All Hallows Eve tradition, and the staff needed to keep their wits about them. She hoped the ball would sufficiently preoccupy the mischief-makers. At least having the students all in one place would make it easier for the teachers to keep an eye on them.

She'd heard of the troubles that other colleges suffered on Halloween, including the pranks at Lafayette College a few years back, where the boys poured molten lead in the keyholes of the chapel doors and smeared the pews with molasses. The administration at Hartford Women's College would not take kindly to any monkeyshines this year in light of what had already been going on.

Concordia hadn't the heart to get involved in the excitement. She wasn't sure she would bother going to the ball in costume. She would act as chaperone, of course, as was expected of all of the women faculty. But Sophia's imprisonment and the lack of progress Concordia had made in finding an answer still weighed heavily on her. How was she going to find the truth? And with Amelia away, what else could she do? Should she sneak out again and go back to the Adams' house, perhaps this time to speak with Mrs. Adams? But Concordia was nearly caught last time; she would be summarily dismissed if she tried it again and failed to evade Miss Grant's watchful network of spies.

The strain of having to deal with the lady principal, on top of everything else, was taking its toll on her spirit. She felt so tired.

After her Romantic Age class she went to her office to grade student themes. The slanting stacks of paper littering her desk was daunting, but she determinedly sat down to work.

By the fourth theme she was struggling to keep her eyes open. The scent of lemon wax in the stuffy air, the drone of a fly trapped in the windowsill, the scattering of dust motes as they drifted lazily along the arc of light....

She shook herself awake. A bracing dose of fresh air was in order. Certainly, the Romantic poets would approve:

There is pleasure in the pathless woods,
There is a rapture on the lonely shore,
There is society, where none intrudes,
By the deep sea, and music in its roar:
I love not man the less, but Nature more...

She headed for Rook's Hill, on the eastern side of the campus grounds. There was a little time before Mr. Harrison expected her at their first rehearsal this afternoon. The roles had been assigned, and the costumes and sets were underway. Perhaps they *could* be ready before the Christmas recess.

She huffed a bit in climbing the slope. Deep breaths of crisp air, mingled with the scent of fallen leaves, lifted her mood. The view was worth it: the heavily-wooded side of campus was still a lovely-but-thinned sweep of burnt oranges and reds and golds. People walking about below her were part of an indifferent landscape, rather than impetuous students to be responsible for, troubled friends who needed rescuing, or difficult administrators to appease.

As she completed the circuit, descending the hill and passing by the pond, the chilled, constricted lump of worry that had been plaguing her began to soften and ease. She deliberately put aside her worry about Sophia for just a little while longer and sat.

Her solitude was soon disturbed by the sound of Dean Pierce's wheelchair along the sidewalk, crunching dried leaves in its wake. "Hello, Miss Wells!" he called out. "Getting some air?"

"It was just what I needed," Concordia answered. The dean seemed never to be in a black mood, she thought, noting his relaxed expression and bright eyes. No lines creased the smooth, bald head, stiffened the shoulders, or tightened the hands. Pierce was more at peace with his lot than some of the more fortunate people she knew.

"I understand you've had a lot on your mind lately. That was quick work, saving the boy—Eli, is it? What a tragedy that would have been."

Concordia nodded. "But Miss Grant was rather harsh on the students. It wasn't their fault, really. Eli can't even read a 'Wet Paint' sign."

"You've had a little bit of trouble over the boy, too, I understand," he said.

Concordia gave a hollow laugh. "You heard, of course. Miss Grant has restricted me to campus for 'overstepping my authority'."

She looked down at her lap, absent-mindedly plucking off a leaf that landed there.

Peering closely at Concordia, Pierce said, "But there seems to be more on your mind than student pranks or Miss Grant. Can I help?"

Concordia looked up the path, which was empty of students. With this rare opportunity for privacy afforded her, she confided her dilemma about Sophia to the dean. Actually, it all came out in a flood, as if held back too long. Perhaps it was too great of a burden to carry without sharing it, or perhaps she felt more relaxed after her walk. Whatever the reason, Concordia told him a good deal of it: the murder of Colonel Adams, the missing items, Amelia's mutism, Sophia's confession, the gaps and inconsistencies in the stories, and Concordia's recent talk with the servants—although she hoped the dean wouldn't realize that the visit had occurred *after* Miss Grant restricted her to campus.

Pierce listened attentively, then thought a while before he spoke. "You do appear to be at an impasse. The police have a self-confessed culprit, so—not to distress you further, my dear, but one must face reality—they will not be looking farther afield for another suspect. And you have already interviewed the staff and gotten nowhere. That leaves Mrs. Adams, but you have no official authority to be questioning anyone, and no personal relationship with the woman, correct? So you may not get anywhere in that regard."

He was quiet for a while longer. "Perhaps you need to know more about the colonel himself. If we are to assume that your friend is innocent, then it must be someone with a grudge against him, yes?"

"True. But how would I learn more about him? As you said, I have no official authority to talk with anyone about Colonel Adams. I considered asking the lawyer about the colonel's will, but I doubt he would break confidentiality to talk to *me*."

Dean Pierce was a quick-witted man. He gave Concordia a sharp look. "So, you suspect the widow? Isn't that a bit of a cliché, Miss Wells? A younger woman marrying an older man for his money, then killing him to inherit? Sounds like one of those penny dreadfuls our young ladies like to read."

"Maybe it's a cliché for a reason," Concordia retorted. She felt a little silly considering the possibility in the first place. She knew she was grasping at straws.

"I suppose," the dean answered, "but perhaps there's another approach." He hesitated.

"What approach?" Concordia asked.

"You said that some of the colonel's Egyptian relics—ones that he didn't donate to our exhibit—were missing from his study. Although it's possible that they were sold before the colonel's death, the police haven't found any proof of that, correct?"

Concordia nodded.

"So perhaps someone knowledgeable about these artifacts is involved. Colonel Adams associated with such individuals, I understand. Perhaps someone was after these items, and the Colonel merely got in the way?"

"But how would I—" Concordia stopped. *Her father.* He and the colonel had been partners. The Adams' cook, Mrs. Lewis, had also mentioned it.

Dean Pierce, a slight smile touching his lips, watched Concordia making the connections. "Yes! You already have the means to learn more about the colonel's past, and how his dealings in Egyptian relics might be connected now. Your father's own past is intertwined in his."

"How did *you* know about my father?" Concordia asked.

Pierce cleared his throat uncomfortably. "I hate to admit to listening to scuttlebutt, but you understand how rampant gossip is on a college campus."

"I see," Concordia said. Heaven only knows what other gossip about her had been bandied about. She pushed that thought aside for the moment. "But I know very little of my father's work as an Egyptian scholar, and nothing about his business relationship with Colonel Adams."

"Are there no papers of your father's that you could look through? Any close family members?" Pierce suggested.

"Well... I *could* ask my mother," Concordia said. She didn't relish such a conversation. Their relationship was not as close as could be desired, and for some reason the subject of Papa was a touchy one. But for Sophia's sake, she would do it.

"There you go," Pierce said. "Ask your mother and see if you can find any relevant family papers."

"There's just one problem with that," Concordia said. "Miss Grant's restriction, remember?"

Dean Pierce nodded sympathetically. "I think I can prevail upon Miss Grant to set that aside. I'll speak with her today." He winked. "We can't have our professors slipping through fences, now, can we?"

Concordia started. For a man confined to a wheelchair, the dean seemed to know everything that went on.

Concordia checked her watch. "I have to get to rehearsal. Thank you, dean, for your help."

He patted her hand. "Anytime, my dear. A fascinating little puzzle, I must say. You'll solve it. Would you mind telling me what you find? You have my curiosity piqued."

Concordia's conversation with Dean Pierce, though enlightening, had made her late for play practice. She hurried over to the auditorium, where the students were already assembled and being addressed by Mr. Harrison.

Charles Harrison made a great show of checking his watch and grimacing, although he said nothing. Concordia knew the very precise mathematics teacher was punctual in the extreme, while she was... not.

"Miss Wells, if you would be so good as to work with our Hamlet here. Miss Rhodes." He pointed to the tall, gangly senior standing beside the curtain, who giggled at the mention of her name. "I shall be planning the choreography for the final scene."

"Don't you need Hamlet for your choreography?" Concordia asked.

"I have a stand-in for the job. Once I have the movements worked out, we can teach it to her later. For now, she needs to work on her lines." He looked over at Miss Rhodes in exasperation. "You must apply yourself, young lady. Focus!"

Suitably chastened, Miss Rhodes followed Concordia to the far side of the stage, while Mr. Harrison issued mock-armaments and proceeded to shuffle bodies around.

Concordia pulled out her copy of *Hamlet*. "Let's see what you know so far. What part are you working on, Miss Rhodes?"

"Act One, scene two," the girl muttered.

"That's all?" Concordia said. *Oh, dear.* They had a lot of work ahead of them.

"All right. This is the scene where Horatio tells Hamlet that he saw the ghost of the king, Hamlet's father. Hamlet has made the decision to stand watch with him tonight, to try and speak with him. I'll read Horatio's part. Ready?"

Miss Rhodes nodded.

"'*My lord, I think I saw him yesternight,…the king, your father,*'" Concordia began. Miss Rhodes responded hesitantly at first, then with more confidence as the scene progressed.

"'… *If it assume my noble father's person,*
I'll speak to it though hell itself should gape
And bid me hold my peace—'"

Miss Rhodes stopped as Concordia abruptly dropped her book.

"I beg your pardon," Concordia said, stooping to pick it up. Her hands shook and her mind raced, back to her conversation with Dean Pierce, and even further back, to the séance with Madame Durand. Could ghosts really exist? Was her father trying to communicate with her, just as Hamlet's father had in the play?

She shook off the feeling but resolved to talk to her mother. Tomorrow.

"Let us proceed," she said, opening the book again.

Finally they stopped for the evening. It was getting close to curfew, otherwise known as the "ten o'clock rule," when all students were supposed to be in bed with their lights out.

As Concordia helped Mr. Harrison stow the props in the storage chest, she noticed something was missing.

"Mr. Harrison, do you know what happened to the queen's diadem? I don't see it." She pulled out the rest of the trunk's contents, just to be sure.

Mr. Harrison came over to look. "I didn't notice, really," he said. "I was focused on whether we had enough swords, and they were at the top. When did you last see it?"

"Two days ago, when I first checked through to see what we could use. These are left over from last year's play. I know I should have checked earlier, but I've been…busy." In fact, Concordia received quite a scolding from the lady principal when she went to her for the key to the chest.

"Is it valuable?" Harrison asked, frowning.

"No-o, I don't think so. I suppose we could make another." And that had better be soon. *Drat.* She sighed. "I hope Miss Grant won't hold *me* responsible. At her request, I just turned in an inventory of the trunk's contents, with the diadem on it." It would be just her luck if the lady principal came and checked before they had a replacement made.

"Really?" Mr. Harrison looked more concerned than Concordia would have expected. The man didn't strike her as all that compassionate. "I'll ask the custodian," he offered. "His son is very handy with metalwork. I'm sure he could make a replacement."

"Thank you," Concordia said, relieved though a bit puzzled by the generous offer from a man who barely seemed to tolerate her presence. But then again, joining forces against the lady principal made for unlikely allies.

Chapter 15

Do not forever with thy vailed lids
Seek for thy noble father in the dust.

I.ii

Week 6, Instructor Calendar
October 1896

Concordia awoke to the sound of rain beating against the windows. The walk to chapel was going to be miserable. And after chapel, the trolley ride to her mother's house would be even worse. But there was no help for it.

Even if Concordia didn't learn enough in her visit to her mother to catch the real killer, perhaps she could find sufficient evidence to convince Sophia to retract her confession and give Capshaw an additional lead to pursue. Thank goodness the dean had managed to coax Miss Grant into lifting the off-campus restriction. Concordia would have been a muddy mess crawling between a fence today.

After chapel, Concordia didn't bother to change into a dry skirt and stockings—she would only get wet again. It was Saturday, so she had no classes or responsibilities until dinner, and her absence even then was permissible. The students were engaged in quiet activities and housework in the cottage. Ruby shooed her out.

"Don't you worry about the girls," she said, "I can handle 'em. You just go and have your visit, though it's a shame to travel in such a downpour."

At the Wells' home, the housekeeper opened the door to a bedraggled young lady she barely recognized—hat plastered to hair, hair plastered to head, skirts sodden and dripping.

"Miss Concordia!" she exclaimed, opening the door wider. "Why didn't you tell us you were coming? We could have sent someone to get you."

Concordia had debated that point but thought it best to catch her mother unexpectedly. "It's fine, Mrs. Houston. I just need to dry out a bit."

"Why don't you go up to your old room. I'm sure there are some clothes of yours still in the wardrobe. Then I'll get these dried proper before you have to go back. I'll tell your mother you're here." She turned toward the kitchen, shaking her head and muttering, "Young ladies these days; so harum-scarum... catch her death of cold. Not even that ferr-eigner, Madame Doo-rand, is coming out in the cold and wet today..."

Concordia interrupted the housekeeper in mid-mutter. "Did you say 'Madame Durand'? Was she supposed to come here today?"

Mrs. Houston pressed Concordia's damp jacket against her chest in a protective gesture and shivered. "The woman gives me the creeps, she does. She's been a reg'lar here, doing 'readings' and 'consultations' a couple o' times in the past week, burning stuff that leaves a stink like a bordello. Yer mother *asked* her to come, can you believe it? You'd think she had no more sense than a lump o' sugar. But ever since Miss Mary died, she's not like herself anymore." She sighed.

This was alarming news, indeed. Concordia felt a familiar surge of anger toward Madame Durand, exploiting the grief of others for her own gain. She was going to have to try and make her mother see reason.

Thanking the housekeeper, she hurried upstairs to change.

The parlor looked much the same as Concordia remembered, except for the new drapes and rug. It was a decidedly formal space for visitors. The stiff arm chairs with their ornately-turned legs, the regimental arrangement of portraits along the far wall, and the matching, evenly-spaced candlesticks on the mantel spoke of her mother's love of order.

The one disruption to the primness of the atmosphere, however, was a large glass bowl on top of the piano, generously filled with orange chrysanthemums that seemed to glow in the light. Mrs. Houston's doing, Concordia guessed.

Mrs. Wells stood beside the parlor fire.

"Mother, how have you been? It's good to see you." Concordia could tell she was angry. She hadn't approached Concordia or even clasped her hand in greeting. This did not bode well for their talk.

Mrs. Wells gestured to the other chair and stiffly seated herself. "And you as well. Except for seeing you at Madame Durand's college demonstration, I haven't seen or heard from you since the term started. Are you that busy that you could not visit or write?"

Concordia flushed at the reprimand. She looked at her hands in her lap. "I know. Since Mary died, I know we've been… trying… to get along, but I feel as if I'm always waiting for you to criticize my work."

Mrs. Wells narrowed her eyes. "You are not quite the woman of the world you make yourself out to be if you cannot take a little criticism, particularly when it is for your own welfare. A child should heed her parent. I have greater knowledge of the ways of the world—even without a fancy college degree. I want you to be guided by my experience of how the world works for women."

Concordia sighed. "Please, let's not go down that path again."

"So why *did* you come, Concordia?"

"Actually, to take advantage of some of that knowledge of yours," Concordia said, trying unsuccessfully to keep the edge from her voice. It wouldn't do to antagonize her. Especially when she needed information about her father, already a sensitive subject. Mrs. Wells had always resented the special bond that Concordia and her father had shared.

Mrs. Wells raised an eyebrow, but folded her delicate hands in her lap and waited.

"You know of Colonel Adams' murder?" Concordia asked. Her mother inclined her head in agreement.

"Then you also know that Sophia has confessed to it and is in prison even now?"

Mrs. Wells sniffed, and put a delicate handkerchief to her nose. "Yes. It's incomprehensible. I don't believe it of her."

Concordia knew that Mother had a soft spot for Sophia, despite her settlement work and progressive ideas.

"I don't believe it, either. I want to help her, but I need information." Concordia recounted what she knew of the murder and Sophia's inexplicable behavior afterward. She pulled out the bracelet that had been found in Colonel Adams' safe.

"Papa left this for me. Colonel Adams' lawyer found it in the safe after his death." She passed it over to her mother, who took it reluctantly but barely glanced at it. "Do you know why Papa would have done this, and why it was only to be given to me after the colonel's death?"

For a while, Mrs. Wells didn't answer. Concordia waited.

Mrs. Wells handed back the bracelet. "This has no connection to the murder. You are wasting your time."

"Perhaps there is no direct connection," Concordia countered, "but how can you be so sure that the association between Papa and the colonel was not the reason for the colonel's death? Colonel Adams' donation to the school seems to have started a chain of ruinous events. One of the artifacts disappeared right under the nose of the curator, and then, only days later, the colonel was killed and more artifacts are missing. Now Sophia's sister has been rendered mute from the shock, and Sophia herself has confessed to the crime. We have to get to the bottom of this."

When Concordia's mother said nothing, she continued. "The colonel's cook, Mrs. Lewis, has been in that household for a long time. She remembered that Papa and the colonel went on an expedition together in Egypt more than twenty years ago.

She doesn't remember that the two of them had any dealings with each other after that. Did they have a falling out?"

Mrs. Wells continued to look silently at the fire.

"And why did Papa never mention his Egyptian scholarly work?" Concordia went on. "I read one of his essays that a colleague showed me. He was well-respected in his field at one time. Why did he abandon his success, and pretend it had never happened?"

"Enough!" Mrs. Wells abruptly stood. "Leave the past alone, Concordia. It can have nothing to do with Colonel Adams' death in the here and now. You will only cause pain. I am sorry for Sophia, but I cannot help you."

Concordia also stood. "I *will* find out, Mother. A woman's life and sanity are at stake." She walked out of the room and slammed the door.

It was a dismal evening. The rain had worsened, coming down in sheets and saturating the ground to such an extent that several large trees in the neighborhood, their roots unable to keep hold in the crumbling ground, toppled into houses and blocked nearby streets. Concordia would be staying the night.

Concordia felt badly about how the talk with her mother had gone. Not only had she failed to learn anything about her father, but she had yet again antagonized her mother.

And, in the heat of the moment, she had forgotten to ask her about Madame Durand. What was the extent of her involvement? Her mother was usually such a sensible woman. She should be consulting with a minister, not a psychic. Had Mary's death changed her so utterly?

Perhaps Concordia should have anticipated this when she saw her at Madame Durand's college demonstration. Had the parlor tricks been enough to convince Mother that the medium was genuine? Had Lydia Adams been instrumental in persuading Mother to turn to her personal spiritualist? Whatever the case, it seemed that Madame was intertwined in Concordia's life, through both her college and her family, and there wasn't anything she could do about it at the moment. She would have to wait for another opportunity to speak to Mother and caution her about placing trust in such quackery.

Mrs. Wells remained in her room, taking a supper tray. Concordia, not wanting to sit in the enormous dining room by herself, ate in the kitchen with the housekeeper. As she ate, she fiddled with the bracelet her father had given her, wondering if she could unlock the clue she was sure it contained.

"May I see it, miss?" the housekeeper asked, the bracelet catching her eye. "It looks familiar."

Concordia passed it over. "Do you recognize it?"

The housekeeper's brow puckered.

"Ah," she said, face clearing, "I do. Your father was working on this, using pliers or such-like on it."

"When was this?"

"Near the end of his life, poor man. I'm not sure how much you remember of that time. He did a lot of journal writing, sketches and drawings, that sort of thing. And tinkering, like this. This was after the doctors diagnosed his heart condition. He knew he didn't have much time left. News like that can make a man introspective, that's for sure."

Concordia certainly remembered that painful time. She was sixteen. Her father, usually so welcoming of her presence in his study, kept his door shut even to her in the last few months of his life. Apparently, he occupied himself with solitary pursuits such as "tinkering." Reading and writing, too…

See if you can find any relevant family papers, Dean Pierce had said. Concordia put down her fork and leaned forward eagerly. "Do you know where Papa's effects would be now?"

Concordia hated attics. They were the most dreary places. Except for cellars, which were worse. The rain was drumming steadily against the roof tiles as she set down her lamp and started peering into boxes.

After two hours, her neck ached and she was ready to give up for the night. She'd found all sorts of items from childhood: spinning tops, hoops, baby dolls, old clothes for dress-up. She'd even found a woman's bright red hooded cloak that gave her an idea for a costume to wear to the masquerade ball. She set it aside to take back to school with her. But she found no papers of any kind from her father; in fact, not many of his possessions were here.

Concordia sighed. His clothes and personal items must have been given away long ago.

Hot and tired from her exertions, Concordia sat down on a trunk to catch her breath. Now what?

She leaned forward and rubbed her throbbing temples. She knew why her father had given the bracelet to Colonel Adams. He couldn't have trusted Mother to give it to her. If Mother was so adamant about not discussing that period of Randolph Wells' life, she certainly wouldn't have passed along the bracelet.

Concordia knew the bracelet was a message. There was something Papa wanted her to find and the bracelet was the clue. But why stipulate that Concordia receive it *after* the colonel's death? If the bracelet—or whatever its message was—had anything to do with the murder of Colonel Adams, eleven years after her father had created this puzzle, she couldn't say, but she was on this road now. There was no going back.

Concordia tried to put herself in her father's position. How could he be sure that what he'd hidden would stay in place for years after his death? How would he know his wife wouldn't find and destroy whatever it was?

His study. It was the only room her mother didn't bother with. Of course, the draperies and rug would have been replaced over time and the desk cleaned out, but the books...

Concordia pulled the bracelet from her pocket and looked at it again. Two of the symbols were definitely familiar to her. She closed her eyes and concentrated.

Then she had it. They were *book engravers' marks.* She pulled the lamp closer. It made sense now. The bead with the shield symbol, a "T" and "F" in the middle, was most likely the publisher Ticknor and Fields. Then there was the bead with the "W" against a looped background that Miss Phillips had pointed out earlier. Of course. C. H. Webb! Her heart pounded in excitement.

Dusting off her skirts and clutching the bracelet, she went down to the study. A wave of nostalgia washed over her as she turned up the wall sconces and looked around the room. This was the first time in years that she'd been in here. The dark mahogany desk, the tufted wing chairs, well-worn and mismatched, the hassock she loved to sit upon as a little girl... they all brought back memories. Was it her imagination, or could she catch the faint scent of her father's pipe tobacco from his favorite reading chair?

Concordia stepped back and looked over the entire wall of floor-to-ceiling bookcases. Where to start?

Finally, after much clambering up and down the ladder provided for the upper shelves, she found the Webb symbol stamped upon a number of matched volumes along the right side of the wall. Soon she found the one for Ticknor and Fields, too, on the left side, again part of a matched set of volumes. But what about the others? Were they printer's marks at all? She wasn't sure. She held the bracelet up to the wall sconce. One of the beads looked to have a spray of branches behind a tiny flag. That didn't belong to any publisher she knew of, but spines were often stamped with marks related to their content. Perhaps she was looking for a United States history book. Not that it narrowed the field; her father's reading interests were eclectic in the extreme.

Many of the books were faded with age. Concordia's eyes watered in an attempt to decipher the markings on the spines.

At last, she found the flag symbol, on a book entitled *Pen Pictures of the War.* It looked to be about the Civil War conflict, more than thirty years ago.

She held the bracelet to the light again. The last bead looked to be a fan, or perhaps a peacock. She stepped back from the shelves, taking note of the position of the three she'd found so far. Where was the fourth?

After staring a long time, she finally found it—a single volume, down nearly at her feet. It too, was crumbling with age. She felt a flush of triumph, much like what she had experienced as a girl, when she'd successfully worked out a cipher her father had crafted for her.

There was nothing unique about any of the books. Perhaps it was a positional clue. It must be at the intersection of these volumes, Concordia reasoned. Pulling out the books a little way from their shelves, she stepped back for a careful look. She ran a hand in an imaginary line with the top and bottom shelves, then on a diagonal with the side shelves, until...

There. A dark blue spine, with faded gilt letters. Milton's *Paradise Lost.* Was that how her father had felt in his remaining weeks of life? Or was it a warning, his ghost imparting a secret and a mission to his progeny? She couldn't get away from ghosts. The presence of Madame Durand in her life was turning her into a mystic.

On the other hand, Papa had always had an ironic sense of humor.

Concordia was in for another surprise when she pulled out the book. Its pages had been glued together, and the interior hollowed out and reinforced with thin balsawood. In the recess, she found tightly-rolled papers and a pouch. She opened the pouch and nearly dropped it in her shock.

It was the heart amulet, stolen from the college's exhibit.

Chapter 16

O, answer me! Let me not burst in ignorance...

Week 6, Instructor Calendar
October 1896

C oncordia couldn't be sure until she checked with Miss
Phillips tomorrow. She had only a glimpse of the
amulet from the back of the crowd during the exhibit opening,
but it *looked* the same. Remembering what Miss Phillips had said
about its magnetic properties, she pulled out a letter opener
from the desk drawer. Sure enough, it was drawn to the stone
with a soft *click*.

She sat back in her father's chair and stared at it for a while.
How could this be *here*? If her father hadn't put it here, then
who had? Was it connected to Colonel Adams' murder?

Then she remembered the papers, and eagerly unrolled
them.

January 13, 1884

My Dear Concordia,

*If you are reading this, then you are truly the clever woman I
knew you would grow up to be. You always loved a good puzzle.*

*But, alas, this is not a game; it is very real. Your mother would
have never given you these pages willingly, for they reveal a painful
incident from my past. You know her ways—not discussing
something is as good as it having never happened. But it did
happen, and you need to know about it. It could affect your future.*

As I write this, you are the tender age of sixteen: too young to understand. If I were honest, I would acknowledge that I haven't the courage to tell you to your face.

As things now stand, I won't be here to tell you when you are old enough: the heart specialist has pronounced his sentence. It is time to get my affairs in order. I regret that I will not see you fulfill your dreams, my dear, but I am confident that you will.

My passions and pursuits have changed since you were a little girl, and for good reason. You have known me as a scholar of the arts and letters. Before you were born, however, and for the early part of your life which you were too young to remember, I was an avid scholar of Ancient Egypt. My expeditions were moderately successful, and I made a few key discoveries that benefitted archeologists greater than myself. Artifacts which I have unearthed are in museums in both Cairo and London. I once had a small collection of my own.

I had two business partners in this enterprise; Colonel Adams, whom you know, and a dealer/ art expert who lived in Cairo. Everyone called him Red. It was an apt name, for he was red-haired, red-complected from the pitiless heat of the desert, and had a red-hot temper, too. The association between the three of us lasted nearly a decade before it soured. We shared an excitement for the chase—to be the first men to find the secrets of the ancient dead, long-hidden and long-forgotten, in places where no man had thought to look. Sun-stroke, thirst, contagion, unscrupulous guides—none of that mattered to us. Adams provided the necessary funding, but never joined our expeditions, until our final one. I was the scholar, interpreting the ancient writings; Red was the planner, coordinating our transportation, our supplies, and our strategy. It seemed a beneficial arrangement.

What caused the rift at the end had been there all along, for Red and I had entirely different goals. I was arrogant enough to want fame, yes, but as a scholar I wanted to preserve the ancient places from the grave-robbers and relic-hunters. Unfortunately, I was too blind to see that Red was the worst of the treasure hunters. By the time I realized what he really was, the damage had been done.

The events that transpired afterward are recorded in my journal. I have included those pages for you and destroyed the rest. I cannot bring myself to recount it here, for what I had done was a terrible thing, and nearly cost Red's life. Despicable as he was, he did not deserve such a fate. After you read the account, you must decide what to do with the information. Use it wisely, my dear, but be warned: I have made an enemy, who may now be your own.

Your loving father,
Randolph Wells

Concordia pulled out her handkerchief, dabbed her eyes, and blew her nose noisily. She still missed Papa.

She looked at the other pages. The writing on these was different; it looked to be a sort of shorthand she didn't recognize. There was also a sketched map. Perhaps, when Concordia brought Miss Phillips the amulet tomorrow, she could make sense of these pages.

"What have you found there, Concordia?" a voice said.

Concordia gave a yelp and nearly jumped out of her chair, papers sliding to the floor. Her mother, clad in a dressing gown and carrying a lamp, stood in the doorway.

"Mother! You gave me a fright."

Mrs. Wells ignored the remark. "What do you have?" she asked again, coming closer.

Concordia scooped up and protectively hugged the pages to her chest. "Papa left these for me. They are papers from his last Egypt expedition."

Her mother's eyes narrowed. "He concealed them from me, all this time?"

"I only just found them tonight. The bracelet I showed you was his clue to help me locate them. I supposed he guessed that you wouldn't give them to me if he had asked you." Concordia gave her mother a long look. "And he was right, wasn't he? Who was *Red*, Mother? What happened?"

"If you have his papers, you don't need *me* to tell you," Mrs. Wells said acidly.

"The journal pages themselves are in some sort of script I cannot read," Concordia said reluctantly.

"Concordia, please, trust my judgment," her mother pleaded. "It is all past, long ago. Leave it be."

"Trust your *judgment?*" Concordia said harshly. "You are allowing yourself to be duped by a charlatan. How can you go in for all this séance mumbo jumbo with Madame Durand and still claim you have good judgment?"

Concordia knew she had gone too far. She had meant to sit down with her mother in a quiet time, and gently point out the ways in which Madame was taking advantage of her grief. She had planned to suggest that she speak with their minister or a friend. Instead, Concordia had been cruel and mocking.

Mrs. Wells clenched her hands together. "You have never lost *a child*," she said through gritted teeth. She turned to leave. "Keep those things, for all of the good they will do you."

Concordia watched her leave in silence, not knowing what to say.

Chapter 17

My soul is full of discord and dismay.

IV, i.

Week 6, Instructor Calendar
October 1896

Concordia struggled to leave behind the guilt she felt about last night's argument. She would have to give careful thought about how to mend the damage.

In the meantime, there were the amulet and papers to think of. This morning Concordia had realized that, despite her discovery, she was no closer to learning the identity of Colonel Adams' killer. So instead of returning directly to the college she decided to stop by the Adams' house. It was an early hour for calling upon the family, but she could at least talk with the staff again and learn if Amelia had returned.

The Wells' housekeeper was very obliging in culling goodies from the larder for Concordia to bring to Mrs. Lewis: a tin of Darjeeling tea; a generous chunk of sponge cake, and a jar of her delectably tangy lemon curd. Mrs. Houston wrapped the whole in a large napkin for Concordia. She gave her a hug.

"You come back soon, now, miss. Try not to worry about your mother. She'll snap out of it, I'm sure."

Mrs. Wells had not come down to say good-bye, but Concordia hadn't expected her to. Perhaps she was a little relieved, too.

"Keep an eye on Mother, will you? And let me know if Madame Durand makes a return?"

The housekeeper promised. Concordia thanked her and left.

"Miss Wells, why what a pleasure to see you again!" Mrs. Lewis said, opening the back door at her knock. "The rest o' the house is at the Sunday service, but yer welcome to come in for some tea."

"Oh dear, what happened to you?" Concordia asked, as she watched the cook hobble on a cane and bandaged foot.

"Ah, my gout is botherin' me," she said. "Doc drained it yesterday. That's why I'm a'tome today, instead of at church." She looked at her curiously. "Shouldn't you be at service, too, if you don't mind me askin'?"

"Ours at the college is a bit later on Sunday," Concordia explained. "I only stopped by for a short stay, but I brought some lovely things from my mother's larder."

"Aye, how is your mother? I haven't seen her in ages."

"Oh, fine," Concordia said vaguely. But Mrs. Lewis wasn't paying much attention, as she untied the napkin.

"Oh, my! You brought Dar-jee-eeling tea! Oh, I adore that; we haven't had it in a dog's age around here."

"You sit; let me make you some," Concordia offered.

The cook didn't demur, but propped her foot up comfortably and pointed to where everything was. Soon they were both sitting with the fragrant tea between them, and slices of Mrs. Houston's sponge cake.

"So you've heard about Sophia. I suppose that's why you're here," Mrs. Lewis said. "But she's nowt back yet. Later today, she comes home."

Concordia almost choked on her tea. "Sophia? They are letting her go?" *Thank goodness.*

Mrs. Lewis shook her head. "She's not out o' trouble yet, poor dear. They's just letting her stay in the house, but she canna leave it. Miss Amelia is back, you see. Poor bairn's been crazy frantic without Miss Sophia. Tried to run away from her uncle's house, twice. They could'na keep her. The missus pleaded wi' the coppers to let Miss Sophia come back to take care o' her sister." She sniffed. "Lord knows the missus could'na trouble herself to do it, even if Miss Amelia woulda let her anywhere near."

Concordia took a moment to digest this information. At least Sophia wouldn't endure the humiliation of prison. For the time being.

"Is Amelia talking?"

The cook made a face. "Not like you and I would call 'talking.' When she isn't dead quiet, she rambles. Cries a lot, too, poor li'l thing. The missus is hoping her sister can calm her down. Mrs. Adams isn't what you'd call 'patient'."

Concordia hoped Sophia could calm the child and get her to talk, and not only for the girl's welfare. They needed answers.

"What'cha got there, miss?" Mrs. Lewis asked in a change of subject. She pointed to the hooded red cape, which Concordia had folded neatly and set aside while making the tea.

"I found it in Mother's attic last night—don't you think it would make a good costume for Red Riding Hood?" Concordia said, reaching over to fluff out the folds. "The college is having a Halloween ball for the students and staff next week."

The cook's eyes brightened. "Ah! I remember All Hallows back home, when I was a wee one. We'd go 'guising'—wi' blackened faces and old clothes to fool evil spirr'ts, and folks would give us sweets. But my favorite thing was dookin' for apples. Will your students be playin' any o' those sort o' games?"

Concordia nodded. "The girls have convinced some of the staff to sponsor several of the traditional activities in the smaller rooms at Sycamore House. There will be dancing, too, in the president's dining hall."

Mrs. Lewis leaned forward in interest as Concordia ticked off the list with her fingers.

"The plan so far is to have Miss Banning read tea leaves, Madame Durand to work the planchette board, Miss Phillips to oversee what you call 'apple dookin,' and Mr. Langdon to supervise the nut-casting."

The latter activity, nut-casting, was quite popular with the students. Each girl took turns throwing two nuts in the fire— one to represent themselves, and one a potential beau—to predict the future of their relationship. It was all harmless nonsense, of course, but sometimes the students got a little over-eager and drew too close to the fire. Last year, one girl got hit right between the eyes when a nut popped back out of the hearth. The young lady was less distressed by the injury than by the resulting prediction that the object of her affections was false. Concordia hoped President Langdon could keep the crowd in check.

"Aye, I remember that custom of burning the nits," the cook said. "The ones that popped were bad, but if they burned brightly, you've found your true love." She closed her eyes and quoted:

The auld guid wife's well-hoarded nits
Are round an' round divided,
An' monie lads' and lassies' fates'
Are there that night decided.
Some kindle, couthie, side by side
An' burn thegither trimly;
Some start away w'i' saucy pride,
And jump out-owre the chimlie

Concordia was surprised at first to hear the cook quoting a Robert Burns verse, but realized that any Scotswoman worth her tartan had her kinsman's poetry committed to memory from a young age.

The doorbell rang.

"That could be Miss Sophia now!" Mrs. Lewis said, frantically removing her apron, brushing crumbs off her chest, and struggling to her feet.

"I'll answer it," Concordia offered. It would be excruciating to wait for the hobbling cook to make it all the way to the front door. With as much decorum as she could manage, she made her way quickly down the hall and opened the door.

Lieutenant Capshaw was supporting a thin, weary-looking Sophia on the step.

"Sophia!" Concordia cried, embracing her friend. "Thank heaven you're out of that dreadful place. Hello, lieutenant," she added.

"Lieutenant Capshaw was the one who pleaded my case to his superiors," Sophia said, "although it isn't over."

"That will come with time," Capshaw said, "but no more secrets, miss."

Sophia inclined a weary head. From Concordia's angle, the circles under Sophia's eyes and the slight twitch along her jaw were alarming signs of profound exhaustion.

The hobbled Mrs. Lewis had caught up to them. "Miss Sophia, you are a sight fer sore eyes, I must say."

Sophia gave her a hug. "It's good to be back. Where's Amelia?"

"Sleeping," the cook said. "The doctor gave her something. Why don't you lay down for a bit, too, miss? You look tuckered out."

"I think I will. But you'll let me know when she wakes?"

The cook promised, and led Sophia up to her room. Although who led whom was questionable, with one hobbling on a cane and the other so tired she could barely stand upright.

Concordia turned back to the lieutenant, expecting to say good-bye, but instead, Capshaw continued on to the parlor and gestured to her. "If you please, Miss Wells, we have a number of things to talk about."

"Now," he began, when they were both seated and the parlor door closed behind them, "we have made progress in the investigation of Colonel Adams' murder, but not nearly enough." He coughed delicately, as if to coax the next words out. "I need your—" *cough* "—help, miss."

That was a first, Concordia thought, suppressing a smile. "What do you want me to do?"

"Let me first explain where we are."

Concordia settled the folds of her skirt and waited.

Capshaw got up and paced the room as he talked. "We know Miss Adams is innocent of the murder of her father. She made a false confession and tampered with evidence in order to protect someone else." He stopped and looked over at Concordia. "I didn't have to look far for that person. There is only one individual Miss Adams would go to such lengths to protect."

Concordia nodded. "Her sister, Amelia."

"Correct," Capshaw said. He continued his pacing. "But then the question I had to ask was *why* Miss Adams would so readily suspect her eight-year-old sister of murdering their own father? Because even if Miss Adams saw the girl standing over the body, gun in hand, nightgown bloody—and I'm sure that what Miss Adams burned in her fireplace was her *sister's* bloody nightdress, not her own—why did she jump to the conclusion that it was purposeful? Miss Adams would not have acted as she did had she thought it was an accident. No, she thought her sister had *deliberately* killed their father."

Concordia felt a chill run through her at these words. "How could that be?" she protested. "What possible motive could such a young child have? It's incomprehensible."

Capshaw gave a heavy sigh and, finally, seated himself again. "That is the line of inquiry I have been pursuing since Miss Adams' arrest. And I am sorry to say that I have found an ugly truth in this household, which provides *both* sisters with plenty of motive." He hesitated.

"What, lieutenant?" Concordia prompted. "What ugly truth?" As dearly as she did not want to be told, she knew it was necessary.

Capshaw shifted in his chair. "The more I looked into the colonel's past, the more I realized what a scoundrel he was: ruthless—and at times unscrupulous—in his business dealings. During his military career, he exacted severe punishments upon those under his command, and sabotaged rivals in order to get ahead. I even found that he and your father had worked together long ago, Miss Wells, with Adams providing the funding for tomb expeditions in Egypt and even going on their last one. It went badly, I understand. I wouldn't be surprised if Adams had a hand in that, too. Perhaps you know more about it than I. But none of this prepared me for—" He stopped, gathering his composure.

Concordia kept her patience in check as best she could.

Capshaw continued. "It took a while, talking with the staff, the family doctor, the lawyer. Many reluctant people, but finally, I was able to piece it together."

He looked Concordia square in the eye. "The colonel ill-used his daughters, Miss Wells," he said quietly. "He methodically beat both of his girls."

Concordia's heart hammered hard in her chest. She couldn't get a full breath. Snippets of memory came back to her from their childhood when Sophia would come to play. Sophia had seemed happier during the colonel's assignments that called him away from home. Concordia remembered a smattering of injuries Sophia had suffered, explained away as a collision with a door or a stumble down the stairs. Then there was the scary time when Sophia was said to have fallen, cracked her ribs, and later developed pneumonia. As a child, Concordia had never suspected. Now it fit together.

Capshaw was watching her closely. "You have been friends with Sophia for a very long time, haven't you? You see it now."

Concordia took a shaky breath and met the policeman's eyes. No wonder Sophia had left the house as soon as she was able. But she didn't go very far, because of Amelia. How could Adams have been so cruel to his own daughters?

"So Amelia has also been a target of the colonel?" Concordia asked.

"When I confronted Miss Adams about what I knew, she told me... some of it. She had hoped that Amelia would be spared, but she tried to keep a close eye on her. She thinks it started recently, after her mother's death."

Concordia thought back to Amelia's appearance the day after the murder. "I saw no bruises on her, except for the bump on her head."

Capshaw sighed. "At my request, the doctor examined Miss Amelia thoroughly. He found a number of old bruises, along the ribs. The colonel learned on Miss Adams, remember. He would know how to do it by now so it wouldn't show."

A blaze of white-hot anger burned in Concordia's chest. She stood and paced the room. "*Why?* Why didn't someone do something to protect these girls? The mother? The doctor? The servants?"

"The servants were in no position to speak out," Capshaw said, also standing, "although, when I finally got the truth out of Mrs. Lewis she said that both the staff and the mother tried to keep the girls out of his way. Their mother is dead now, but during her lifetime she feared her husband's temper. Her declining health made it difficult for her to intervene and she had nowhere to turn. According to the law, a man has the right to discipline his children as he sees fit.

"By the time Miss Adams was fifteen, however, she was strong enough—and determined enough—to deter the colonel's… proclivities. That's when she said the beatings finally stopped. For her, that is."

"What about the doctor? Why didn't he do something?" Concordia asked.

Capshaw shook his head. "The family doctor of Miss Adams' childhood passed away a number of years ago. The current one had his suspicions, but wasn't called in often enough to be sure."

"So you believe that this gives Amelia sufficient motive to have killed him. What about her head injury? Could Adams have struck her, and she grabbed the gun to protect herself?"

"And shot him in the *back*?" Capshaw asked skeptically. "More likely, she fainted and hit her head on the desk as she fell, for all we know. I wish the child could tell us."

"I have trouble believing Amelia deliberately killed her father. But if it's true, what would happen to her?" There could be no good answer to this, Concordia knew.

"A child this young would not be formally charged," Capshaw said, "but—" His voice trailed off.

"—she would be quietly locked away," Concordia finished for him. "Dear heaven." She shuddered. A vulnerable, traumatized young girl at the mercy of strangers, surrounded by the violently insane? If the child weren't already mad, she soon would be.

They were both quiet for a few moments.

"The only hope for Amelia is if we can find that someone else is responsible," Capshaw said. "Once I confronted Miss Adams with what I knew about her father, she admitted that she'd lied."

"So what really happened?" Concordia asked.

"By Miss Adams' account, she awoke to Amelia shaking her. Her nightdress was bloody. At first, Miss Adams was panicked, thinking that Amelia had been grievously injured. While checking the girl for any cuts, she found the bruises on her ribs. Amelia was still frantic to lead her back to the study, so Miss Adams got Amelia a clean gown and followed her back there. When she saw their father had been shot, she assumed that her sister had just been beaten by the colonel and had shot him to stop it."

Concordia closed her eyes to regain her composure. It was all so horrible. "How did Sophia come to have the gun?" she asked, finally.

"Miss Adams isn't sure about that. She thinks that Amelia must have crouched over the body—that's how the nightdress got so bloody—picked up the gun, and in her panic, ran to her sister's room for help with it still in her hand. Whether the child was panicked because she had just shot her father, or had just found her father, we do not know. She probably set the weapon down in the bedroom while she was shaking her sister awake. Miss Adams didn't see it in her room until it was too late to put it back. That's when she hid it."

He sighed and shook his head. "If only Miss Adams hadn't tampered with the evidence. Especially burning the girl's nightgown. We might have been able to tell from the bloodstains if Amelia had done the shooting or not."

Concordia remembered the night after the murder, when she searched Sophia's room. The stiffened fabric, wrapped around something heavy, and shoved under Sophia's bed. It had to have been Amelia's gown and the gun. Sophia couldn't risk destroying the gown until the police were out of the house. Concordia could kick herself for not taking it out and examining it at the time. But there was no point in volunteering *that* piece of information to Capshaw. She'd never hear the end of it.

"You said I could help, lieutenant. What can I do?"

"I'm thinking of the two Egyptian relics that are missing. Nothing else is gone. I'm skeptical that they've been misplaced or sold. They were so valuable that the colonel was reluctant to donate them to the college, so it's unlikely that he would have been careless with the receipt of sale. I've found a number of receipts for valuable acquisitions and sales of such."

Maybe there was hope, Concordia thought. She remembered something else, too. "You told me that the outer door of the safe was open and the colonel was lying right next to it. That could also indicate an intruder's attempt to secure valuables."

Capshaw nodded. "But I'm specifically thinking of *Egyptian* valuables. The missing artifacts were most likely acquired while Adams collaborated with your father. That's where I need your help. I was hoping you could tell me more about the projects your father and Adams worked on together, any associates they had, and so on."

To Capshaw's alarm, Concordia laughed aloud. That she and the lieutenant had been simultaneously trying to find answers to the murder, through the unlikely avenue of her father's Egypt expeditions, was the oddest piece of luck she had seen in a while.

She rummaged through her satchel, pulling out the amulet and papers she had found last night, along with the bracelet. "Perhaps these may help, lieutenant."

Chapter 18

Time be thine, And thy best graces spend it at thy will.
I.ii

Week 6, Instructor Calendar
October 1896

Concordia barely returned in time for Sunday service. As she made her way into the pew, hymnal in hand, she saw Miss Grant give her what the students had dubbed "the Ogre Eye." She was in for it later, she knew.

She tried not to squirm as she waited for chapel to conclude. She wanted to talk with Miss Phillips right away, to try to make heads-or-tails of her father's journals. It looked to be in a special kind of shorthand that Miss Phillips, accomplished in all things cryptogram, might be able to decode.

Lieutenant Capshaw had perked up considerably when Concordia showed him her father's letter mentioning a third man, "Red." Could this man have broken into the house in search of something valuable in the colonel's collection? Had the colonel walked in on him, perhaps, and was killed? But why now, after more than two decades?

She had to decipher her father's journal. She was sure the answer lay there.

Concordia looked for Miss Phillips when chapel was over. She hadn't seen her at the service.

"Where is Miss Phillips?" she asked Miss Jenkins, the infirmarian, as they filed out the doors and into the chill, late-October sunshine.

"She's caught a nasty chest cold. I sent her to bed."

"How unfortunate," Concordia murmured.

Concordia knew it was tactless of her, but she needed answers, so she walked over to Miss Phillips' quarters in Hemlock Cottage.

The house matron, balancing a tray of broth and toast, answered her knock. She frowned in disapproval. "She's not to have visitors, Miss Wells. Miss Jenkins' instructions."

"Nonsense, Gertie," a voice croaked through the open door of the instructor's quarters. "She can bring me the tray. You go on."

The housekeeper hesitated. "Well, I *do* have a lot to do. All right, miss, go ahead in, and take this. But don't stay long or Miss Jenkins'll have my hide."

Concordia carried the tray into Miss Phillips' room.

The history professor's quarters was a suite of two rooms on the first floor of the small dormitory building. It was much like Concordia's own, with a cozy outer room to use as a study. There was space for a writing desk and chair, along with the reading chair and table flanking the hearth. Beyond the study was the bedroom, simply furnished with an armoire, bed, night table, and dry sink. The clutter of books, artifacts, and tools, most still in boxes, made Miss Phillips' rooms even more cramped than Concordia's.

"I have yet to finish getting settled in," Miss Phillips said apologetically, gesturing vaguely at the tallest stack.

"How are you feeling?" Concordia asked.

Miss Phillips coughed, then grimaced. "Rather miserable, actually. I don't know what's worse, the coughing, or the 'remedies' Miss Jenkins comes up with. Or the boredom," she added.

"Well, if you're up to it, I have something that will pique your interest," Concordia said, passing over what she'd found secreted in her father's study.

Dorothy Phillips' mouth formed a small "o" of disbelief when she saw the amulet. "You found it?! But where?" She sat up and turned it over in her hands.

"So that *is* the missing amulet?" Concordia asked.

Miss Phillips, holding it up to the light, sighed and shook her head. "I thought it was at first; it's nearly identical. Do you see, here?" She pointed to a series of diagonal scorings on the back of the piece. "The original didn't have those markings. But this is amazing, nonetheless. So there *are* two of them. It proves my theory that these type of amulets, the ones with magnetic properties, were made in pairs. They were probably used...in healing... rituals." She set it down as a fit of coughing overtook her.

Concordia poured her a glass of water. Miss Phillips drank and leaned back against the pillows.

"Where did you find it?"

For the second time that day, Concordia related how she'd pieced together the clues from the bracelet, connecting them to printer's marks on the spines of books in her father's study.

"Ah, printers' marks. I thought they looked familiar." Miss Phillips nodded in approval. "Very clever, my dear."

Concordia flushed. "My father and I often composed riddles and codes for each other when I was a child, although I doubt mine were much of a challenge to *him*." She smiled at the memory.

"Why did he go to so much trouble to set up such a puzzle, rather than just give it to you?"

"Perhaps he thought I was too young to have it. He died when I was sixteen."

"He could have left it with your mother to give you later," Miss Phillips pointed out. She looked at Concordia's expression. "Ah. I take it that your mother would not have respected his wishes. Do you know why?"

Concordia shook her head. "She refuses to discuss any of my father's past. She was quite angry when she saw that I had found these."

Miss Phillips smiled in sympathy. "Mothers can be difficult. Heaven knows mine was. I'm much older than you, and attending college back in my day was even more unusual than it is now. It caused a rift that wasn't mended for years."

Miss Phillips stared thoughtfully at the amulet in her hand. "Well, now we know there are two: this one, which had been in your father's possession, and the other, which was part of Colonel Adams' collection and donated to us, although we're fairly certain the donation was accidental. Unfortunately, we still don't know where it is."

That question wasn't as important to Concordia as understanding why her father left her *this* relic, who the third man was, and what had happened on that expedition.

"I was hoping you could look through these notes of his. I found them with the relic." She showed Miss Phillips the letter. "This was the only writing I could read. The rest is in some sort of shorthand."

Miss Phillips read through the letter, calmly at first, then became more animated at the end. "A third man," she said. "That could explain the exhibit theft, and perhaps it explains the colonel's murder."

"It cannot explain both; they cancel each other out," Concordia said. "If the 'third man' stole the amulet at the exhibit, then he wouldn't have needed to go to Colonel Adams' house in an attempt to steal it, and kill him in the process. However, if he *wasn't* the one who stole the amulet from the exhibit, and thought the colonel had it –which you had thought at first, remember?—that would make sense."

"That's assuming the man visited Colonel Adams in order to steal the amulet," Miss Phillips pointed out. "He may have been after something else."

"Good point. Two other Egyptian artifacts—a statuette and a necklace—*are* missing. Capshaw is trying to determine if they were sold by the colonel, or stolen when he was murdered. It isn't clear."

Miss Phillips looked troubled.

"What is it?" Concordia asked.

"I just realized. Whoever we're talking about—this 'third man'—must be someone we know. Someone who attended the exhibit opening."

Concordia shivered. "Someone who knew the amulet was missing—or stole it himself." She remembered that the newspaper reporter, Ben Rosen, showed an inordinate interest in Colonel Adams' collection, and had even visited the colonel the day of his death. She would have to find out more about the man.

"But there's a problem with that line of thought, too," Concordia said. "You discovered it missing after everyone had left. Only you and I and Miss Pomeroy knew about it before the colonel's death. You didn't tell the lady principal until after the murder, remember? We're missing something here."

Miss Phillips drank some more water before speaking. "We are missing a great deal. It's all a confused muddle."

"Can you decipher the other pages?" Concordia asked. "They may give us the answer."

Miss Phillips wheezed and squinted at them. "I'm sorry. I don't recognize the shorthand system. My faculties aren't working to their full capacity, to say the least. I can work on it when I'm better."

Concordia swallowed her disappointment and patted Miss Phillips' hand. "I understand."

"You'll want to be careful with the amulet your father left you," Miss Phillips said, giving her a troubled look. "The 'third man' may be after that one, too. We can assume that, one way or the other, he has the colonel's by now."

Concordia left the papers and map with Miss Phillips and returned to Willow Cottage. She looked around her quarters. Where could she hide the amulet? Someone determined enough to kill Colonel Adams would easily tear through her rooms and find whatever hiding place she'd naively decided upon. Her best course, she decided, was to keep it upon her person. She slipped it into her skirt pocket. It felt a bit heavy there, but wasn't cumbersome. She would have to remember to take it out when she changed skirts. Sometimes remembering that she'd left her spectacles on top of her head was a challenge.

With that settled she wrote a couple of letters and then sent for Eli. He came quickly.

"Yes, miss?" He was looking better these days, Concordia noticed. His face no longer had that pinched look of a child perpetually without enough to eat. His unruly hair was at least somewhat combed, and his neck and ears were clean. His clothes were a trifle large on him, but at least they were tidy and free of tears. Staying with the Durands was having a good effect on the boy. The Cat, however, which Concordia could see twining about the boy's legs, looked as disreputable as ever, and now had fur missing from the end of its tail.

"How have you been? I haven't seen you in a while," Concordia said. "Are they keeping you busy with errands?"

"Oh, yes, indeed," he said, "I'm ever so busy, with my duties here, and workin' for Madame Doo-rand, too. And Mr. Clyde has been teachin' me carpenter stuff in his free time. I do have to go to school in the morning, but that ain't so bad. I can write my name now, and read a little, too," he added.

"How wonderful! I'm so proud of you. I have a couple of messages that are *very* important. Can you deliver them for me? Make sure you hand each one only to the person it's addressed to." She passed one over. Let's see what he can read, she thought.

His eyes perked up when he recognized Sophia's name. "I can do that. It would be nice to see Miss Sophia again."

That reminded Concordia of something. "By the way, the parlor maid, Clara, wanted me to ask you to return the Adams' back door key. They've been missing it."

Eli shook his head. "I don't have it. Last time I used it was a while ago, miss. And I put it back, I know I did."

"Hmm. Well, tell Clara so she knows to look elsewhere." It wouldn't be good for the household to have a key loose. Concordia gave him the other envelope. "And I also want you to deliver this one. Into his hands only."

She shooed the cat from the ottoman, where it had taken up residence when her back was turned. With an air of wounded dignity, it jumped off and dodged behind the coffee table. She sighed.

Eli was puzzling out the address on the second envelope in the meanwhile, lips silently forming the letter sounds, before he had it. "P-police, miss? Must I?"

"It's only Lieutenant Capshaw, Eli. He's a nice man, remember? He saved us when the railing collapsed. You don't have anything to worry about from him. I would trust him with my life."

Eli looked doubtful. Concordia understood his reluctance, since he'd seen the inside of a police station far too often in his short life. "Amelia's welfare depends upon it," she added.

That seemed to do the trick. Eli straightened, squared his thin shoulders as if girding for battle, and left to do the deed, the cat trotting at his heels.

Her notes to Lieutenant Capshaw and Sophia *were* very important, Concordia reflected. They explained the delay in deciphering her father's journal, and asked Sophia and Capshaw to stall for time before Amelia was brought before an examining panel of doctors—and possibly committed.

"Miss Wells?" came Ruby's muffled voice through the door. Concordia opened it. The matron was holding a bright red garment.

"I think this will do," Ruby said, passing it over. "It's a bit of an antique from my sister's trunk, but I re-did the laces for you."

It was a pretty red velvet over-bodice, heavily-boned at the sides and front, with a profusion of black silk lacing.

"Oh, Ruby, it's perfect! Thank you," Concordia said. That should complete her Red Riding Hood costume for next week's Masquerade Ball.

Ruby raised her head, and sniffed. "Do you smell something?"

They both looked toward the staircase that led up to the student rooms and saw a gray haze of smoke.

As if on cue, a voice from upstairs yelled "Fire!"

Ruby rushed to the kitchen for a pan of water while Concordia grabbed the hall mat and ran upstairs.

The sharp smell of burnt sugar was overpowering. Coughing, she pushed past students clustered around a low table, as they ineffectually tried to put out the fire. Sugar and chocolate had spilled onto the burner the students had been using—illegally, of course—and ignited paper wrappers and napkins. Their attempts to blow out the flames had only made it worse. Now the tablecloth had caught, too.

"Run down and fetch more pans of water, quickly," Concordia ordered. She started beating at the flames with her mat.

Some of the girls were shrieking, which further grated on Concordia's already frayed nerves. "Stop that caterwauling!" she called out sharply. "Do you want to bring Miss Grant down on our heads?"

That shut them up plenty fast.

Ruby came up with a full pan of water sloshing over the sides, and dumped it on the flames. Several other girls followed with more pots of water, until the fire was completely out. But the smoke, accompanied by the sickening burnt-sugar smell, was still oppressive.

"Open the windows, and we'll air out the room until tomorrow. Miss Bentham, move your things in with Miss Rochester for the time being. Count yourselves *lucky* that the lady principal wasn't here to see this," Concordia admonished.

"Um, Miss We-ells..." one girl said nervously, tugging on her sleeve and pointing to the hall.

Oh, no.

There stood Miss Grant, hands on hips, her tiny dark eyes snapping in anger. Her gaze took in the blackened tabletop, the burnt fragments of tablecloth, and the sodden, *squishy* carpet.

"It seems that your luck has just run out, Miss Wells," she said.

It was a subdued cottage of wretched girls when Miss Grant finally left. Even though only five young ladies were involved in the illicit hot cocoa preparation, the lady principal had seen fit to punish the entire house. No one in Willow Cottage would be attending the Halloween Masquerade Ball. No one, that is, except for Concordia, whom Miss Grant still needed as chaperone.

Concordia sighed. She would have preferred to stay here with the girls on Halloween, and at least make the time a little more agreeable, with stories around the fire and goodies from Ruby's kitchen. They could be reckless girls, to be sure, but they didn't deserve such a penalty.

The front door bell rang.

Now who could that be? Since Ruby and the girls were still occupied with cleaning up, Concordia answered it.

It was Eli and the Cat—would he ever leave the beast behind, she wondered—with replies to her messages. She'd forgotten about them in the tumult.

The boy sniffed the air. "Is somethin' burnin'?"

Concordia grimaced. "It's a long story. You have messages from Sophia and the lieutenant?"

"Jus' Miss Sophia. They were both at her house." He passed it over.

Concordia sat, pushing the purring animal's face out of her lap as she read her friend's note.

> *My dear Concordia,*
>
> *I have attempted to persuade Lydia to abandon the commitment proceedings against Amelia, but without success. Not even the lieutenant, with his theory that the perpetrator is an enemy from Father's past, has been able to convince her that Amelia is innocent. Amelia's own erratic behavior has not helped, and she becomes hysterical in our step-mother's presence, although she is calmer when she is with me. Of course, my earlier actions have not helped, either.*
>
> *I think Lydia wants to get on with the comfortable life of a rich widow, and be done with the irksome encumbrance of a traumatized child. I will refrain from saying more on that front, as I do not wish to be un-Christian.*

Lieutenant Capshaw and I have been hatching a plan to delay Amelia's commitment proceeding, to give you more time to translate your father's journal. I know you'll send us word as soon as you know something.

Leave it to us, and do not worry.

Yours,

Sophia

Concordia let out a breath she didn't realize she'd been holding. A burden had been lifted, at least temporarily. And once Miss Phillips had recovered, that lady would be able to unlock the secret in her father's journal.

Eli had been anxiously watching Concordia. "You look better now, miss."

Concordia stood and patted him on the shoulder. "I am. You've been a big help, too. Are you hungry?"

She looked down at the boy and smiled. Silly question.

Chapter 19

O day and night, but this is wondrous strange!

I.v

Week 7, Instructor Calendar
October/November 1896

It was the night of the Halloween Masquerade.

Concordia smoothed her skirts. Except for her boots and cloak, she was ready. She checked the mirror to assess the result. Did she look like an early-era village girl setting out for the forest? About to meet a Big Bad Wolf?

She'd chosen a simple skirt of soft navy wool and her only ruffled-yoke white blouse. Over top she wore an apron of white muslin along with the bright red over-bodice that Ruby had lent her. It was a bit tight. While flattering to her figure—especially the bosom—it certainly wasn't comfortable.

Concordia grimaced at her reflection. But it should work. To complete the effect she had brushed out her hair and plaited it into pigtails, with red bows at the ends. How odd it would feel to walk out of the cottage with her hair down. She draped the red cloak about her shoulders and sat to put on her boots.

The cottage doorbell rang.

Drat. With Ruby and the girls occupied in the kitchen making consolation treats, she was going to have to answer that. Concordia hobbled into the hallway and opened the door.

There stood David Bradley.

Concordia's mouth opened of its own accord as she stood there and stared, balanced on one foot, boot in one hand and doorknob in the other.

He grinned as he took in the sight. "Aren't you going to invite me in? I promise I'm not a wolf, Miss... Riding Hood?"

"Oh! I'm sorry. I had no idea you were back in town! Please, do come in." She opened the door wider. "We can sit in the parlor. I have to leave in a minute, though—" she broke off when she noticed his attire. Her heart beat a little faster as she realized that he was dressed to attend tonight's ball, too: not in costume, but in evening dress. The effect was quite handsome. His crisply starched white shirt, sharply creased and well-tailored trousers, and black tail coat fit him just as well as she remembered from last year's Spring Dance, when her heart had been in her throat as he'd swept her along the dance floor.

"*You* are going? But the dance has been restricted to students and staff," Concordia finally said.

"I *am* on the staff," he said, smiling.

Concordia was confused. "How—"

He steered her over to a chair, then pulled a nearby stool closer and perched himself on it. "I should have written you about it first, rather than surprising you this way. It all happened rather quickly."

He peered at her closely. "You don't look happy to see me."

Concordia shook her head. "It's not that... I'm trying to understand, that's all."

She *was* glad to see him. Actually, a bit disconcerted by *how* glad she felt at the very sight of him. His presence always made her feel reassured, as if everything would turn out fine. She wasn't sure whether to trust that feeling.

David gave her a long look before continuing. "When Amelia was sent away, I went back to Boston to teach my classes. But I was worried about her the entire time. And Sophia."

Concordia noticed the *And Sophia,* and wondered yet again if he had formed an attachment to her friend.

"It was appalling to me that she was in prison and I was so far away. I couldn't do anything for either of them," David continued. "I never believed Sophia's story. I'd just decided to give my classes back to the fellow who had taken them over before—and he was happy for the work, believe me—when I got word from Sophia that she and Amelia were back at the house. That decided it for me, and here I am."

"You said you were on the staff here," Concordia reminded him.

"Oh, yes, that. I didn't like the idea of just kicking around Hartford, hovering night and day around Sophia and Amelia without anything else to occupy me, so I went to my old friend, Professor Grundy. You must know him, if only by name: he's head of your Chemistry department. He put me on the staff just yesterday as his assistant. I'll be running some labs for him and grading student work. And it appears that my timing is fortuitous. I get the distinct pleasure of attending your ball." David Bradley looked at Concordia appreciatively. "You make a charming Red Riding Hood, my dear. Shall I call you 'Red' for short this evening?"

Red. Concordia's cheeks grew hot and her hands grew cold. She trembled.

"Concordia? What's wrong?" He gently took her hands in his.

It was too much. She burst into tears.

A moment later, Ruby walked into the parlor to a startling scene: that of Mr. Bradley—where had *he* come from?—with his arm around Miss Wells' shoulders as she sobbed into his shirt.

The house matron, charged with the propriety of the ladies under her care, raised an eyebrow at the man. He grimaced apologetically at her over Concordia's shoulder.

Ruby rolled her eyes, backed out of the room, and quietly closed the door behind her.

Sometimes, the rules have to be bent a little.

Once the storm was reduced to mere sniffles, David handed Concordia his handkerchief. "Better?" he asked, smoothing back a strand of hair that had fallen across her face.

She nodded. "I'm s-sorry for losing my composure. The past few weeks have been dreadful." She looked at the closed door. "Did someone come in? Oh, dear. Not one of the girls, I hope."

David smiled. "Just Ruby, don't worry."

Concordia sighed, and dried the last of her tears. "Your shirt is wet."

"It will dry," David said. "Now tell me what's wrong."

So she did. She started with the suspicion centered upon Amelia, and Capshaw's investigation of enemies from the colonel's past. This brought her to the surprising Egypt connection between the colonel and her father and the puzzle he'd left. She described her discovery of a second amulet, her father's papers, and the man named Red.

"Something untoward happened on the expedition, but I don't know what. The account is written in some sort of shorthand. My mother refuses to discuss anything about Papa's Egypt days. And Miss Phillips has been too ill to work on decoding the journal entries."

"I can write to a friend of mine in Boston who may be familiar with that shorthand system," David offered. "Just in case Miss Phillips is not up to the task." He looked at her closely. "But it's fair to say there's more going on, isn't there, Concordia? Not just trying to solve Colonel Adams' murder, although that's bad enough. This is the most agitated I've seen you. It doesn't look as if you're getting much sleep lately."

He knew her better than she realized, Concordia thought.

"Yes, there's more." She told him about Madame Durand's pervasive influence upon her mother, the railing scare of nearly losing Eli over the side, and Miss Grant's hostility towards her.

"The woman hates me," Concordia added.

"Aren't you exaggerating just a bit?" David said gently.

Concordia gave a bitter laugh. "This is only your second day, David. Give her time. You'll see. On top of everything else, she has punished all of the students here at the cottage for a— well, maybe not *mild* infraction, there was a fire—"

David looked startled. "You had a *fire* here?"

"Just a *little* one. As a result, the entire cottage has been prohibited from attending tonight's ball."

"I imagine that isn't popular."

Concordia shook her head. "The students in the *other* cottages were quite upset when they learned about it. There's a great deal of ill-feeling toward Miss Grant these days."

There was a discreet knock before the parlor door opened and Ruby walked in. "It's getting late, miss. And the girls want to see you before you go."

"Mercy!" Concordia exclaimed, jumping up. Miss Grant wanted the chaperones in place ahead of time. She was going to be late, *again*.

David held out an arm. "Shall we?"

At least she had an ally to help her beard the dragon in her den. Or, more aptly, the big bad wolf.

The decorating committee had outdone itself this year, Concordia reflected as they approached Sycamore House. It was dusk, but the walkway was illuminated by cheery pumpkin lanterns placed along both sides. The students had liberally festooned the entrance with seasonal décor: cornstalks, bittersweet vines, and chestnut branches. Ribbon-and-raffia swags were affixed along the room and around the supper buffet tables, which would be laid for the meal later. At the moment, only horn-of-plenty centerpieces graced the table tops. Lanterns and candelabras illuminated dark corners and added to the cheeriness of the room, but Concordia knew they would soon add to the heat of it once the room was fully occupied.

The musicians tuned their instruments while clumps of faculty and staff, many in costume, chatted and looked around. Concordia spotted Lady Principal Grant, dressed as a queen—Elizabeth, she presumed, judging by the ornate ruff and white face powder she sported along with a truly monstrous farthingale-hooped skirt. Miss Grant, at that moment, fixed glowering eyes upon *her* from across the room. Whether Miss Grant disapproved of Concordia's lateness, her costume, or the presence of a man she didn't recognize standing beside her, she didn't know. Perhaps it was all three. Miss Grant began her advance upon them.

David followed her stare. "Is *that* the lady principal?" he murmured.

Concordia could only nod, watching Miss Grant in fascination as she maneuvered around the growing crowd. The extreme side hoops of her costume had a will of their own and whacked more than one person in the lady's path.

In a moment, she was upon them. "You are *late*," Miss Grant snapped. She turned to David. "And who are *you?*"

Miss Grant had made an unfortunate costume choice, Concordia thought. Setting aside the hooped-skirt malady, the face powder was already forming creases along the lady's forehead, mouth and eyes. Ill-temper and heat would only make that worse by evening's end.

David gave a formal bow. "Mr. Bradley, ma'am. I was recently hired to assist Professor Grundy."

"Hmph. Well, I suppose that's acceptable," Miss Grant said grudgingly. "Your before-supper chaperone assignment will be right here, in the ballroom. Are you competent enough to make sure these heedless girls don't knock over any candles and start a fire? Good. We've had enough fires to last us a while, haven't we?" she added, giving Concordia a coy look. Concordia flushed.

"You will be on rotation, Miss Wells," Miss Grant continued, "assisting the smaller groups in their activities. Pay special attention to Miss Pomeroy. She had to step in at the last minute to replace Miss Phillips, who is still in bed. She is in charge of the apple-bobbing game on the back porch. The woman doesn't know her head from a hole in the ground, if you ask me."

Charles Harrison, the mathematics professor, walked up to them. "Miss Grant, the band doesn't know if they are supposed to start with a quadrille or a two-step. I cannot find Mr. Langdon or Mr. Pierce to ask. And the kitchen staff wants to know when to lay supper."

The lady principal shook her head, clearly harried. She turned away without a backward glance and stomped toward the musicians' platform.

"I begin to see what you mean," David whispered.

"Who are you supposed to be, Mr. Harrison?" Concordia politely enquired, noting the man's curled wig, dark frock coat, and white cravat.

Mr. Harrison looked surprised. "Blaise Pascal, of course," he answered.

David nodded. "The famous philosopher and mathematician."

"Ah," Concordia said. She would never understand the appeal of mathematics. But she had to admit that Charles Harrison was surprisingly competent as the director of the Shakespeare play. The students were coming along nicely.

"If you'll excuse me, I have to help Madame Durand set up in the parlor," Mr. Harrison said, and left.

"I suppose I should check on Miss Pomeroy," Concordia said reluctantly.

"See you at supper, then. But watch out for wolves," he added.

"I intend to."

Concordia struggled across the ballroom to reach the hallway. The room was rapidly filling with girls, in all manner of dress: elegant, imaginative, and even bizarre. A headdress of spangled bats adorned one girl's head. It quite spoiled what would have been a pretty effect, as her gown was a charming black Brussels net over orange silk.

One sight stopped Concordia dead in her tracks just as she was about to clear the ballroom floor. At least a dozen girls had just entered the room dressed in identical costume.

"Are they supposed to be knights of some sort?" Concordia asked Miss Jenkins, who had just walked by.

Miss Jenkins glanced back at the entrance. Each student in the group was wearing a simple red tunic under a white cape decorated in a gold *fleur de lis* pattern; each wore a mock sword strapped around the waist and a coif of shimmery material over the hair. The effect, multiplied, was stunning. Except for variations in height and build, one couldn't tell the girls apart.

"How odd," Miss Jenkins said. "I think each girl is supposed to be Joan of Arc. See the *fleur de lis* on the capes? Much like the standard carried into the Battle of *Orleans*."

"Really? A dozen Joan of Arcs? Or would it be *Joans* of Arc, I wonder? Why would they dress as the same historic figure?" In Concordia's experience, the young ladies took great pains to avoid duplication, rather than actively plan for it.

"Ever since that series about Joan of Arc came out in *Harper's* last year—you remember, the one that turned out to have been written by Mr. Clemens—she has become quite a popular figure," Miss Jenkins said. "Still, it looks a little silly, a dozen of them dressed exactly the same."

"And suspicious," Concordia added.

Miss Jenkins nodded. "They're up to something. But I have to go. I'm late for my tea-leaf readings."

Concordia laughed. "Do you know anything about reading tea leaves?"

Hannah Jenkins snorted. "What is there to know? I'll make it up as I go. Miss Banning will be doing 'readings,' too," she added. "Probably channeling quotes from dead statesmen and philosophers for her predictions."

They parted ways in the hall. Just outside the porch, Concordia found a number of students lined up for the apple "dookin."

"Miss Pomeroy isn't here yet?" she asked one girl.

The girl sighed and pointed around the corner. There stood Miss Pomeroy on a stool, looking down at a number of girls crowded around a washtub. Strands of her hair were coming loose and her glasses slid perilously close to the tip of her nose.

"Oh, Miss Wells, thank goodness," she said, climbing down.

Concordia could see the problem. She tapped one of the girls who was bent over the tub. She straightened, teeth triumphantly clenched around an apple stem. Her shirtwaist was soaked.

"Miss Drury, go to the kitchen. Have the staff bring back towels, extra washtubs, and pitchers of water to fill them. This should have been set up already."

The girl hurried off.

Soon the situation was under better control, with simultaneous groups of girls clustered around the basins, hands behind backs, trying to catch an apple. Towels sopped up the spillage.

During the next hour, Concordia saw several of the Joan-of-Arc-costumed girls. When she asked one about it, the young lady confirmed she was, indeed, Joan of Arc, but merely shrugged when asked why so many girls had identical costumes.

Undoubtedly up to something, Concordia decided.

The students tried to get Concordia to give the "dookin" a try, but she declined. Miss Pomeroy, however, was game, except she forgot to remove her glasses in advance. They promptly slid off her nose, and with a little *splish*, dropped right into the tub.

"Oh. Oh, my," Miss Pomeroy blinked uncertainly. One of the girls fished them out.

"Thank you, dear," Miss Pomeroy said.

Eventually, the room emptied as the girls moved off to other games and dancing. Concordia felt a little restless.

"Can you manage when more come?" she asked Miss Pomeroy.

"Of course. You run along and see what the others are up to. You're supposed to be a floater, are you not?"

Once she was in the hallway, Concordia paused. Where should she go next? The tea-leaf reading? The nut-burning?

The sounds of raucous laughter penetrating the music decided her. Nut-burning it is, then.

The parlor was crowded with girls, each eager to try her hand at throwing nuts—or "nits" as they were referred to in Scotland, where the tradition started—into the fire. The ever-patient President Langdon was overseeing the activity, and was so occupied with keeping the ladies out of the hearth that he didn't notice Concordia come in. He was dressed in evening attire that was just as ill-fitting as his customary day wear: trousers rumpled, shirt beginning to pull away from his pear-shaped middle, once-shiny patent leather oxfords scuffed and dull. He made an unlikely-looking administrator, but there was more to him than met the eye. Concordia had long admired his compassion and quick intellect.

She took off her cloak almost at once and set it aside. Although every window was open in the room, the fire, candles, and press of bodies made it unbearably warm. Sweat was glistening on Langdon's face and he had abandoned his jacket long since, but he was still good-naturedly playing along. He handed one girl a couple of nuts. "So, who will it be, my dear?"

"Stephen," the girl murmured, but not softly enough, for one of the girls chimed in: "Ooh, I know *him*! Madge is sweet on *Steph-en!*" which led to more laughter.

The girl threw them in. They all quieted, watching the nuts within the flames, absorbed by the play of light. Concordia found herself drawn into the game, too. Would they burn side by side, which meant the couple was destined for marriage? Or would one pop and crackle, meaning the man was faithless? Funny how we look for signs of our future in the most unlikely places, she thought. She tried not to consider what her romantic future held; for a woman, a romantic future and a professional future were mutually exclusive. Which did she really want? She thought she knew the answer.

One nut caught and burned brightly. The other at first did nothing but smoke; then it, too, caught fire, leaning into the first. The girls clapped their hands in delight.

Concordia noticed movement in the back of the room. A burly, broad-shouldered figure separated from a gloomy corner and moved toward her. Mr. Rosen, the newspaper reporter. Although he'd no doubt been invited for the sake of writing an account of the college event, he was dressed in proper evening attire—black trousers, jacket, tie, and white shirt with the customary high collar points. The whole looked a trifle dusty, though, as if it had sat in someone's closet for too long. Without his usual bowler atop his head, Concordia could see he had a full head of thick, wavy gray hair. He wiped his reddened face as he moved closer to the light. She caught a hint of reddish stubble along his chin.

She gave a start, remembering her father's letter.

Everyone called him Red. It was an apt name, for he was red-haired, red-complected from the pitiless heat of the desert, and had a red-hot temper, too.

"Good evening… Miss Wells, isn't it?" he said.

"Yes, good evening to you as well, Mr. Rosen," she said, her thoughts going a mile a minute. He was the right age to be her father's former partner-turned-rival. He looked to be red-haired before he had aged. Was that enough to suspect a man?

Concordia gestured toward the group. "Getting enough material for your article?"

"So far, but I have other areas to cover. I would like to see Madame Durand's demonstration later. President Langdon has graciously invited me to stay for the supper buffet before that event." He looked over her costume, pencil in hand. "I'm doing an inventory of the different costumes for my article. Are you that fairytale character…Little Red Riding Hood, I believe?"

Concordia, and in a moment of inspiration, held out her hand in mock-formality. "This evening, you may call me *Red*."

The man looked startled, but played along, taking her hand and making an awkward little bow over it. "My pleasure, *Red*." He let go of her hand and started scribbling.

Concordia suppressed a disappointed sigh. She wasn't very accomplished in this detective business. The man's mild reaction was certainly no conclusive indication of whether or not he was Red. She tried another approach.

"Do you get to travel much in your profession?"

He was still looking down at his notepad as he answered. "Here and there," he murmured. "I've been at it for a long time."

"Oh? Were you always a reporter?"

He finally looked up at her, puzzled by her not-so-subtle inquiry. "Not always. Many of us fall into this line of work after pursuing other endeavors."

Concordia had to tread carefully. "Do you enjoy your work?"

"Mostly."

"I assume you have to cover some disagreeable stories," she added sympathetically. "The murder of Colonel Adams, for example?"

The man narrowed his eyes suspiciously. "What are you getting at, Miss Wells? I know when I'm being 'interviewed,' believe me."

"I-I apologize," Concordia stammered.

"Why so curious?" Rosen said. "Did you perhaps hear that I saw the colonel the afternoon before his death? As I told that blasted policeman, I needed more background information before writing my article. I had no opportunity to speak with him in depth at the time."

His face reddened as he leaned over her. "'Curiosity killed the cat,' young lady. I would be very careful of where I stick my nose, if I were you."

Concordia shrank back.

"Is there a problem here?" a voice asked.

She whirled around to find Dean Pierce, nearly at her elbow. She hadn't even heard him approach.

For a man in a wheelchair, the dean conveyed an imposing presence. Tonight, dressed as the powerful Cardinal de Richelieu—red cardinal's robes, ecclesiastic skull cap, and enormous cross of Lorraine sitting on his chest—he looked even more commanding. Rosen cleared his throat. "Not at all. If you will excuse me."

Pierce inclined his head in mute dismissal.

"I didn't want a reporter here but the president insisted," Pierce said, when Rosen had gone. "Mr. Langdon is looking for good press to counteract the notoriety of the stolen amulet and the railing collapse."

Concordia nodded. "It *has* been a trying term."

They heard the supper bell. Eager girls with youthful appetites started filling the hall, heading for the buffet.

"Coming?" the dean asked, pivoting his chair.

She shook her head. "I'll join you later."

With a smile and a wave to Concordia, the dean wheeled himself to join the stream of girls.

Concordia lingered in the parlor and helped President Langdon put the room to rights. No point in rushing to the buffet when there was sure to be a line.

"How are your classes going, my dear?" Mr. Langdon politely enquired, as they straightened furniture and picked up debris.

"The students are coming along well," Concordia answered. "The senior Literature majors should be ready for their examinations by spring, and some of the more impulsive sophomores from last year—you remember Miss Landry?"— Langdon nodded—"are finally settling down to be responsible young ladies." She shook her head. "There were times when I doubted it was possible."

Langdon laughed. "Even parents have doubts about their own progeny, Miss Wells. But these girls are thriving under your influence."

Concordia gave him a skeptical look.

Langdon's expression grew serious. "Do not let anyone— even someone in authority over you—make you doubt yourself," he said quietly.

She looked down at her hands. "It's too late for that, I'm afraid."

"Nonsense," President Langdon said briskly. "Our lady principal doesn't know you as I do. I have not yet seen fit to override her authority, but you can always come to me if things get out of hand."

Concordia flushed and nodded mutely. She wasn't sure how much Langdon knew about her difficulties with Miss Grant. But she wanted to deal with the issue herself rather than run to him for rescue.

"Let's get some supper." Langdon patted his large middle. "I'm starving."

The sight of all that food on the buffet tables made Concordia realize how hungry she really was. The multiple *a la carte* offerings made it difficult to choose. Among the favorites were *aspic de foie gras, canard roti a l'orange*, and cold sandwiches of chicken salad. Then there were the desserts of baked apple, stuffed with brown-sugared nuts, pumpkin *crème brulee*, and *petit fours*. Cider, tea, and lemonade were plentiful. She loaded her plate to the tipping point, wondering if there was a way to surreptitiously loosen the laces of her over-bodice.

"Here, allow me," someone said. Concordia turned abruptly as David made a grab for the sandwich sliding off her plate. "I've saved seats for us," he added.

And a good thing, too, Concordia thought, looking over the crowd. With no seats left, many of the girls were perched upon windowsills and the porch steps outside.

"There was no help for it," David murmured as he helped her into her seat. Concordia quickly realized what he meant when she nodded to her table mates. Besides Miss Pomeroy, Mr. Harrison, Dean Pierce, and Miss Banning, Miss Grant and Madame Durand were also part of their group. They each acknowledged her greeting with varying degrees of cordiality except Margaret Banning, who was diving into her aspic with great gusto and ignoring everyone.

Being seated with both Miss Grant *and* Madame Durand might be enough to take the edge off her appetite, Concordia thought.

As they ate, Concordia noticed that the lady principal appeared rather mellow, introspective even. She had obviously tired of the white face powder and had wiped most of it off, except for what clung to the furrows of her face. At the moment, she was holding up a spoon and staring at her reflection in it. At least Miss Grant wasn't tormenting *her*, so Concordia had no quarrel with whatever the woman did to keep herself occupied.

Since Concordia had been away from the ballroom before supper, this was the first time tonight that she had seen Madame Durand. The lady looked stunning in her gypsy costume— dressed as Carmen, Concordia guessed. Madame's black hair, full and lustrous, was loose about her shoulders, pinned back only at one ear, behind which a red silk rose was appended. She wore the characteristic loose-ruffled white cotton blouse of a peasant gypsy, with a heavily-fringed silk shawl of Prussian blue.

What Concordia could see of the skirt was voluminous black satin, richly embroidered in a profuse floral pattern. Madame looked her most exotic this evening.

"Where is Monsieur Durand?" Concordia asked politely.

Madame blotted her lips before answering. "He conveys his apologies, but says he does not care for such entertainments." She gave a little shrug.

A student approached their table. Looking back at her friends, who kept waving her on, she tentatively addressed the medium. "Excuse me, Madame. When will you be giving your planchette reading? We're all wild to see it."

"What's a planchette?" David Bradley asked.

Madame Durand turned her light blue eyes to David. "It is a device used for automatic writing, *Monsieur* Bradley. People also call them 'talking boards'. It is a shield-shaped, flat piece of hardwood, about this big"—she held out her hands six inches apart—"with three small wheels underneath, and a hole for a pencil. A sheet of paper is placed under the device, and two people rest their hands *lightly* upon the planchette. If the spirits wish, they will move the board and communicate with us through what is written upon the paper."

Concordia gave a little shiver.

Then Madame looked up at the student, still hovering at her shoulder. "Soon, *ma cherie.* When it is closer to the witching hour of midnight, we will gather. That is the optimum time for the spirits to traverse the boundary between the dead and the living."

Satisfied, the student thanked her and went back to her companions.

David raised a skeptical eyebrow. "Isn't it more feasible to assume that those resting their hands upon this piece of wood are doing the moving themselves?"

"I've heard of these boards, too," Miss Pomeroy interrupted. "I thought it was a child's toy. In fact, aren't they sold in toy shops?"

Madame shook her head vigorously. "No, no—it is not a *toy;* it is a *spirit board.*"

The kitchen staff had begun clearing the plates from the table, which seemed to rouse Miss Banning—no longer eating—to join the conversation.

"Hmph. *'Calling a tail a leg doesn't make it a leg.'* Abraham Lincoln." She thumped her cane beside her in emphasis.

"It has been tested many times, and sessions are closely observed," Madame retorted. She pushed back her chair, and all of the men—except for Dean Pierce—rose politely.

"If you will excuse me," Madame said, "I have some preparations to complete." She turned to the dean. "Would you mind assisting me?"

Dean Pierce looked startled, but recovered well. "Of course."

With an irritated flounce of her skirts, she stalked out, Pierce wheeling himself to catch up. Their departure seemed to be everyone's cue to get up from the table, too.

Which was just as well, since the band had just struck up a lively melody. Girls were pairing off along the floor, spacing themselves evenly apart for the two-step.

David had a gleam in his eye as he turned to Concordia. "May I have this dance?" He reached out a gloved hand.

"Delighted," she said, thrilling to the feel of his other hand upon the small of her back as he guided her around clusters of people.

He led her out on the floor and they started the dance, weaving and twirling with the other pairs. Some of the Joan of Arcs were dancing, too, but Concordia noticed that they weren't *all* there on the floor. As she spun and faced different directions throughout the dance's movements, she looked for the rest of them. Six, seven, eight....

But she had to focus on the intricate movements. Concordia reached out with both gloved hands, stepping forward toward her partner again to complete the round. David clasped them, smiling warmly, his eyes crinkling in the corners the way she always loved. She felt giddy, happy. She smiled back.

Then she caught sight of Lady Principal Grant and her smile faded. As they locked eyes, Concordia could see that the woman's expression was more than a scowl of disapproval.

It was hatred, raw and powerful.

Chapter 20

By heaven I charge thee, speak.

I.i

Week 7, Instructor Calendar
October/November 1896

It was finally the "witching hour," and Madame Durand was ready.

While not quite *everyone* was interested in "spirit automatism," it was a very popular demonstration, judging by the crowd. Concordia, David, and several other faculty members worked the back of the room, keeping the girls quiet and seated.

Madame stood to address them.

"Our Spirit Club has been growing nicely. Your interest warms my heart"—here she pressed both hands to her bosom and bowed her head in humility—"and I am deeply grateful. Tonight, we conduct a little experiment, to see if the spirits will speak with us. Some may call it a parlor game"—this said with a sharp glance over at David Bradley, who merely grinned back— "but powerful evidence has shown that this phenomenon defies human explanation. Psychical forces are at work."

She walked into the crowd of eager girls, hands upon her hips, skirts swishing, head high, looking the very part of the passionate gypsy she was dressed to be. Finally, she stood before Mr. Rosen and whispered to him. He bowed and moved to the front. Then she walked all the way to the back of the room and stopped beside Concordia. She looked at her intently with those ice blue eyes.

"Miss Wells, please to join us at the table?"

Concordia heard the envious sighs of the young ladies around her. She wanted to say no, but thought that would sound churlish. Besides, it might help to see Madame up close again during a performance. Perhaps she could see how the lady worked some of her tricks. And convince her mother to abandon such foolishness.

She followed Madame to the table at the front of the room. Taking up most of the surface was a large piece of white paper. Upon it was the planchette Madame had described: flat, wooden, its shield shape ending at a point, an upright pencil pushed through a hole near the pointed end. Tiny wheels were affixed beneath the board.

Mr. Rosen helped Concordia into her chair as Madame explained the process.

"Miss Wells and I shall sit across from each other, placing our fingers lightly upon the wood. Mr. Rosen will stand beside the table to observe; he will also call upon the young ladies in the audience for questions that we can ask the spirits. Some of the answers may not be legible, or make sense; some might be in the form of a prediction, the veracity of which may be evident at a later time."

Mr. Rosen seated her in the chair opposite Concordia. In the dim light, Madame's heavily-lashed eyes looked shadowed, mysterious. "Do not try to push or move the board in any way," she instructed. "We will simply rest our hands upon it in a relaxed fashion."

"Does anyone have a question?" Mr. Rosen called out. Several hands were raised. "Yes, young lady," he said, picking one of the girls dressed as Joan of Arc.

"Will Professor W. find true love?"

Startled, Concordia jerked her hand and the planchette slid off the table. She murmured an apology and picked it up as some of the girls tittered. She felt her face grow hot. The girls could be mischievous brats at times.

She and Madame placed their hands back upon the board. At first, nothing happened; then, she could feel tremors under her fingers. The board began to glide, of its own accord, around part of the page. She could see the pencil tracing small loops. She looked at Madame's hands. It didn't look as if she was doing anything to cause this, either. How was this happening? It was an unnerving sensation. Then the board abruptly stopped. Mr. Rosen bent over for a closer look.

"*Yes*," he intoned, clearly puzzled.

The audience applauded in delight. Concordia turned a few more shades of red.

Mr. Rosen picked another upraised hand.

"Will Miss *G.* find true love?"

General laughter followed this question, but as there was more than one "Miss G" on campus, Lady Principal Grant could say nothing in objection. But everyone knew to whom the question referred.

The planchette began to glide once again. This time, it did not seem to spell a name, but instead to outline a form. It stopped.

Mr. Rosen squinted at it. "It's not a word, it's a picture. An animal?"

Several girls chuckled at that.

The board moved again. This time, there *was* a word. *Horse.*

"*Horse*," Mr. Rosen quoted. He frowned.

Two more times, the planchette wrote "horse," and then it stopped. Several girls exchanged glances.

As other questions were asked, with a variety of success, Concordia was getting an idea. She knew the spirit world wasn't *really* speaking to them, of course, even though she still didn't know how Madame was working the trick. But here was an opportunity to learn something about Colonel Adams' murder. If the murderer was not a member of the colonel's family, then perhaps, as Miss Phillips had suggested, it was someone *here*, from the college. Maybe *Red* was here. She felt a shiver settle along her spine.

She looked over at Ben Rosen, still convinced that he was hiding something. He could *be* Red. But he'd thwarted her earlier attempt to question him as closely as she wanted.

She couldn't ask directly about the murder. But she could try something else.

Concordia looked over at Madame Durand. "May *I* ask a question?"

"Of course," Madame said.

In a dramatic voice meant to project throughout the room, Concordia intoned, "Who is *Red*, and is he *here?*"

The talking board abruptly skidded across the table, and fell to the floor with a clatter.

"Concordia, that was beyond reckless," David whispered fiercely.

David had pulled her into the arbor just outside Sycamore House after the planchette session, in order to talk with her privately. A private tongue-lashing was more like it.

Concordia balled her hands into fists. "I had to try it."

The results had been disappointing, though. There was such a commotion when the planchette sailed off the table that she'd had no opportunity to observe Mr. Rosen's reaction to her question, or that of anyone *else* for that matter. And when she'd turned back around, the reporter was gone.

She sighed.

David grabbed her shoulders, angry. "You told me that your father's letter called Red his enemy and yours. If Red was truly here tonight, you have tipped your hand. He now knows that you are aware of his existence. You could be in danger."

Concordia had never seen him so angry before. While she was touched by his concern, she didn't appreciate being talked to in this way. She shook off his hands. "It's not your responsibility. It is *mine*, and I will do as I see fit."

"You are a *damnably* stubborn woman," he said. He pulled her to him, and brought his lips down upon hers.

The kiss was born of frustration and anger, and, with fury on her own part she tried to push him away. He had kissed her once before, last spring, but not like this.

The kiss softened. She found herself kissing him back. *Mercy, what was she doing?*

Finally, she pulled away from him, and put a hand to her lips in shock.

"I don't want anything to happen to you, Concordia," he whispered.

She couldn't trust herself to speak.

The sound of nearby voices brought Concordia back to her senses. "I have to go. A group of us are walking back to the cottages. It wouldn't do for anyone to see us together like this."

"Let me go with you," he said, taking her hand in his.

"You've taken enough liberties for one evening," Concordia snapped.

She was about to pull away when Miss Grant stepped through the arbor, eyes gleaming with malice. Actually, only *part* of her could step through, as her enormous skirt hoops, attached to an already wide build, prevented her from clearing the wicket gate, which shook in protest. But she got far enough.

"I might have known I'd find you here, Miss Wells. And alone with a young man! Hardly the model of propriety, is it?" she sneered.

Concordia flushed a deep red.

Do not let anyone—even someone in authority over you—make you doubt yourself, President Langdon had told her. He was right.

Ready to come to her defense, David stepped toward the lady principal. Concordia stopped him. "No. I have something to say." And she was going to have her say, even if it meant losing the job she loved. Enough was enough. She turned to face the lady principal. Her heart thumped hard in her chest.

"Miss Grant, you see impropriety because you look for the ill in people." She held up a hand, forestalling that lady's interruption. "In fact, it is *you* who have been outraging the propriety of our sex all this semester: your heavy-handed punishments, your malicious delight in the pain of others, your rank disregard for the welfare of those committed to your keeping. You leave misery in your wake, as tangible and malodorous as a plague."

Concordia paused to catch her breath. Miss Grant's face went white, then red-blotched.

A chorus of clapping, whistles, and cheers erupted from the far side of the shrubbery.

Land sakes, they'd had an audience. Concordia glanced uncertainly back at David, whose mouth was hanging open.

Miss Grant had finally recovered her voice. "You are *finished,*" she said, between gritted teeth, and flounced out.

Chapter 21

How weary, stale, flat, and unprofitable
Seem to me all the uses of this world!

I.ii

Week 7, Instructor Calendar
October/November 1896

It was a subdued walk from Sycamore House to the cluster of student cottages. The path took them through the quadrangle, past Founder's Hall, the chapel, and the classroom buildings. Miss Grant maintained a stony silence, marching slightly ahead of the group of students, which included the Joan of Arcs. All of the girls had heard Concordia's outburst. Concordia herself trailed behind them, Miss Jenkins at her side. That lady had also heard the interchange and cast anxious glances her way.

Concordia felt utterly weary. The days to come would be no better. She would have to pack her things and leave in disgrace. Explain to her mother what happened. *Live* with her mother until she figured things out.

The clouded and waning moon cast a faint, intermittent light upon the quadrangle scene, giving the buildings ghostly forms. Concordia's teeth chattered in the chill air and she wrapped her cloak around her more tightly. There would be frost upon the pumpkins tonight, for sure. Strange how, when everything in one's life was falling apart, the rest of the world went on unaffected.

The dim pathway lights provided only modest illumination. All other lamps were out at this late hour.

Except for one.

"Look!" Miss Jenkins pointed to Founder's Hall library. The main door was ajar, and a light burned within.

Miss Grant's face puckered in anger, those currant eyes burrowing further into her face under the force of lowering brows. She put on a surprising burst of speed for a woman of her size, and waddled full-tilt toward the building. Concordia and Miss Jenkins followed close behind. The students stayed where they were on the path: some gaping, some grinning ear-to-ear.

Miss Grant let out a little *oomph* as she batted at something against her face and slipped on the floor. When Concordia and Miss Jenkins reached the door, they too were swatting at something sticky. Strips of ribbon, coated with molasses, dangled from the transom. They clung to Concordia's cheeks and hair as she fought to pull them off.

"Miss Grant, are you all right?" Miss Jenkins called out. They stepped farther into the room. Moving away from the dangling stickiness, Concordia groped for the electric lights and snapped them on. They froze at the sight.

There was *a horse* in the library.

It seemed a particularly *large* horse, although any horse would have looked enormous inside a library. He was munching contentedly on what was left of a bale of hay the thoughtful pranksters had supplied. How the animal had been coaxed up the steps and through the door was anyone's guess, as was the impending problem of how to get him *out*. As Concordia knew from sad experience at her aunt's farm in the country, *down* was much more difficult than *up* when it came to farm animals.

At the moment, all Miss Jenkins and Concordia seemed able to do was stare at the beast. He must have been in here a while, judging by the mess; books strewn and stepped on, carts knocked over, hay covering *everything*.

"Help me up, if you please," Miss Grant snapped.

With considerable effort, they pulled the lady principal to her feet, only to find that she had slipped on one of those disagreeable barnyard deposits commonly left by a horse.

Concordia's eyes watered from the exertion of not laughing at the sight of the hopping mad Lady Principal, a smear of manure up the back of her gown, farthingale hoops now twisted at ludicrous angles. Miss Grant stomped back outside to yell at the students, getting smacked yet *again* by the molasses-coated booby trap in the doorway. Once she was out of the building, Concordia and Miss Jenkins collapsed against each other in hiccupping laughter, tears streaming down their cheeks. It was wicked, it really was, to be laughing at the lady principal this way. But they couldn't help it.

Once they recovered sufficiently for speech, Hannah Jenkins walked over to the horse, careful to sidestep additional droppings. Concordia, never fond of horses, nonetheless decided it was safer to stay with Miss Jenkins and the animal than go outside and observe the lady principal's tirade. With her luck, Miss Grant might find a way to blame *her* for this.

"Well, they certainly pulled a memorable one this time," Miss Jenkins said, patting the animal's neck, whereupon he started licking the molasses from her hair.

"And to do it while everyone was busy at the ball," Concordia agreed. "I suspect our Joan of Arcs were responsible. That would explain why nearly a dozen of the girls wore identical costumes. A few could then slip out to pull the prank while the others created the impression that all were still in attendance."

"Using coifs to cover their hair, which would have been a distinguishing feature," Miss Jenkins added, with a hint of admiration in her tone. "Diabolical." She looked the animal over as he whinnied softly. "At least they picked the most placid horse from our stable. If he panicked he could have injured himself."

"But it's still quite a feat to sneak him out of the barn and into here," Concordia said. She looked around. "The librarian isn't going to like this."

"The students will be doing the cleanup, obviously. With the sharp-tongued Miss Cowles to answer to, I don't envy them that task."

"In the meantime," Concordia said, as she stepped around a fresh dropping, "how do we get it out of here?"

Miss Jenkins didn't answer. She stared at the horse with a troubled frown.

"What is it?" Concordia asked.

"That talking board," Miss Jenkins said slowly, turning to look at her. "The answer to '*Will Miss G. find true love?*' It was a *horse.*"

Concordia shook off the uneasy prickle at the base of her neck. "Well," she answered with a bravado she didn't quite feel, "either the girls shared their secret with Madame Durand, or the spirits have a mischievous sense of humor. Which would you rather believe?"

Chapter 22

There is a special Providence in the fall of a sparrow.

V.ii

Week 7, Instructor Calendar
November 1896

The next day Concordia began her packing. No sense in waiting until the lady principal, gloating in her triumph, walked in to hand-deliver her termination notice. The cause for dismissal, of course, would be insubordination. She was flagrantly guilty, and in front of witnesses, too.

Witnesses who had applauded.

She couldn't help but smile briefly at the memory. She'd been wanting to do that for weeks. Odious woman.

As Concordia amassed piles on her bed, she realized that the cottage was strangely quiet. Even on class days there were usually students in and out all the time. She hadn't heard Ruby bustling about, either. Concordia had hoped a few of the girls in her charge would have stopped by and offered some words of sympathy or support, but there'd been no one. Had she made so little difference in their lives? Was she to be forgotten so easily when she was gone? Her eyes stung as she blinked back tears.

After she had most of her things sorted, Concordia realized that she still had to tackle the contents of her office. But of course, Miss Grant's office was just down the hall from hers. The thought of seeing the woman again settled like a cold lump in her stomach. But there was no help for it.

She locked the door to her rooms, went down the hall, and opened the front door. Eli was standing on the porch step, reaching a hand to the bell.

"Oh!" Concordia jumped back in surprise. "What are you doing here?" Had Miss Grant, with her twisted sense of humor, given the boy her termination notice to deliver?

"I've been sent to fetch you, miss," the boy mumbled, not meeting her eyes. "Mr. Langdon wants to see you."

Concordia's heart sank. So this was it. She closed the door behind her. "Let's go, then."

All of the faculty offices, including President Langdon's, were in Founder's Hall. At least, she thought wryly, she could start packing up her books right after talking with him. Her office was on the floor above.

As they approached the Hall there looked to be an unusual amount of bustle and activity. She passed students in a long line: outside the building, up the two flights of stairs, and ending immediately outside the president's office. They smiled as she walked past.

"Do you know what this is all about?" Concordia asked Eli. The boy shrugged. Taking a deep breath, she rapped on the door.

"Come in."

She opened it.

The sight that greeted her made her draw in a quick breath. *What on earth?*

Ruby Hitchcock and *all twenty-two* of her cottage students were crammed around the president's desk. Langdon himself stood behind it, as if barricaded in. Concordia never imagined that his office, spacious though it was, could hold so many people.

He waved a hand at everyone else. "All right; she's here. Give us some privacy, please."

Ruby and the students murmured in discontent, casting concerned glances at Concordia as they left. Finally, the room was cleared. Langdon pointed to a chair. "Have a seat."

"What is going on? What were my girls doing here?" She gestured to the hallway outside the door. "There are more students out there, by the way. Are they all waiting to see *you*?"

Langdon gave a weary sigh and sat down. "I imagine so. Nearly two-thirds of the campus has already passed through my door this morning, wanting to talk to me about you."

Concordia looked incredulous. "*Me?*"

"More correctly, you and the lady principal," Langdon said. "Miss Grant, of course, had come to see me *early* in the morning"—he winced—"with a litany of complaints against you, culminating in the incident last night, of which I was not a witness. She recommended I dismiss you for insubordination, moral turpitude, and dereliction of duties."

Concordia felt her stomach clench. With such charges against her, she would not be hired *anywhere*.

"But my day had only begun," Langdon continued. "Since my interview with the lady principal, I have been... *haunted* is as good a word as any, I suppose. That young man who works for Grundy—Mr. Bradley?—was one of the first. He tried to take sole responsibility for you being out in the arbor with him to begin with. Not that I believed you capable of anything sordid. Since then, there has been a steady procession of students, teachers... even the cook and the messenger boys. Each of them with grievances regarding the lady principal, and staunch support for *you*."

Concordia felt a lightness in her chest. So *that's* what the students had been doing today. Not ignoring her but *defending* her, pleading her case to the president. And David Bradley, trying to protect her. She didn't know whether to laugh or cry.

"Several students were quite distraught," Langdon added. "It seems Miss Grant had been coercing a few of them to spy upon you, in order to stay in her good graces. A troubling pattern has emerged about the lady. I have some difficult decisions to make." He shook his head at Concordia. "Why didn't you come to me?"

She looked down at her hands. "I guess I thought I could handle things myself."

He shook his head. "I regret allowing the situation to continue. I didn't want to undermine her authority, but I had no idea how bad the conditions had become."

"What will happen now?" Concordia asked.

"Even before this perpetual visitation upon my office, I did not take the majority of Miss Grant's claims at face value," he continued mildly, "but your behavior toward her last night must be addressed."

Concordia, flushing, looked at the floor.

"I impressed upon Miss Grant how burdensome it would be to find someone to assume the entirety of your duties so late in the semester, both in teaching your classes and overseeing the girls in your cottage," Langdon continued. "With the prank in the library still painfully fresh in her mind, I also pointed out how your dismissal could foster an additional wave of ill-feeling from the students. We want the pranks to stop, not add fuel to the fire. So, Miss Wells, you will *not* be dismissed, but you will write a pretty little note of apology to the lady principal, and future dealings between you two will be civil. I have said as much to Miss Grant on that score as well. Agreed?"

Concordia felt nearly giddy with relief. "What will you do about the student prank?" she asked.

"The students responsible—there has been a startling upsurge of confession and contrition today—are cleaning up the library, even now. In addition, until the Thanksgiving recess, all club activities, meetings, frolics, teas, and visits of any kind on campus are suspended. Curfew will be moved two hours earlier, to eight o'clock. I am giving the lady principal the authority to restore privileges earlier, if she sees fit."

That was highly unlikely, Concordia thought. She sighed. No diversions outside of the classroom? Early curfew? She didn't relish dealing with the students over the next few weeks.

Langdon stood, as did Concordia. "I imagine we shall both have our hands full in the near future. Send in the next student on your way out, would you?"

Chapter 23

How, now, Horatio! You tremble and look pale.

I, i.

Weeks 8 and 9, Instructor Calendar
November 1896

The campus was, indeed, a cheerless place after the horse prank. The restrictions imposed by President Langdon last week were beginning to make themselves felt. As a result, Concordia and Ruby had two dozen grumbling and restless girls to deal with on a daily basis.

Miss Phillips' cold had developed into bronchitis and she had been moved to the infirmary under the watchful eye of Miss Jenkins. She was in no condition to decipher Randolph Wells' journal.

Concordia wondered if she should ask David to write to his cryptologist friend. She hadn't seen much of him since the disastrous incident in the arbor, although she thought of him a great deal. She suspected he was avoiding her, but didn't know if that was the result of embarrassment or caution. Of course, she imagined that his laboratory work and frequent visits to Amelia took up a great deal of his time.

Sophia wrote to Concordia nearly every day to report on Amelia's progress. The child was calmer now, and beginning to talk normally, unless asked about what she had seen or remembered the night of the murder. Sophia was convinced that, given more time, the girl would recover. Mrs. Adams, however, insisted upon going forward with the commitment proceedings. Sophia was able to stall sufficiently by having the family doctor declare that Amelia first undergo the expert examination of child specialist Dr. Bridgers, who was currently on a steamer on the far side of the Atlantic. He wasn't due to return for another month.

While that was a relief, the worry was taking its toll. Concordia felt just as trapped as the students, with nowhere to go, and no progress to be made.

Finally, after another day of shrieking, arguing, and a spilled pot of illicitly-cooked fudge in a student's room—when would these girls stop *cooking?*—Concordia knew she had to step out for a break.

"I'll be back in a little while," she said, grabbing her jacket. Ruby nodded in sympathy—or was that envy?—as Concordia walked outside into the quiet, chill November air.

She walked around the grounds for a little, finally sitting down on the bench beside the pond, watching the birds peck at the dried leaves and warm themselves in the sun.

"You look awfully gloomy today," said a familiar voice. Concordia looked over to see Dean Pierce wheeling his chair toward her. She got up to help him, but he waved her off. "I've been doing this for a long time, dear. I'm perfectly capable, thank you." His voice held a bit of an edge, or was that her imagination? His expression seemed pleasant.

Concordia wondered again what circumstances had landed Dean Pierce in that chair. Some sort of tragic accident long ago, she had heard. Rumors suggested a fall from a horse. Of course, it would be vulgar to inquire.

"Is something on your mind, Miss Wells? Or are you just mirroring the general gloom of the campus?"

"A little of both, I suppose."

"I remember the last time we talked, you were going to look for more clues about your father's past, isn't that right? Don't be discouraged. I'm sure you'll find the answers you're looking for."

"Actually," Concordia said, leaning toward him, "this is rather confidential, so please don't tell anyone—"

"Of course, of course," he said eagerly. "You've found something?" His eyes gleamed with interest. He smiled paternally at her.

He really was a nice man for an administrator, Concordia thought. Except for President Langdon, very few of them took the time to listen to the troubles of a junior faculty member.

Concordia related what she had found in her father's study, along with her frustration in not being able to decipher his journal. "We really think it contains the answer to Colonel Adams' death," she said.

"'We'?" he asked.

"Sophia, Miss Phillips, Mr. Bradley, and the policeman know," Concordia said. "Although Miss Phillips has been too ill to take a good look. But I'm hopeful that she can decipher it when she's better."

"How fascinating," the dean said. "But that was so very long ago. How is it that this is all happening *now*?"

"I don't know," Concordia admitted.

"What will you do with the amulet?" he asked.

"My father took great pains to make sure I got it," Concordia said. "I'll keep it for now and decide later, after all this settles down."

"A wise decision, I think," Pierce said. In a change of subject, he asked, "How are you and Miss Grant getting along these days?"

"Hmm… well, there are no *open* conflicts. That's something, I suppose. Let us just say we don't seek out one another's company."

Concordia had written and delivered her "pretty little note of apology," and Miss Grant had made no further mention of the incident. In actuality, the lady principal did not talk to her at all. Concordia didn't find this a relief, however, for the lady principal's silence was often accompanied by barely-disguised looks of utter hatred. Concordia felt it whenever they passed one another in the hall or attended the same meeting.

Why did Miss Grant hate her so?

"Perhaps you two struggle because you don't understand each other," the dean suggested.

Concordia sighed and let her eyes rest on the nearly-bare trees in the distance, the earlier sweep of reds and golds having faded to brown. "Do *you* understand her, Dean?"

Pierce gave a little chuckle. "Perhaps not entirely, but I've been making a point of observing her. She is under a great deal of strain. Belligerence seems to be how she copes with it."

"She should take up a more congenial hobby," Concordia retorted. "Like lawn tennis. Or knitting."

Pierce laughed aloud. "Shall I tell her that when I see her later today?"

"Certainly *not.*" Concordia checked the watch on her jacket lapel. *Drat!* It was getting late, and she still had a lesson plan to write before supper. "I have to go."

Concordia felt Dean Pierce's paternal gaze follow her as she hurried along the path toward Willow Cottage.

She finished her work just in time to dress for supper. There was quite a commotion going on upstairs as the girls, too, changed into dinner dresses.

Concordia smiled. She'd noticed that with the students' activities restricted, more of a fuss was being made for those things which they *could* do, namely, classes and meals. Unfortunately, this made them unusually chatty in the classroom as well as the dining hall.

Ruby tapped on the partly-open door and stuck her head in. "This came for you while you were out, miss." She held out an envelope.

"Just set it down over there, thanks," Concordia said, struggling with a boot.

After Ruby left and the struggle was resolved successfully, she opened the letter. It was from Miss Phillips.

Concordia,
Although I'm still recovering from this horrid illness, I had a burst of energy today and was able to get the first part of your father's journal translated. (Shh...don't tell Miss Jenkins). I've

enclosed it here. He used an early shorthand that had fallen out of popularity more than twenty years ago.

I hope to get to the remainder of it soon.

Yours,

Dorothy

Concordia's heart beat faster as she pulled out the pages, written in Miss Phillips compact hand, with quavering lines here and there.

> *The Journal of Randolph Wells, Ph.D.*
>
> *23 October 1873*
>
> *He must be stopped.*
>
> *It is with a heavy heart that I write this, for Red was my close friend through difficult expeditions, and has saved my life more than once.*
>
> *He is also a liar and a plunderer. I know that now, having just received answers to letters I'd sent weeks ago. They confirm my suspicions. Red has been stealing relics behind my back and selling them in back-alley markets.*
>
> *The timing of the news is disastrous, as we are already underway. I did not think to ask for any letters that might have reached the boat just before our departure, and the careless servant only remembered to distribute them to us on the second day of our Nile journey from Cairo to Amarna. There is no turning back.*
>
> *Why did I not realize the truth about Red sooner, before I shared my translations of the stelae, before I told him of the high priest's tomb? He would strip it of every valuable antiquary, as I now know he did with our discovery at Abydos. Worse yet, should we find the tomb, the wall-writing within it could provide clues to the location of the Royal Tomb of King Akhenaten and his family. This would yield no end of treasure.*
>
> *Adams has joined us on this expedition. It is his first. But now I need his help to stop the thief in our midst.*
>
> *24 October 1873*
>
> *Adams and I have plan. The arrangements have been made.*

Perhaps the most difficult part at the moment is having to smile at the villain, pretending I know nothing of what he has been up to.

Adams and I have decided that, when we dock the boat, at which point the land portion of our journey begins, we will confront Red and tell him we are leaving him behind. I will take personal satisfaction in telling him why. It may be necessary to physically restrain him. Either way, we'll be leaving an extra man behind on the boat to keep him there. We certainly don't want him to follow us.

Our intent, should we be so fortunate as to find the tomb, has always been to catalogue its contents, sketch some of the major pieces, and pack a few of the less-fragile items to bring to Mariette in Boulaq as proof of our find. As the head archaeologist for Egypt's premiere museum, Mariette will have the manpower, heavy equipment, and other resources to properly secure the tomb. Our team, however, will get the credit for the find and the enormous satisfaction that comes from unearthing Egypt's treasures.

The one troubling aspect to this is that Red already knows the contents of the map, and could probably find it himself. What is to prevent him from going back to the site later and plundering it then? It would be impossible to post guards at the tomb until such time as Mariette secures the site.

Adams has pointed out, however, that once our discovery and cataloguing are complete, Red wouldn't be able to get away with stealing anything, even if he were given free reign over the tomb. We would have ample proof against him.

It is hard to argue with such logic as this. And yet, I am uneasy.

❦

25 October 1873

Adams wants to amend the plan. He is concerned that we are destroying Red's reputation on the basis of only two letters. While he agrees that we need to leave Red behind until we know for sure, his sense of fair play makes him reluctant to publicly humiliate the man in front of the entire expedition party. Adams is a noble man and I am impressed by his ethics in this regard.

Adams proposes to slip a sleeping draught in Red's drink, and when he cannot be roused, tell the rest of the party that he is too ill to make the land journey. We will leave two of Adams' most reliable men to keep him on the boat when he awakes.

I do not like it, but we have to consider the reputation of the expedition as a whole and not compromise it with scandal.

27 October 1873

We are moored at our destination and the unpleasant task has been accomplished. We have left Red behind on the boat. There is more unpleasantness to come, when we must confront him with what we know and report to Mariette what I have learned about his activities. But for now, I look forward to the search for the tomb.

Miss Phillips' translation ended there. Concordia was grateful to her for copying out so much of it, ill as she was. She was hopeful that they would have more answers soon.

Even with this much, Concordia felt as if she had learned a great deal about these three men. She wished her father hadn't trusted Colonel Adams so much. With what she now knew of him, she suspected his proposed "amendment" to the plan was not in her father's best interests. But she would have to wait for the rest.

If only they could find Red. Was he really here? She wished her father had provided her with his full name and a better description. Although the passage of more than two decades may have altered his appearance greatly.

Nonetheless, she should share what she had so far with Lieutenant Capshaw. She had just sat down to compose a note when she heard the thunder of two dozen pairs of feet coming down the stairs. She sighed. It would have to wait until after supper. Stuffing Miss Phillips' envelope in her skirt pocket, she walked out.

The dining hall was clamorous with the chatter of girls greeting each other like long-lost soul-mates. Thanksgiving recess couldn't come soon enough.

Concordia seated herself at one of the staff tables and looked around. "Where is Miss Grant?" That woman never missed a meal.

Miss Pomeroy craned her neck for a better view of the other staff tables. "I don't see her, either. That *is* odd. Do you suppose she's ill?"

"One could only hope," another teacher muttered, for which she got a kick under the table from Miss Jenkins.

"Ow!" she exclaimed, giving the infirmarian a black look.

"Miss Grant has eyes and ears everywhere," Miss Jenkins murmured, inclining her head toward Mr. Harrison at the next table.

"How do you know?" Miss Pomeroy asked.

Concordia looked over at the gentleman in question. Mr. Harrison seemed rather nervous today. The usually prim, turned-down mouth was white-lipped and drawn; beads of sweat stood out on his forehead. She could see his hands trembling as he put his napkin to his lips. What was wrong with him?

Hannah Jenkins nodded to Miss Pomeroy and leaned forward so as to not be overheard. "I have seen the two of them together quite often lately. They seem very...cozy. Once, he came out of her office when I knew she wasn't even in there and slipped something into his pocket."

That was an interesting development, which Concordia resolved to find out more about later, but she drew the discussion back to the subject at hand. "When did anyone see Miss Grant last?"

"She stopped by the gymnasium this morning," Miss Jenkins said, her voice still under the hubbub of the students' noise. "I'd reported some of my badminton shuttlecocks missing. The woman made me go through the entire inventory with her to see if I 'misplaced' anything else. She was in fine form then, I'm sorry to say."

Concordia noticed Dean Pierce wheeling himself into the room. He had said he'd be seeing Miss Grant today; he might know. Something was not right here. Excusing herself from the table, she walked over to greet him.

"Mr. Pierce, hello," Concordia said. "I was wondering, did you see the lady principal this afternoon?"

"I did not," Dean Pierce snapped, wheeling himself around to look up at her. "If you must know, I was indisposed, something a healthy young lady like yourself would never consider in others, would you?"

Concordia was taken aback by the unexpected anger. He did indeed look unwell, his face pale and drawn.

"I-I beg your pardon, dean," she stammered, and retreated back to her seat. What was wrong with everyone? She hoped there wasn't a contagion of some sort brewing.

"That didn't go well," said Miss Jenkins, who missed little.

"No, it did not. He's usually quite kind."

When the meal was over, still with no sign of the lady principal, Concordia said, "Anyone want to go with me to check on Miss Grant?"

A number of eyes dropped. There appeared to be no takers.

"I'll go with you," Miss Pomeroy finally offered. Concordia gave her a grateful look.

Gertrude Pomeroy, who had been teaching at the college for ages, lived in Delacey house with the other women senior faculty, which included administrators such as the lady principal. She used her key to unlock the front door, Concordia trailing behind.

Miss Pomeroy knew exactly which door belonged to Miss Grant's private quarters, which was a time-saver, as Concordia would have had to ask and then explain herself.

Miss Pomeroy tapped on the door. "Miss Grant?"

No answer. They waited a few moments.

She knocked with more vigor. "Miss Grant, are you in there?"

After another minute, Concordia said, "Should we try the door?"

Since Miss Pomeroy looked *very* reluctant to do so, Concordia grasped the knob. It turned easily. She pushed it open, bracing herself for the Ogre's blast. *How dare you enter my inner sanctum!*

But there was nothing. The room was empty.

"Miss Grant?" they called out together.

Miss Pomeroy looked at Concordia. "I think we have to check the bedroom."

"Yes."

Cautiously, both women crept tentatively toward it.

"Oh, *no*," Miss Pomeroy breathed.

The woman was sprawled on the floor, face purple.

"*Miss Grant?!*" Concordia exclaimed.

Miss Pomeroy rushed over and felt the woman's pulse. "She's still alive. Barely." She pointed at the lady's disarranged collar. "Look at these marks on her neck. She's been strangled."

Concordia ran to the outer door and called for help. The housekeeper rushed in. "Well, what's this about, then?" She stopped and sucked her breath in sharply at the sight of the lady principal.

"Call a doctor," Concordia ordered. "And the police. Ask for Lieutenant Capshaw. *Hurry.*"

The housekeeper ran as fast as her arthritic legs could carry her.

Concordia went back to Miss Pomeroy, who was chafing the lady principal's wrists, loosening her collar, and gently probing her neck. "Nothing appears broken, thank goodness."

"The room is a mess," Concordia said, looking around at the pillows tossed to the floor, the mattress partially lifted off its frame, and the contents of Miss Grant's desk, which had been swept to the floor. "Perhaps she surprised an intruder?" She picked up an object she recognized.

"This is the diadem we were going to use for the play," Concordia said. "But then it disappeared."

Miss Pomeroy, having done all she could for Miss Grant until the doctor arrived, joined her, looking at the desk's open drawers. "Hmm, those are the shuttlecocks Miss Jenkins said she was missing. And look, here's my gilt-illuminated bookmark." She picked it up. "It was a gift from the French Society students. I thought I'd lost it weeks ago."

Concordia looked at her. "What does it mean?"

Miss Pomeroy frowned. Then her face cleared in understanding. "Ah. Yes. This explains a few things. We have a cousin in the family with this problem."

"What problem?"

"I'll explain later," Miss Pomeroy said, as the outer door opened. Help had arrived.

The housekeeper had the good sense to summon Miss Jenkins as well. Under the infirmarian's take-charge style, the room was cleared quickly and a stretcher brought.

"You instincts were excellent, Concordia," Miss Jenkins said, before shooing her and Miss Pomeroy into the hall. "If she hadn't been discovered until morning, she'd be dead."

"Well, I didn't imagine *this* happening," Concordia said. "Will she recover?"

Miss Jenkins shrugged. "It's too soon to say. But at least she has a chance now. Ah, lieutenant," she said, looking over Concordia's shoulder to see the policeman hurrying down the hall, "this way. We haven't moved her yet, but we must do so quickly."

Lieutenant Capshaw, stoop-shouldered and gloomy as usual, shook his head as he moved past Concordia. "Miss Wells. Why do I always find *you* in the midst of these events?" He held up a hand to forestall her retort. "If you two would wait for me downstairs." Without waiting for an answer, he followed Miss Jenkins.

The harried-looking housekeeper appeared in the hall. "Miss Wells, the policeman wants you and Miss Pomeroy to wait for him in the solarium. Can you see your own way? There's an uproar below-stairs I have to see to." Then she, too, hurried out of sight.

"What problem did you mean, when you were talking about Miss Grant being like your cousin?" Concordia asked, as they walked down the stairs.

Miss Pomeroy sighed. "Our cousin Arnold. A 'human magpie' we called him. He couldn't resist things that were pretty, shiny, or had some sort of novelty. He would just slip it into a pocket when no one was looking. Rarely was the item of any monetary value; he just liked to have it. The impulse seemed to plague him most when he was under stress."

"I'd never heard of such a thing," Concordia said.

"Oh, it's not as unusual as you might think, Miss Wells. 'Kleptomania,' it is called. From the Greek 'kleptein,' meaning 'to steal,' and—"

"Yes, I see," Concordia interrupted, wanting to curtail the etymology lecture, which she knew Gertrude Pomeroy dearly loved. "So you believe that our lady principal has klepto... klepto..."

"Klepto*mania*," Miss Pomeroy said. "Yes, that seems clear."

"How could she function in such a visible administrative position? Wouldn't someone have said something by now, from other schools?"

"It took our family a long while to realize what was happening with Arnold. Turns out, his mother knew all along and was trying to protect him, by putting back the items he stole before anyone noticed. Maybe that's what happened here?"

Concordia didn't respond. Her mind was hard at work, gauging the possibilities. This changed everything.

Chapter 24

Be wary, then; best safety lies in fear.

I.iii

Weeks 8 and 9, Instructor Calendar
November 1896

"What enemies did Miss Grant have?" Capshaw asked, pulling out his oft-folded wad of notes and nub of a pencil.

Concordia snorted. "You've met the woman. No one liked her. If that were the criterion, lieutenant, we'd all be guilty."

Capshaw leaned toward Concordia. "We have to start somewhere, Miss Wells. By the way, I have also heard of the... er... incident in the arbor last week. Count yourself lucky you have witnesses to account for your whereabouts today, or you would be my prime suspect."

Concordia decided to ignore the jibe.

"Could it have anything to do with her kleptomania?" Miss Pomeroy asked.

"Her *what?*"

Miss Pomeroy explained to Capshaw the rash of missing items that the school had experienced since the lady principal's arrival this semester, some of which they had found in her rooms, and her theory that someone could be helping Miss Grant stay ahead of trouble.

"I noticed a clutter of objects when I examined the scene, but had no idea they were stolen," Capshaw said. "And you think, Miss Pomeroy, that someone has been shielding her?"

"I do, now that I've been thinking more on it," Gertrude Pomeroy said. She turned to Concordia. "Remember the librarian's teapot that went missing, only to be found later, in the infirmary, of all places? Not the faculty lounge, or the library, where one might reasonably expect it to turn up? And how about Ruby's lambskin gloves, the ones she thought she'd left in the dining hall, which turned up on a bench outside the arboretum, somewhere that Ruby never goes?"

"I see," Capshaw said. "Who do you think could be covering for her?"

Miss Pomeroy shrugged.

Concordia had an idea. "I think Miss Jenkins knows, Lieutenant."

It took a while to track down Hannah Jenkins since she had been kept so busy with Miss Grant. Once Capshaw talked with that lady, however, he immediately sent for Mr. Harrison and called Miss Pomeroy and Concordia back to the solarium.

Judging by his white, stricken face, Mr. Harrison had obviously heard the news. "Please, can I go see her?" he asked Capshaw.

"We can take you over there shortly, Mr. Harrison," Capshaw said. "But first, I want to know why you have been sneaking into Miss Grant's office and putting back items that she had stolen. What is your relationship to the lady?"

"You know—?" He looked defeated. "I suppose it was bound to come out. Yes, I was aware of her thefts. I tried to put back everything I could find. When her back was turned. I'd learned long ago that there was no use arguing with her."

"You have a history with the lady, then, Mr. Harrison?" Capshaw asked.

Harrison looked down at his immaculately-manicured nails. "She is my half-sister."

Miss Jenkins' eyes widened. Miss Pomeroy nodded. Concordia just kept looking from one person to another.

"You two are *related*?" she said in disbelief. She had never encountered a more unlikely pair: Miss Grant, hot-tempered, malicious, gluttonous and nosy; Mr. Harrison, cerebral, distant, meticulous, and controlled.

Harrison stared down at his hands. "She had to move around a great deal. She changed employment nearly every year. We've tried doctors, medicines. Nothing worked. Finally, I decided to get myself hired at the same schools to try to keep her out of trouble. No one was to know that I'm her brother. It was easier that way."

"Do you have any idea who would have assaulted your sister, Mr. Harrison? Or why?" Capshaw asked.

He hesitated.

"Yes?" Capshaw prompted.

"There has been one item that I am sure she took, which she has hidden from me very cleverly. I haven't been able to find it," Harrison said. "I wonder if her attacker was after it."

"What item is that?" Capshaw asked.

Harrison looked right at Concordia. "I've heard rumors that you possess one, too. I would be careful, Miss Wells."

Concordia suppressed a shudder.

"What item?" Capshaw repeated.

"The heart amulet from the exhibit. My sister stole it."

Concordia and Miss Pomeroy looked at each other. At least, Miss Phillips would be relieved to hear *that*.

"And you said nothing earlier, in order to protect her?" Capshaw asked.

"Yes, that—and I didn't see her actually *steal* it," Harrison said. "But she was right beside the table it was set upon, when there was a great deal of commotion... Colonel Adams had walked into the wrong lavatory, I believe—" at this, Miss Pomeroy blushed profusely—"and my sister is very good at sleight-of-hand."

"How do you think the amulet is connected with her attack? Was it a valuable item?" Capshaw asked, taking notes in a rapid hand.

Harrison cleared his throat. "Not to my knowledge, but... well, you see, er... Madame Durand said the amulet was *cursed*."

"Indeed?" Capshaw said. "I wasn't under the impression that college people believed in such—" he appeared to choose his word carefully—"phenomena."

Harrison flushed. "I know it sounds absurd. It's just that I have not been able to shake the sense that someone desperately wants that amulet, and it has brought misfortune to its possessor." He looked at Concordia. "Possessor*s*," he corrected.

Concordia felt a chill run up her spine. She hadn't considered herself a target before, and now Mr. Harrison was giving her goosebumps. She remembered Madame Durand's warning at the end of her psychic demonstration, the same night the medium had pronounced that Miss Phillips had lost something of value. Then, when the railing had given way, Concordia saw her chanting *doom, doom,* over and over, in the midst of the crowd below.

But really, Madame Durand had been making dire pronouncements ever since she'd set foot on campus. With all the bad things happening lately she hadn't been far wrong.

"Well, whatever the reason," Capshaw said briskly, stuffing his notes back in his pocket, "we can at least check to see if the amulet is in her quarters. Thank you, sir. The patrolman is waiting outside to escort you to the hospital."

As the others got up to leave they heard a disturbance outside.

"You cannot go in. Lieutenant's orders!" they heard through the door.

Capshaw sighed and opened the door. There was Ben Rosen arguing with the patrolman.

"You," Capshaw pointed to the reporter, "out."

Rosen, bowler tipped back on his head, ignored Capshaw. He was writing furiously as he got a good look at the room's occupants. "Hmm, interviewed Miss Wells, Miss Pomeroy... is that one 'm' or two?... and... What's your name, sir?" he asked Mr. Harrison, who blanched and took a step back.

Capshaw exchanged a meaningful look with the patrolman, who promptly took Rosen by the elbow. "You heard the

Lieutenant—move!" Still protesting and scribbling, Rosen was forcibly ushered out the side door.

"I hope he doesn't spell my name wrong," Miss Pomeroy murmured.

"How did he find out so quickly about Miss Grant?" Concordia said.

Capshaw shrugged. "A hospital attendant, a maid here at the college, an errand boy? Most of these newspapermen offer money for a tip like this." He looked over at Harrison. "I'm sorry, sir. It would all come out, sooner or later, in the papers. Looks like it will be sooner."

Harrison, who had recovered some of his color, nodded stiffly.

Soon, everyone else had left but Concordia and Capshaw.

"Was there something else you wanted, miss?" Capshaw asked, seeing her linger.

"How are Sophia and Amelia?" Concordia asked.

Capshaw gave a great sigh. "It's still a bit of a mess. As you know, Miss Adams has been able to delay the mental evaluation of the little girl until the expert returns from Europe. Between Mr. Bradley's visits and her sister's presence, Miss Amelia is more calm—unless we try to bring up the subject of the colonel." His face softened. "She is a brave little girl. As is her sister."

Concordia realized with a start that Capshaw seemed emotionally involved with the sisters. She had never seen the softer side to the policeman before.

"Well, I have something promising," Concordia said, "look at this." She pulled out the translation of her father's journal that Miss Phillips had accomplished so far.

Capshaw's expression brightened as he reached for them. Concordia watched him read with increased absorption until he got to the abrupt end of the passage.

"I will telegraph the museum in Boulaq," Capshaw said. "It might take some time. It's unfortunate that your father never gives the man's proper name."

"I know, but we can't be sure, even if he's in the area, that he would be using his given name," Concordia pointed out. "He might have used an alias to avoid tipping his hand and putting Colonel Adams on his guard."

"You'll let me know when Miss Phillips has deciphered the rest of it?"

Concordia nodded, and turned to leave.

"Miss Wells? You may want to secure that amulet of yours. I'm going back to check the lady principal's quarters and office now, but if Mr. Harrison is correct about what his sister's attacker was after... you are a target as well."

It was well past curfew when Concordia crossed the grounds. Although the half-moon was out behind the clouds, it did little to illuminate the barely-lit path, instead casting threatening shadows that made her pick up her pace and glance over her shoulder more than once as she headed to Willow Cottage. Her breath came out as ghostly wraiths in the chill November air. She shivered. Why hadn't she waited for Lieutenant Capshaw to escort her back? Pride? Fatigue? She just wanted to crawl into her bed and forget the sight of Miss Grant's strangled form.

She stopped short as she approached the science building, where the door had opened, and a light was snuffed out. She uttered a little squeak of alarm as a man's shadow approached. Her heart hammered in her throat.

"Concordia—it's just me," a voice whispered.

She let out the breath she was holding. "David! You scared me to death! Whatever are you doing out this late?"

David Bradley looked down at her. In the moonlight, she could see his brow creased in worry. "I heard about Miss Grant. Is it true you found her?"

Concordia nodded, shuddering.

He removed his jacket and put it over her shoulders. "Let's get you home."

She pulled the soft wool collar more firmly around her, breathing in the faint scent of his shaving soap. The silence stretched uncomfortably between them. Concordia sensed there was a great deal David wanted to say. As did she.

"Thank you for speaking to President Langdon last week," she said at last.

He looked down at his hands. "I'm sorry about my behavior that night. You had enough to be distressed about."

Concordia sighed. "I know you were concerned for my welfare. Heaven knows I can be stubborn." She must drive him crazy with her pig-headedness. But what exactly was he sorry for: kissing her, or putting her in a compromising position with the lady principal?

They had reached the porch of Willow Cottage. She handed back his jacket. There was one thing she needed to make clear. "David. Can you accept that, right or wrong, I must make my own decisions? I need a friend, not a protector."

"Is that all you need, Concordia?" David held her gaze for a moment before her eyes dropped.

"Such things are seldom simple," was all she could trust herself to say.

One thing she *did* know: he was not in love with Sophia and that thought made her feel like a giddy schoolgirl. *Land sakes.*

"Good night," he said.

After he left, she quietly undid the latch and slipped into the cottage. A curious sight greeted her in the front hallway: that of the house matron, sleeping upright in a chair and snoring like a lumberjack. She was clad in a threadbare old nightdress, wrapped in a shawl and shod in homely felt slippers. A Winchester rifle lay across her knees.

Obviously, Ruby knew about the attack on Miss Grant and had taken matters into her own hands to protect her lambs. Where on earth did she get such a weapon? The woman was enormously self-sufficient.

And yet, it was an oddly comforting sight.

Careful not to wake her, Concordia secured the latch and tiptoed into her room.

Sleep, when it did come, was uneasy, riddled with visions of Miss Grant's swollen, purple face.

Chapter 25

This above all, to thine own self be true.

I.iii

Week 10, Instructor Calendar
November 1896

Lieutenant Capshaw and his men visited every day the week following the attack upon Miss Grant, questioning staff and students. Capshaw had not found the amulet in the lady principal's quarters, nor in her office. He sent several telegrams to officials in Egypt looking for more information about Red, and combed through lists of men with known associations to Colonel Adams, to see if anyone matched Red's description.

With the active police presence on campus and Rosen's front page story in *The Courant* about the attack, worried parents began scooping up their girls and taking them home. Since normality could not be restored under such circumstances, President Langdon bowed to the inevitable and suspended all classes until after the Thanksgiving recess.

Miss Phillips was feeling much better but had a backload of work from her illness. She promised Concordia that she would finish her father's journal during the holiday break. Concordia tried not to chafe at the delay.

Miss Grant remained in the hospital, still unconscious. Her recovery was uncertain. Mr. Harrison spent most of his time with her.

So it was with great surprise that Concordia found him ringing the bell of Willow Cottage one afternoon just before Thanksgiving.

"Mr. Harrison, hello!" Concordia exclaimed. "Please, come in." She led him into the parlor. He perched on the edge of the seat in his usual meticulous manner, careful of trouser creases, hands together in his lap. Except, Concordia noticed, his hands were pressed together to keep them from trembling. The man was under a terrible strain.

"How is Miss Grant?" she asked politely.

"No better, but thank you." He cleared his throat. "I have come to ap-apologize for my sister's treatment of you."

Concordia shook her head. "None is necessary, I assure you, Mr. Harrison. You are not responsible for her behavior." She looked at him searchingly. "But can you explain something that I've never understood. Why does she *hate* me so?"

Mr. Harrison sighed and looked down at his well-polished shoes. "Please know it is not your fault. Olivia has suffered grievously, Miss Wells. People have no idea how destructive an impulse it is—to want, to steal, to acquire. How anxiety-and guilt-ridden a thing it is. When she came to campus, determined once again to conquer her impulses and make a fresh start, she saw you and felt an overwhelming envy. Her circumstances have made her a bitter woman. You were everything she could never be: confident, young, pretty, well-liked, successful."

Concordia hadn't considered herself any of these things, but she supposed through Miss Grant's eyes it could have seemed so. "I'm sorry for you both."

Harrison acknowledged this with a bow of the head, and said: "I know that others will be taking over my duties once classes resume, but what about the play? Will it still go on?"

Concordia nodded. "Miss Pomeroy—she's the acting lady principal now, being the most senior of the faculty—has pushed back the performance date to the end of term, in late January. And Miss Banning has agreed to help me." Given last year's experience, however, help from that quarter wouldn't be quite as constructive as she would like, but she would manage.

He stood. "I have more packing to do—both for myself and for her—but I wanted to see you before I left. And to thank you. If she ever does recover, it will be because you found her so soon. I am grateful."

Just as Concordia watched Mr. Harrison step off the porch of Willow Cottage, she saw Lieutenant Capshaw approaching. The men stopped and conversed briefly along the path before parting ways, Capshaw heading straight for the cottage. Concordia held the door open.

"Did you want to see me?"

Capshaw was frowning and looking behind him. "What did Harrison want?"

Concordia led him into the parlor. "Trying to make amends for his sister. He seemed to feel responsible for her, which I suppose is understandable. Why?"

Capshaw shook his head. "As we investigate further, Mr. Harrison's story is not holding together. No one can verify his whereabouts during the time before the meal, when we believe Miss Grant was strangled. He conducts himself in a nervous manner under questioning and the maid reported a heated exchange between him and Miss Grant only the day before."

Concordia remembered how pale and agitated Harrison looked when they were in the dining hall that day. It was peculiar, certainly, but not necessarily damning.

"Further," Capshaw went on, "the more I think about his theory that the attacker was after the amulet, the more skeptical I am. How would this person know the lady principal had it? The suspicion that she was a chronic thief would have circulated very quickly throughout campus."

Concordia shook her head. "I have a hard time believing that Mr. Harrison would attempt to murder *his own sister*, lieutenant! He has tried to *protect* her all this time."

"In my sad experience, Miss Wells, the assault or murder of someone in her own home is usually at the hands of a person she's closest to."

What a sordid profession being a policeman was, Concordia thought. "What will you do?"

"My men are keeping an eye on him now. I have asked him to come to the station for questioning once he's finished packing. Even if we don't have enough evidence to charge him, your president has promised me that he won't be permitted to return to the college. For any reason. You are safe."

Chapter 26

We know what we are, but know not what we may be.

IV, v.

Thanksgiving, 1896

President Langdon arranged for a traditional Thanksgiving feast at Sycamore House. The few students who couldn't travel because of distance or finances were invited, along with any faculty members and their guests who wished to attend.

Concordia had extended the olive branch to her mother, inviting her to the college feast as well. In her opinion, such an occasion should be shared with many. It was certainly preferable to just she and her mother staring at each other over the enormous bowl of yams that the housekeeper insisted upon preparing each year. The gaiety of a larger group setting, too, might smooth any lingering awkwardness between them after their argument a few weeks ago.

At first, Concordia thought she would have to wheedle and cajole her into accepting. Mother was usually lukewarm about attending college functions. But then Concordia realized that the Durands also planned to attend the college's "quaint American celebration," as Madame had put it, so the additional incentive was enough to convince her to come.

As Concordia entered the dining room at Sycamore House, she saw that a number of faculty had decided to join them this year. Besides the president, who acted as host, she saw that Mr. Pierce, Miss Jennings, Miss Banning, Miss Pomeroy, and Miss

Cowles were in attendance today. It promised to be a lively group.

Even Eli was there, helping guests with their coats. Concordia looked around for the Cat, but thankfully it was nowhere to be seen. Probably terrorizing the kitchen.

"Are you looking forward to the feast?" Concordia asked the boy, as he took her coat.

"Oh, yes, they got *so much* food back there, miss," he said, his eyes wide. "I'll be having my dinner in the kitchen with Cook and the rest o' them."

She ruffled the boy's hair affectionately and he smiled up at her. Funny, how attached to him she had become. He looked sturdier these days; a succession of steady meals and a warm bed were helping him thrive. And she could swear he'd grown at least an inch since she had seen him last.

"I better go hang these up," he added. And off he went to the cloakroom, arms full, trying not to step on the dragging hems. Concordia watched him, wincing. Well, she could give her coat a good brushing later.

The staff had succeeded in making the room look charmingly autumnal, with acorn wreaths, pinecone arrangements, and boughs of evergreen. A massive cornucopia on the table spilled over with gourds, nuts, and berries. Candlelight softened the whole scene. The aromas wafting from the kitchen made Concordia's stomach rumble.

For the first time in a long while, the general mood was relaxed and happy. Students talked animatedly, helping themselves to the punch bowl and hovering near the kitchen door to catch glimpses of the food preparations. Some of the girls were taking turns at the pianoforte, playing airs for the guests.

It was wonderfully normal. No policemen, no forecasts of doom, no mean-spirited administrator. Concordia exhaled and smiled to herself.

"Concordia."

She turned in surprise to see David Bradley, looking at her with warm brown eyes. She flushed at his appreciative glance, glad she'd chosen her nicest dress for the occasion, an at-the-shoulder green silk with a fitted bodice and sashed waist. How she was going to be able to eat anything was another issue, of course.

"David, how nice to see you! You're not dining with your family today?"

"What, and miss all this?" he gestured toward the pianoforte, where President Langdon and Dean Pierce were now lending their enthusiastic baritones to the song. "My brother is still abroad, and my mother and father decided to extend their visit with friends in New York."

"Well, I'm glad you're here." She smiled.

He leaned closer, taking her gloved hand and bowing over it in mock formality. "As am I," he murmured.

Mercy, was it getting warm in here?

Miss Jennings approached, carrying a tray of hors d'oeuvres. "Here, try these, they're delectable. I believe that asparagus is involved."

"Have you joined the wait staff?" David teased.

"Everything is coming off the burners at once, so I'm helping out. If I like it I may make a career change," Miss Jennings said with a smile.

I wonder what can be keeping my mother," Concordia said, looking around. "I thought she'd be here by now."

"I just saw her come in with the Durands," Miss Jenkins said. "The boy is helping with their wraps." She pointed.

Concordia craned her neck. Ah, there they were. Her mother, eyes bright and her cheeks becomingly flushed, was conversing with Madame Durand. Concordia had not seen her mother this happy and animated in a long while. Since Mary had died.

Concordia heaved a disappointed sigh. Her mother used to have an abundance of common sense. Why was she deliberately abandoning it and chasing an illusion?

But seeing her in the company of Madame Durand today, Concordia had niggling doubts. If this made her mother happy, was that so bad? Who was she to try to take away that hope?

But false hope is no hope at all, she reminded herself. The disillusion would be more crushing the longer the lie continued.

For now, Concordia put on a smile as her mother approached.

"Concordia! Happy Thanksgiving, my dear," Mrs. Wells said warmly. She kissed her cheek, which startled Concordia no end. Rarely was her mother this affectionate in public.

"And Mr. Bradley. So good to see you again," Mrs. Wells added, turning to David. David gave a little bow. "You are well, I trust?"

"Indeed, yes," he answered, nodding to the Durands as well.

Jacques Durand inclined his head in greeting but said nothing. His wife, however, was voluble.

"Miss Wells!" Madame cried, seizing Concordia's arm. "Your mother has been telling me so many stories about you growing up. And especially about the special bond between you and your father. How charming! What a unique man he must have been. After the time his spirit spoke to you in our little session I had been hoping that in my work with *Madame Wells*"—here she smiled at Concordia's mother—"we would hear from him once again." She gave an elegant shrug. "Alas, it has not happened yet, but one has hopes!"

David looked quite startled by Madame's casual mention of communicating with spirits as if they were but a railway trip away. He raised an eyebrow in Concordia's direction. She gritted her teeth and rolled her eyes.

The ring of the dinner bell spared Concordia from further details of how Madame planned to summon long-dead members of the Wells clan. Madame Durand took Mrs. Wells by the arm and led her toward their seats, chattering all the while. The medium looked back at Concordia with a triumphant smile.

Concordia clenched her hands together. It was obvious that Mother was deeply enthralled by the oh-so-charming Madame. Where would this lead? How was Concordia going to get her mother to come to her senses? It seemed a battle of wills between her and Madame Durand, with her mother as the prize.

President Langdon had spared no expense in providing a true Thanksgiving bounty. The table nearly groaned with the weight of it all. Besides the usual roast turkeys, each prepared *a la Reine* style with oyster stuffing, there was cranberry sauce, mashed potatoes, baked yams, cold celery-and-olive trays, cheeses, nuts, and pies of mincemeat and pumpkin. Concordia was full before they were half done.

Just before the dessert course—which she would certainly have to forgo—she felt something snuffle under her skirts and then twine around her ankles.

The Cat.

Thank goodness she wasn't the jump-and-shriek sort of lady. Perhaps she had grown accustomed to the beast. So long as the feline didn't claw her best stockings. Otherwise, she'd make a fur collar out of him.

As Concordia might have expected, Eli came bursting out of the kitchen door, looking anxiously around the room. She caught his eye and pointed under the table.

Concordia's fellow diners couldn't help but notice the boy from the cloakroom diving under the tablecloth at her feet. He gently disentangled the animal from under her skirts as Concordia bent over—at least, as much as she was able, in her tight corset—to help. Both Cat and stockings suffered no ill-effects.

Eli flushed a deep red when he saw all eyes were upon him. "Sorry. He got away," he muttered, retreating with the Cat to the kitchen.

Over the general chuckles, Madame said, "That creature, he follows the young man *everywhere*, doesn't he?"

"Two vagrants finding each other," Dean Pierce said sarcastically.

Concordia looked at him in surprise. That was an oddly disparaging remark, particularly from someone who most likely suffered condescension himself. Of course, he didn't know Eli as she did.

Soon the meal was over, the dishes cleared, and post-feast fatigue began to set in.

Concordia got up from the table and touched her mother on the elbow. "I should go back," she said, "but can we talk for a moment first?"

Puzzled, Mrs. Wells followed her to an inner corridor near the front hall.

"We haven't spoken in a while," Concordia began. "I'm so sorry about our argument before. How are you feeling?"

Mrs. Wells smiled and patted her daughter's arm. "Better than I've felt in ages, thanks to Madame Durand. Thank you for your concern. All is forgiven, dear."

"I'm glad. But Mother, I'm still worried about your growing attachment... to Madame Durand." There. She said it. She waited for the angry outburst.

Her mother gave a little laugh. "Oh, how well Madame can predict these things! She told me that you would be stubborn in this regard. You are too preoccupied with the world of the intellect, Concordia. There is room for little else beyond what you can see and measure."

Concordia, flustered, was silent.

"Let me see if I can put it in a way you would understand, dear. *There are more things in heaven and earth, Horatio, than are dreamt of in your philosophy.*"

Splendid. Now Mother was quoting Shakespeare to *her*.

"While that may be true," Concordia said, "and there *might* be legitimate spirit mediums out there, how do you know that Madame Durand is one of them? Many of these people have been proved the worst of charlatans. I don't want you to nurture false hopes that you will be able to communicate with... Mary."

Mrs. Wells turned hurt eyes to Concordia. "I can see that we are at an impasse. You do not know Madame as I do. Believe what you like, but I will listen to no more of it." She turned on her heel and walked away.

Concordia sighed and turned toward the cloakroom, briefly locking eyes across the room with Madame Durand who was still seated at the table. The medium raised her water glass to Concordia in a mocking salute.

Chapter 27

A dream itself is but a shadow.

II.ii

Week 12, Instructor Calendar
December 1896

The mood on campus was significantly improved when the students returned from their longer-than-usual recess, ready to resume their studies and activities in earnest. Lady Principal Pomeroy reinstated all events, including the play rehearsals, and—whatever her private objections to Madame Durand—the Spiritualist Club.

Madame Durand wasted no time in calling a meeting of its members—of which there was a growing number. Concordia, to her dismay, found their play practice numbers were significantly depleted as a result. Whatever spirits Madame could conjure were apparently more engaging than the ghost of Hamlet's father. She would have to speak with Miss Pomeroy about *that*.

Preparations for the Christmas season had begun in earnest, too, as the girls crafted gifts for family back home and for each other—in great secrecy, of course. The detritus of bright wools, colored papers, paint boxes, fabric scraps, and craft implements littered students' rooms and spilled over into the common area. Concordia was inevitably asked to hold a finger on a bow, mend a tear, locate scissors or paste, or untangle knots. It was difficult to get any work done.

Finally, after the tenth knock on her sitting-room door in the past hour, Concordia scooped up the rest of her ungraded student themes. "Ruby, I'll be in my office," she called toward the kitchen. Before anyone else could intercept her, she shrugged on her jacket and left.

Once settled in the quiet of her office, Concordia made short work of the stack of papers. She had nearly finished when there was a tap on her office door.

"Enter!" she called.

Eli walked in, glancing around the room as if searching for something. Concordia looked for the inevitable four-pawed shadow behind the boy, but the Cat was nowhere to be seen. Probably in an alley fight, she thought.

Concordia noticed that Eli was quieter, preoccupied.

"Is something wrong?" she asked.

"Have you seen him, miss?"

"Cat?" She thought back. "Why no, actually, not since the holiday dinner several days ago."

"It's been that long since I seen him, too," Eli said. "I'm worried. He's never gone more than overnight. I was hoping he was here."

"I'll be sure to tell you if I do see him. I know it's worrisome to have a—pet—go missing. Have you looked in all his usual places?"

The boy nodded, then sniffed.

Concordia got up and put an arm around his thin shoulders. "I'll ask some of the girls to help look. Try not to worry."

Shortly after Eli left, the sound of coughing along the hallway alerted her to Miss Phillips' presence. She got up and opened the door. "Miss Phillips, come in!"

Dorothy Phillips was looking much better. She had a healthy tint to her cheeks and moved once again with her former energy and grace. Only the occasional cough or wheeze gave her away.

"You've finished with my father's journal?" Concordia asked eagerly.

Miss Phillips' expression was somber.

"Something's wrong," Concordia said.

"You'd better read it first," Miss Phillips said, sitting down and sliding the packet toward Concordia.

Concordia pushed her glasses more firmly up her nose and picked up the first sheet.

2 November 1873

Not even the heat and fatigue I feel can suppress my elation over finding the tomb of Meyra, high priest of the sun god, Aten. Now we must dig it out ever-so-carefully. It will be both back-breaking and meticulous work.

❦

8 November 1873

We have the tomb open! Both time and supplies are running low, so Adams and I can only make a quick inventory, sketch the important pieces, and make corrections to the map before we head back to the boat. But what an incredible find! As proof of our discovery, I'll be removing a pair of heart amulets from the tomb. They are unlike any I have seen before: made of a dark stone, rather heavy, with unusual magnetic properties.

We are resting at our encampment as I write this. When we return, I shall visit Mariette in Boulaq and share news of our find. I also have the unpleasant task of turning over the evidence I possess regarding Red's plundering.

I grow tired of the chase, and wish to return to my family as soon as I may.

❦

15 November 1873

I write this in my cabin aboard a Cook's tourist steamboat headed back down the Nile to Cairo. My head has been bandaged, but is still pounding. The doctor on board says that I need to rest. But I must write about the events of the past seven days while they are fresh in my mind. As it is, my head injury is causing gaps in my memory. I fear I shall lose what I have if I don't write it down now.

The day we had finally broken through to the tomb, I decided to return to it in the cooler dusk before losing the light. Upon taking a more careful look through the tomb I grew more excited. The writings on the walls, the treasures, the near-perfect condition of the sarcophagus! There was a heavy, movable interior wall with hand-holds on the outside. After much exertion, I was finally able to push it aside to find a secret inner chamber. But something must have fallen on me, because I don't remember anything until the next morning when Adams and the others were pulling me out of the chamber. Thank heaven they found me.

I remember the next event clearly in my mind, however; Red stepped into the tomb. All of the anger and frustration I had felt became concentrated in one hard point of fury that I could not control. Lord help me, I lunged for the man's throat, and before anyone could separate us, we knocked against a side wall that proved precarious. It collapsed and we brought down the entire roof of the tomb on top of us.

Fortunately, there were others outside who had escaped the collapse and could dig us out. I don't remember much of the process. I kept fading in and out of consciousness. Somewhere in the chaos I lost one of the amulets from my pocket. I could only find one of them later.

Everyone was extricated, except for Red. A solid stone wall had come down upon his back and had him pinned. We did not have large enough winches or enough manpower to move it.

He was still alive, though. The workers were able to clear his head and upper body and revive him. At the sight of me he consigned me to the bowels of hell and heaped invectives upon me that will scar my soul forever.

We had no choice but to leave him and go back to Cairo for help. We left some members of our party behind to care for him, along with all of the supplies we could spare, but it seems doubtful that we will get help to him in time. I am leaving a man behind to die, and it is my fault.

---

30 November 1873

I have been treated and released from the hospital here in Cairo. I am finally well enough to make the long voyage home.

Red did not die out in the desert, but I don't know how fortunate that is, as he is crippled forever. He was rescued by a caravan traveling in the area. They had ropes, pulleys, and a few strong elephants to free him. Red came to the hospital just as I was leaving it, his wife and his pretty little daughter hurrying to his side. I slunk away before they could see me. I am ashamed.

Mariette has still not returned from his trip and now I think, why should I report anything? Red is a broken man, through my fault; do I really want to visit more misery upon him and his family?

As far as the tomb's discovery, I am disenchanted with the pursuit of glory and accolades. Let others discover Egypt's secrets. The workers have been paid and have moved on to other employment. The tomb is collapsed beyond recovery.

Let the sands cover the tomb, perhaps for another thousand years. Adams doesn't care; he, too, has lost his enthusiasm for the hunt. But I'm sure he will buy the collection of artifacts I have accumulated over my career. I will sell them all, except for the amulet. It is a reminder of my failure. I wonder if the other will ever be found.

Once I have disposed of my artifacts, however, I will probably sever my association with Adams. There is a part of me that distrusts him now. I wonder how I came to be struck on the head that night in the tomb, and how Red was able to leave the boat and find the site. Where were the men we left to keep watch over Red? Adams' men.

Tomorrow we sail on a trans-Atlantic steamer for home. I miss my wife and little girls.

Once she had finished reading, Concordia put her head in her hands. It seemed impossible that the journal she just read could have come from the man she'd adored. The Randolph Wells she'd known had been a mild-mannered scholar, content to aspire to no other ambition than successfully completing an obscure translation, and debating key points of philosophy with other scholars. She had never seen him angry or lacking self-control.

But this man, on these pages? Arrogant, devious, quick to anger? Riddled with guilt at the end, yes, but was that enough? His actions had caused a man great pain, and consigned him to a life as a cripple. And what of Red's wife and his "pretty little daughter?" What had happened to them? Had they been reduced to a life of deprivation and want?

Concordia looked up. Miss Phillips was watching her quietly, a look of pity on her face.

"Now we know why he abandoned Egyptology," Concordia said. "He couldn't bear the guilt, the reminders of what he had done."

"It explains other things, too, such as how the amulets became separated," Miss Phillips said. "The one you have—is it safe?"

Concordia took it out of a deep skirt pocket. "I've been carrying it with me for lack of a more secure place for it."

"I would lock it away in a vault somewhere, if I were you," Miss Phillips said. She shivered. "Maybe it *is* cursed, as Madame Durand says."

"What about the other one, which my father lost—somewhere in the rubble of the collapsed tomb, I suppose? How did Colonel Adams get it?"

"I don't know," Miss Phillips said. "Perhaps one of the workers found it after your father and Colonel Adams had gone for help and pocketed it? And later sold it to the colonel? And who has it now... Miss Grant's attacker, I suppose?"

"That seems reasonable to assume. We know it can't be Red, at least not directly," Concordia said. "If he's even still alive. More than twenty years have passed. With someone crippled that badly, no matter how strong he was originally—"

She stopped.

"You've figured out something," Miss Phillips said. "What is it?"

Concordia stood, gathering the papers. "I must see Lieutenant Capshaw—*at once.*"

Chapter 28

Thou hast cleft my heart in twain.

III, iv.

Week 12, Instructor Calendar
December 1896

"Miss Wells, I cannot allow you to do this," Capshaw said vehemently. "Do you realize how dangerous he is? Colonel Adams is dead, and Miss Grant is in the hospital —"

"I must, lieutenant," Concordia interrupted. "You've read the journal entries. You know what happened—as a result of my father's actions."

They were gathered in the Adams' parlor. It had taken Concordia a while to track down the lieutenant. She had finally found him here, with Sophia. He seemed to visit quite often, but she had no time right now to consider the significance of that.

Capshaw spoke softly, and put a hand on Concordia's arm. "Listen to me. It is not your fault. These events had nothing to do with you. Will you just let my men pick him up? You can talk to him down at the station."

Concordia shook her head. She knew now why her father had given her the amulet and the journal. So that she could somehow make up for the wrong he had done and make things right. He could not have anticipated these events, but he wanted her to be prepared if the time should come. Which it had.

The readiness is all.

"I want to talk to Dean Pierce first, *alone*, before you arrest him, lieutenant."

Capshaw turned toward Sophia. "Can you talk some sense into her, please?"

Sophia smiled. "You obviously don't know Concordia very well." Nevertheless, she did pull Concordia over to the settee and sat her down.

"Concordia. *You* think your father gave you his journal and amulet so that you could redress the wrongs he had done. Can I tell you what *I* think? I think he wanted to warn you, because he knew that Red was an unscrupulous man who could cause harm to you someday."

"But Augustus Pierce is in a wheelchair!" Concordia exclaimed.

"Yes, and what has he done?" Sophia asked. "He has killed... my father, and strangled your lady principal—"

"I could be wrong about that. The man is a *cripple*," Concordia said.

Capshaw interrupted, his expression was gloomy with regret. "No, I think you're right, Miss Wells. Which means I was following the wrong thread in suspecting Mr. Harrison. Harrison's account of his whereabouts wasn't the only story we couldn't corroborate. During the time in question, the dean's account of his movements could not be substantiated, either."

He sighed and shook his head. "But I hadn't pursued it because I'd ruled out a man in a wheelchair. I should have realized that with sufficient hand and arm strength and the opportune angle it was possible. Besides, no one knows the extent of his disability, if he can stand or even perhaps walk. As far as the murder of Colonel Adams, I'll have to go back and check Pierce's whereabouts on the night the colonel was shot."

"And with a gun, Pierce needed no strength at all," Sophia added. "But if it *was* him, and he truly is dependent upon that chair, he would have needed help to get into our house that night. An accomplice."

"We'll look into that as well," Capshaw said. He turned to Concordia. "If Pierce is the culprit we seek for both crimes, then this is a bold and desperate man you wish to confront."

"He won't have a gun at Sycamore House," Concordia said. "And there are too many other people around. I'll be perfectly safe." She looked over at the grim-faced Capshaw. "We have more of a chance to get him to talk if I'm alone with him. Besides, he won't hurt me, not if he wants the second amulet. I'm the only one who can get it for him. He must know that."

"Perhaps, but there is something more I wanted to say, Concordia," Sophia broke in. "You think your father did some terrible wrong to Pierce. But look at the circumstances. What is Randolph Wells really guilty of? Employing subterfuge to get around a very cunning man and protect a country's treasures. Lunging at him in the heat of anger. In such a situation, how many other men would have done the same? No man is the paragon of virtue that you have built your father to be over all these years."

Concordia looked down at her lap in silence as Sophia's words hit a little too close to home.

"What happened was a tragic *accident*," Sophia continued. "Pierce's injury was not of your father's creation. Your father, too, was injured and had to get to a hospital. He had no choice but to leave Pierce, yet he did not leave him without providing what care was possible."

Concordia finally looked up. "I understand what you say, Sophia, but I must do it my way."

Capshaw frowned. "I keep forgetting how stubborn you college ladies can be. Very well. We'll do it your way, but with a few precautions in place. Agreed?"

Chapter 29

One may smile, and smile, and be a villain.

I, v.

Week 12, Instructor Calendar
December 1896

The day was overcast and blustery, scuttling dried leaves against the curb as the driver handed Concordia into the Adams' carriage for the ride back to the college. She wrapped her jacket more tightly around herself and shivered from more than the cold.

How could she get the dean to confess to what he had done? What if he denied it all? She had no proof, although Capshaw may be able to confirm the man's identity through replies to his telegrams. But what would that prove? Only that Dean Pierce was actually the man named "Red" in her father's journals, and had been associated with him long ago. The rest of it, what Concordia surmised to be Pierce's single-minded pursuit of the amulets—so single-minded that he was willing to kill to get them—was just conjecture on her part.

And why did Pierce want them so badly? What made them so valuable? None of the experts who examined the one from Colonel Adams considered it a priceless artifact. She was missing something.

One thing was certain: Pierce now knew that she had the other amulet. She should be able to use that for leverage.

Once back at campus, Concordia hurried to her rooms to change before going to see Pierce. Ruby stopped her on her way back out.

"Have you seen the boy, miss?" she asked, looking troubled.
"Eli? No. Why?"

"I've been looking for him, to see if he wanted any of the chicken dumpling soup I just made, and to take some of it over to Miss Phillips. No one's seen him all day."

Concordia felt uneasy. First the cat, now the boy. Something was wrong here. But she had no time to spare for the problem now. She had to hope that he was simply out looking for his pet. "When I get back, we'll make more inquiries," she said, in as reassuring of a tone as she could muster.

With that, she closed the front door behind her and headed over to Sycamore House.

The maid answering the door put Concordia in the front parlor while she went to check on the dean. She returned moments later. "Mr. Pierce said he can join you in twenty minutes. Can you wait, miss?"

Concordia nodded, and settled herself into a chair. The floor-length curtains in front of the deep windows were closed against the draughts and there was a robust fire burning. The room was comfortable enough.

Per Capshaw's instructions, however, Concordia opened one of the windows a few inches.

President Langdon, passing through the hall on his way out, stuck his head in the parlor when he saw a visitor.

"Ah, Miss Wells! For a moment I thought you were Madame Durand. Good to see you, my dear." He looked around at the empty room. "For whom are you waiting?"

Strange that Langdon would have mistaken her for Madame since they looked nothing alike, Concordia thought. "I'm here to see the dean," she answered, trying to keep the tremble from her voice.

The president, however, took note of that and sat down beside her. "Something's wrong. Tell me what's going on."

Her composure crumbling at last, Concordia cried, burying her face into the lapels of his jacket.

It's not usually considered part of a president's duties to have his faculty members sobbing on his shoulder, but Langdon took it in stride. "There, there, my dear," he said, pulling out his handkerchief.

Concordia took a deep breath to recover her composure. *Mercy*, she seemed to be making a habit lately of crying upon men's shoulders in parlors.

"Why don't you tell me about it." Langdon encouraged.

So she did—telling him about her father's past she'd known nothing about, the disillusion she felt about the man she'd idolized, the connection of the amulets to the murder of Colonel Adams and the attack upon the lady principal, and the real identity of her father's associate: Dean Pierce.

"I am here to ap-apologize for what my father had done to him, and to give him the amulet left to me, if only he would turn himself in. I would rather not have him dragged away by the police," she said.

Langdon's expression had turned into an angry scowl during Concordia's account. "Our *dean* did this? I would drag him to police headquarters myself. Why didn't you tell me sooner? Haven't you learned anything from last year's incident, that you shouldn't go rushing off alone?"

"I only figured it out today. I have no proof," Concordia answered. "Lieutenant Capshaw is waiting outside to arrest him if I can get him to confess, so I'm not really alone. I'm sorry, Mr. Langdon," she added meekly.

"Still, I don't like it. Let the police do their jobs," Langdon protested.

Concordia gave one last sniffle and put the handkerchief in her pocket. "You're right. I'm terribly impulsive that way, wanting to do this completely on my own. But Pierce trusts me, and I think I can surprise him enough and coax him to confess. However, if he denies everything, I have no proof, merely suspicion. Nonetheless, I have to try."

Langdon sighed and patted her arm. "Very well." He tapped his chin thoughtfully as he looked around the room. "But I propose we amend the plan slightly."

Concordia nodded as Langdon explained his idea.

Dean Pierce wheeled himself into the room with the ease of practice and powerful hands. Concordia was standing by the fireplace. The man looked as amiable as ever. There wasn't a trace of the anger Concordia had seen in the dining hall a few weeks ago, the day Miss Grant was attacked and left for dead. But she knew it was there, just under the surface. The red-flushed, apoplectic look of a man with a quick temper. His red hair was gone, but the rest remained.

"What can I do for you, dear?" he asked, as he motioned her to sit. She perched nervously on the settee.

"I have made some unpleasant discoveries that I came to discuss with you."

He looked puzzled.

"Miss Phillips has finished transcribing the shorthand from my father's journal entries. About my father's last expedition in Egypt," she added carefully.

The dean's eyes flickered, but that was all.

"I know who you really are, Mr. Pierce—or shall I call you 'Red?" Concordia said.

"I beg your pardon?"

"I know that you hated my father, and the colonel, for thwarting you all those years ago. They deprived you of your plunder. And, of course, the tragic accident that crippled you was the worst blow of all. But why kill Colonel Adams? Was it because my father was dead and out of reach of your revenge? Or because you thought the colonel had the amulet, and you didn't believe him when he denied it?

"And then there's the lady principal," Concordia went on, when Pierce stayed silent. "She had nothing to do with those incidents so long ago. But you found out, somehow, that *she* had stolen the amulet. Did she surprise you in her quarters when you were searching for it? Is that why you attacked her?"

Dean Pierce was quiet for a long while. Concordia waited.

He sighed, wheeling himself closer, so that their knees were nearly touching. "Concordia. Yes, your father and I were in business together, and I *was* called 'Red' back in those days. But I am innocent of what you accuse me. I never killed Adams— much as I would have dearly wanted to at one time, after he had double-crossed me. And you must believe me; I didn't touch a hair on our lady principal's head."

Concordia wanted to believe him, but knew she dare not. A man capable of fooling her father was a very cunning one indeed. She pulled her skirts back and inched away on the sofa. "Why did you pretend, then, that you didn't know my father? Those times when I confided in you, you feigned ignorance. Why?"

"I apologize for the subterfuge, dear. I have forgiven your father—truly I have—but those incidents are a painful memory."

The dean pressed on with his case. "You accuse me of horrible deeds based upon my past association with your father, recounted by him in an old journal, but think about how little sense it makes. How would *I* know that Miss Grant had the amulet? Why would I want the colonel's artifacts or the amulet? They are of little value. I have a large enough collection."

This wasn't going well. The man sounded so reasonable. She was missing something here.

"So you wanted nothing from that tomb?" Concordia asked skeptically. "My father believed otherwise."

Pierce laughed. "At one time, of course. Your father was correct in his suspicions of me. Back then, I dealt in, shall we say, *irregularly* acquired antiquities? But your father actually had more to fear from Adams than from me. The good colonel double-crossed us both. But that doesn't matter now."

He was silent for a moment, before continuing. "After my injury"—here his face flushed with emotion—"there were no more digs for me. Even the tomb that had collapsed upon me was reburied later in a massive sandstorm. The markers were obliterated. Mariette did not even *believe* that it was the tomb of Meyra. Without corroboration from your father—which was never given—he could not be bothered to go look for it. So it was all for nothing. Even my family abandoned me. My *loving* wife didn't want to be saddled with a husband in a wheelchair. She left, taking our only child with her—my daughter, who had been the light of my life."

Concordia felt a pang of pity for the man, but still didn't believe he was innocent. "How did you come to be *here*, at this school?"

"When I was well enough to earn my living again, I acted as curator to local exhibits in Cairo and then in London. I also taught university courses. After a while, I moved back to the States, to Boston, and taught there, in addition to serving on several college boards. Then I saw mention in the newspaper of Adams donating his collection. Hartford Women's College needed someone to fill the dean position. It seemed serendipitous." He smiled paternally at Concordia. "It is nice to see you all grown up. Your father talked about you all the time."

Concordia wasn't about to be distracted. "That doesn't answer my question. Why would you uproot and relocate here, from idle curiosity?"

He shrugged.

Concordia took the amulet and papers out of her pocket. She passed him the smooth stone. "As I mentioned before, my father left this for me. Now I want you to have it."

Pierce gave it barely a glance before setting it aside. "I don't care about the bauble. It's not at all valuable."

He picked up some of the sheets. "Ah, Randolph Wells' shorthand. I'd recognize it anywhere. And what's this? A map?" His eyes gleamed as he reached for the page that had drifted to Concordia's feet.

In that moment, Concordia realized what she had been missing all along. She snatched the map before he could grasp it.

"You never wanted the amulets, did you? Somehow, they were a means to an end. You wanted *the map*. It shows the location of the tomb that Mariette never believed you had found, that is still buried under the sand. That's why you encouraged me to ask my mother about those days and to search through my father's papers. You wanted the fame of discovery, even though you cannot go back there yourself. Or perhaps, you simply want to have it opened and quietly plundered. A man as resourceful as you no doubt has powerful allies back in Egypt."

"Give me the map!" Pierce roared. With a quick push from his chair, he threw himself upon her, pinning her down against the cushions. His large hands closed around her neck. All Concordia could get out was a terrorized squeak before she had no breath to make a noise. Flashes of light appeared around her eyes as she dropped the map and scratched at his hands and arms.

To her immense relief, the pressure on her airway was suddenly gone. Pierce's weight was lifted from her as President Langdon pulled the man away and tossed him to the floor, the wheelchair tipping over as he fell.

The resounding crash brought the housekeeper, maid, and Lieutenant Capshaw rushing in.

"Thank you, Mr. Langdon," Concordia said, in a hoarse whisper. "You heard everything, I hope?"

Langdon nodded, a grim look on his face. "As did the lieutenant, listening at the window. I regret that I got a bit tangled up in the curtain trying to reach you, Concordia, or I would have got him off you sooner. Are you all right?"

She rubbed her neck tenderly. There were sure to be bruises. "I will be," she croaked.

"Still, we should send for Miss Jenkins," Langdon said, looking to the maid, who scurried off.

In the meantime, Capshaw and two of his men had righted Pierce's chair and put him back in it. The man was breathing heavily, and glowered at Concordia.

"This isn't over," he growled.

"Quiet, you," Capshaw said. He turned to his men. "Take him to the station."

Miss Jenkins came in with her medical kit as Pierce was being wheeled out. She gave him a penetrating look before going over to Concordia. After a careful examination, she set to work, probing tenderly and applying rubbing alcohol to a few scratches. Concordia knew she must look a sight.

Capshaw come over to her. "Miss Wells," he sighed. "Are all of you college ladies so single-minded? Did I not tell you he was a dangerous man?"

"Save your voice, it has already been strained. The larynx is swelling a bit," Miss Jenkins said to Concordia. The infirmarian turned to Capshaw. "To answer your first question, lieutenant, yes—we are *all* this stubborn. Get used to it. And as far as dangerous... you'll want to get those scratches on Pierce's arms tended to. Some of them look quite deep." With that, she smiled and turned back to her patient.

After one last look, Capshaw shook his head and left.

Chapter 30

And then it started like a guilty thing
Upon a fearful summons.

I. i

Week 13, Instructor Calendar
December 1896

With Concordia's injury, teaching classes and directing the play were out of the question for the next few days. Miss Jenkins summarily ordered her to rest and not use her voice. At all.

It became clear to Concordia that she wasn't suited to having time on her hands. She had soon finished her backlog of papers and caught up on her reading. She even re-read *Hamlet*, writing notes in the margins about what tips to pass along to students. When she was allowed to talk again.

Capshaw had sent word about their progress since Pierce's arrest. The biggest break in the case had come when Miss Grant finally recovered consciousness. For a woman with a damaged larynx, she had screamed bloody murder and made abundantly clear that Pierce was her attacker. When pressed, she had also reluctantly admitted to stealing the amulet and that Pierce had found it when she surprised him in her rooms.

With such damning witness testimony, Pierce was arraigned in police court for the assaults upon Concordia and Miss Grant and held in custody until the next Superior Court session. There was no clue as yet about what happened to the amulet. "Unfortunately, he had plenty of time to pass the artifact on to someone else," Capshaw had noted. Whether Pierce, because of his past association with Colonel Adams, had anything to do with his murder was still being investigated.

Concordia was also preoccupied thinking about Eli. The boy had been gone for several days now, with no word. No one had seen him at the settlement house, either.

That night, she had a particularly difficult time getting to sleep, tossing and turning so much in her bed that her night dress and sheets were a rumpled mess. She had to get up and straighten everything out before getting back into bed again.

Finally, she did fall asleep but her dreams were strange. She dreamt of herself as Hamlet, listening to her dead father, trying to understand what he wanted. But instead of being dressed in kingly garb, Papa wore his ordinary clothes and an amulet around his neck. Then the dream changed, and Concordia was in the audience watching the play, and Sophia was Hamlet, and the King was a blood-covered Colonel Adams. Instead of the amulet around his neck, he wore a key.

The dream changed again, and Concordia was walking down a long, narrow corridor, lined with mirrors. The strange thing was, she couldn't see herself in them, but every once in a while she'd glimpse a little girl skipping ahead, holding the hand of an unknown person. Concordia followed the girl and craned her neck to see whose hand she was holding, without success. The corridor got colder as they traveled farther. She heard a light *tap* of metal against glass, and the rustle of someone moving around.

This wasn't part of the dream.

The other images faded and Concordia opened her eyes. She saw a shadow of movement. Her heart raced but she remained absolutely still.

There was an intruder in her room.

Whoever was here was being very quiet, navigating carefully around furniture. She couldn't see exactly what he was doing without turning her head and alerting him, so she willed her breathing to stay regular, even when all she wanted to do was gasp in panic. She felt chilled.

She waited. If he crossed the window—which was partly open now, letting in the cold air and probably the reason she woke up—she would be able to see him in the moonlight.

Finally, he stepped into the light, shrinking the distorted shadow to his actual size.

"Eli!" Concordia said, her voice still raspy. She untangled herself from the bedcovers.

"M-Miss Concordia!" He froze.

She turned on the light and lowered her voice, so as not to wake the household. "What are you doing here? And where have you been? We've been so worried about you."

"I been real busy... helpin' at the Durand house. I guess I should have told you." He trembled, and looked down penitently.

"I know you are accustomed to coming and going as you please, but you have people who care about you now. All right?"

He nodded.

"So, glad as I am to see you, why were you sneaking around in my room and scaring me half to death?" Concordia asked.

"I'm right sorry 'bout that. I was trying not to wake you up. I thought... I saw Cat go in here."

"Really? He's still missing?" Concordia turned on more lights and explored various nooks, including under the bed. No sign of the creature. "Well... he's not here now," she said. "But no matter what the reason, young man, you shouldn't be letting yourself into people's private residences."

Eli hung his head. "I'm sorry," he mumbled.

Poor boy. To be missing his pet for so long did not bode well for the Cat's future. She smoothed his hair in a gesture of sympathy.

"I should let you get back to sleep," he said.

"I don't want you walking around at this time of night," Concordia said. She went to the wardrobe and pulled out an extra pillow and blanket. "Come with me."

She put together a makeshift bed for him on the parlor sofa for the night. "We'll talk more in the morning," she said, after tucking him in—a strange feeling, really, tucking in a child all cozy for the night. Oddly comforting to the adult, too. Eli settled down contentedly.

Concordia went back to bed, turned off the lamp, and thankfully fell into a dreamless sleep.

Chapter 31

O villain, villain, smiling, damned villain!

I.v

Week 13, Instructor Calendar
December 1896

C oncordia slept heavily and woke late the next morning. *Mercy—nearly eleven.* Was Eli still here? She didn't hear anything but the usual chatter of girls upstairs and Ruby's humming as she went about her work.

She dressed quickly and checked the parlor. No Eli, although the blanket and pillow were neatly stacked against a corner.

"Have you seen Eli this morning?" Concordia asked, as Ruby came into the room. "He came into my room last night so I made up a bed for him here."

"He—*what?* That boy's got a wild side, still." She shook her head. "Haven't seen 'im, but I'm glad he turned up, finally. I was gettin' a little worried."

"I guess he woke early and didn't want to be caught in a house full of girls," Concordia mused. They would have to go over some basic etiquette with the boy.

"How are you feelin' today, miss? Can I make you somethin' to eat?" Ruby asked.

"No, no, I'm fine, really. You're busy enough. I'll go over to the dining hall and see what they have left," Concordia said.

She went back into her room for her boots and jacket and noticed a key lying on her glass-topped vanity table. She'd never seen it before.

Upon closer inspection, it looked to be no more remarkable than an ordinary house key. But it hadn't been here when she went to bed last night, of that she was sure. So where had it come from?

Then she remembered the sound she'd heard, which had seemed part of her dream: the faint sound of metal against glass. Eli. But why would he leave a key? She stuck it in her pocket for the time being.

She reached for the amulet and papers, as she always did.

The amulet was gone.

Her first reaction was anger; she'd already been through so much with that artifact. It was the last thing her father had given her. But then she felt a growing sense of unease. Eli had never stolen anything but food before, and that out of dire necessity. He had barely given the amulet a passing glance in the past. Why steal it now?

With Pierce's arrest, Concordia had thought that their troubles were over. Now it looked as if someone else was involved, somehow coercing Eli to steal. A former accomplice of Pierce's, perhaps?

Possibly. As Sophia had pointed out, Pierce would have needed help to gain entry into the Adams house unnoticed. But Pierce hadn't wanted the amulet. He'd wanted the map all along. Concordia now understood it to be Pierce's way of reclaiming some of the glory of the old days and enjoy a final triumph over Randolph Wells.

But suppose someone *else* wanted the amulets. He would have allied with Pierce, for their mutual benefit. The accomplice would get the amulet, and Pierce would exact his revenge upon Colonel Adams after all these years. And possibly get the map, too.

Revenge was a powerful emotion. Pierce had said that he'd been "double-crossed" by Adams. With Randolph Wells long dead and out of reach, Adams was the only target left.

Except the plan had not gone well. Yes, Adams had been killed, but he did not have the amulet. Lady Principal Grant had already stolen it. The safe could not be opened to search for the map. And Pierce and his associate had to flee when they heard Amelia coming, although now Concordia wondered about the blow to the poor child's head.

Whoever Pierce's accomplice had been, he must be feeling *very* nervous about Pierce's capture, Concordia thought. At any moment, his identity could be revealed.

The rumble in her stomach reminded her that she hadn't eaten. She should grab something leftover from breakfast first before figuring out her next step.

In the dining hall, Concordia found she wasn't the only person absurdly late to breakfast. Miss Phillips sat by herself, lackadaisically spooning a lumpy, watery substance in her bowl. She looked up. "I cannot recommend the oatmeal this morning. That's what I get for coming so late."

"Are you feeling unwell?" Concordia asked anxiously.

The lady shook her head. "I was up early, in fact, and went over to the gallery to continue with the cataloging. I was so absorbed in the work I lost track of the time."

Concordia looked around to make sure they couldn't be overheard. But they were alone. "The amulet has been stolen," she said. Miss Phillips sucked in a breath.

Concordia told her about Eli's visit the night before and her suspicions. "Pierce is in jail now. He couldn't possibly have had contact with Eli since then. Someone else is involved and pressured the boy to do this. And now Eli has disappeared again."

"But how is he being coerced?"

"I don't know," Concordia said. "I'm trying to figure this out from the other direction. Whoever it is has both amulets now and has achieved his aim. What would he do next? Sell them? Are they valuable as a pair, when they had not been singly?"

Dorothy Phillips tapped a finger against her lips thoughtfully. Concordia could almost see the history professor going through an inventory in her head: *No, those are made of clay... no, they are never made in pairs....*

Miss Phillips looked up. "Something about these is nudging at my memory. I have to look into it further."

"We don't have time. I need to find Eli."

"You could talk to that policeman. Maybe he could start a search for the boy and also keep a watch out for those amulets being sold, although I strongly suspect that's not what the intent is," Miss Phillips said.

With a quick murmur of thanks, Concordia got up from the table, grabbing a roll from the bread basket on her way out.

Concordia took the trolley to the Pratt Street stop, practically in front of the police station.

"Yes, miss, can I help you?" the sergeant at the desk inquired politely, as she entered the lobby.

"Is Lieutenant Capshaw here?" she asked. "It is quite urgent that I speak to him."

"I'm sorry. He's out on a case right now," the man said. "Would you care to leave him a note?"

That would have to do for the moment. Concordia accepted pencil and paper with thanks, and sat on a dusty bench to compose her note. She tried to make it as succinct as possible, recounting the loss of the amulet, emphasizing how the boy could not be held culpable, but that he was in danger from an unknown accomplice of Pierce's.

Pierce. He was here in the jail, wasn't he?

She folded the note, and put Capshaw's name upon it, marking it *URGENT.* As she passed it to the sergeant she said, "Do you have a prisoner here by the name of Pierce?"

"Ah, are you from the college, too, miss? He had another lady visitor here. Quite pretty, she was." He smiled.

"Really? Do you know who?" How odd. Who from the college would have come to see Pierce?

He checked a clipboard. "A Miss Duncan."

She didn't recognize the name. Perhaps Capshaw could look into that. "May *I* talk with the prisoner, please? It's a college matter. Just for a few moments."

The man hesitated. Concordia gave him her sweetest smile, along with her best approximation of a helpless female, which involved some hand-fluttering, grasping of her hanky, and trembling lip.

"Oh, very well, but just for a minute, mind," he grumbled, getting up to escort her.

"Thank you, sergeant."

Pierce's wheelchair couldn't fit through the doors of the usual holding cell, so he had been put in an unfurnished office down the hall from the cell block. A cot, pillow, blanket, and pan were in one corner; a small table with water jug and basin were in another. An orderly had been assigned to tend to his needs, and that man was the one who unlocked the door and opened it for Concordia.

She stood, just inside the doorway, near the orderly. Her heart was racing.

"Ah, Miss Wells, how charming of you to visit me in my ignominy," Pierce said mockingly. "Why are you here? To gloat? That's rather unseemly, my dear." He ran a hand over his stubbled scalp. On a rather heathen level, Concordia was gratified to see that his arms were adorned with several sticking plasters from where she'd scratched him.

"Where is Eli?" Concordia asked abruptly. She had no intention of trading false pleasantries with the man.

"How is your neck?" he asked solicitously. "Healing up, I hope. Your voice *does* sound a bit raspy, though. You want to be careful about that."

Concordia, furious, stepped farther into the room. "Tell me where Eli is," she said, through gritted teeth. "Someone you're in league with has taken him. You know who, and where."

Pierce made a derisive sound. "*In league with...* how quaint!"

"I'll give you the map and my father's journal," Concordia said. "Do what you want with them. I do not care. But tell me where the boy is."

He laughed in her face. "How is the map of any use to me now? I won't be publishing any papers of my brilliant discovery from prison. And I cannot exactly *run* away," he said bitterly.

He was a man with no morals and nothing left to lose. There would be no negotiating with him. Without a word, Concordia turned to leave. The door thudded shut behind her.

"You will *never* find him!" he taunted through the door. She didn't look back.

She had to reach Capshaw. Eli's life depended upon it. Now that Pierce's accomplice had the second amulet and Pierce was in jail for murder, the life of one small boy would not be a consideration. He was a street urchin, eminently dispensable. Who would miss him, really?

Well, she would, and she was going to find him. But how? She couldn't even find *Capshaw*, for goodness sake.

Then she thought. *Sophia.* She would know where the lieutenant was. Concordia had noticed the policeman had been spending a lot of time with Sophia and little Amelia, although she didn't know what to make of that.

Sophia's house was about an eight-block walk from the station. Taking the trolley would have been quicker under normal circumstances, but the afternoon traffic from downtown office workers, combined with the press of early Christmas shoppers, meant the streetcars passed her by, filled to capacity. It would be faster to walk than to wait. Perhaps she could catch a less-crowded trolley at a later stop along Aslyum. She hurried as decorously as she could.

A few blocks later, as she waited for yet *another* crowded streetcar to pass before crossing the corner, something darted between her legs and she almost tripped.

What?

It was Eli's cat.

The unmistakable, bedraggled feline, who looked even *more* bedraggled than usual, if that were possible: thinner, flea-bitten, quivering. She was so happy to see the beast that she picked it up, fleas and all, and hugged it. "Where did *you* come from?" He jumped from her arms and trotted away.

Where Eli is, the cat is sure to follow. Concordia's heart hammered in her chest. Could Eli be nearby?

Where was she? Concordia looked around to orient herself. The corner of Main and Charter Oak.

Now where had the cat gotten to? Concordia caught the flick of its tail half a block away, as it went down an alley. She followed it.

She'd just caught up to it when the animal squeezed itself through a cellar transom window. Then it was gone.

Whose house was this?

Cautiously, she looked in a street-level window of the house. Through the tiny gap in the curtains she could only see a pedestal table with a brass plate of unusual cone-shaped objects.

Hmm… those seemed familiar. Where had she seen them?

The incense at the Adams' séance. She remembered now. So this was either another residence that was having a séance, or, more likely, the Durands' house. She knew the Durands didn't live far from Sophia. She walked down the alley, back around to the front door. The brass plate over the mail slot confirmed it: *Durand.*

Concordia hesitated. What did it mean? Was Eli there? Or was the beast just scrounging for a meal? She went back around to the transom and crouched down. "Eli? Are you in there?" she called softly. She heard nothing. The window was too dirty and the room too dark to see in.

As people passed by, glancing at her in curiosity, Concordia realized that she was drawing attention to herself by bending down and whispering into windows. She made a pretense of looking in her reticule as another man went by, then melted into the afternoon shadows along the side of the house.

She had a choice: go back to the police station for help in rescuing Eli, or get the boy out herself. But going back to the station, especially since Capshaw wasn't there, would be time-consuming. She wasn't even sure she could convince them that Eli was here. For that matter, she wasn't so sure herself. And what would she have the police do? Pound on the door and demand the boy back? Accuse the Durands of kidnapping, a very serious charge, based upon a stray cat? Precious time would be lost in argument.

Her decision was made. She was going in.

As she skirted the house looking for a wider opening than the transom the cat had slipped through, she couldn't help but chuckle to herself.

No matter what the reason, you shouldn't be letting yourself into people's private residences, she'd told Eli, just last night. Well, she'd been wrong, and she hoped she'd have the chance to tell the boy that.

Then she thought of the key, and pulled it from her pocket. Could it be...?

Going to the side door, she tried it in the lock. It fit, but wouldn't turn. What was this key for, then? Why had Eli left it for her? He was trying to tell her something.

So if this wasn't the key to the Durand house, whose was it?

Keys. She'd had a conversation about a key recently. Concordia clenched it in her gloved hand as she thought. A key, and Eli....

Of course. This must be the *Adams'* house key. That's why it fit in the lock of the Durand house but would not turn. Most of the houses in this neighborhood, Sophia's included, were built at the same time and used the same brand of lock. Eli must have found the key, after all. But why would he have left it on a table in her quarters last night instead of giving it to her directly?

Understanding flooded her all at once and she began to see things from the perspective of Pierce's accomplice. The man helping Pierce had to be a frequent visitor to the Adams' house and familiar with the household routine. He knows about the spare backdoor key hidden in the flowerpot. He retrieves it and slips in quietly, letting in Pierce. No doubt he assists him in robbing and killing Colonel Adams.

What would happen to the key after that? The accomplice forgets about it as it languishes in a pocket. Much later, Eli finds that key, recognizing it as the one he used while staying at the Adams' home. But he doesn't understand how it came to be where he found it. He pockets it to ask Concordia about later.

Then, at last, the accomplice gets *one* of the amulets, after Pierce takes it by force from the lady principal and leaves her for dead. It's an easy matter for Pierce to pass it along. But the confederate is still desperate for the mate to it, and knows Concordia has it. But how to get it?

Through Eli. The boy is trusted by Concordia, and he can be made to cooperate. The cat is snatched shortly after the Thanksgiving meal. (No doubt a number of scratches were incurred in *that* process). Eli is frantic to find the cat, the one thing he cares most about in the world. The animal is shown to the boy, and the threat is made. Eli, under duress to steal Concordia's amulet, but cannot tell her why. He steals the amulet and leaves the key as a clue, hoping she will figure it out.

Jacques Durand. He was Pierce's accomplice. It made sense. He was a frequent visitor to the Adams' house, assisting Madame in her séances; Eli was living with them, and he knew the boy's affection for his cat; he was at the Thanksgiving dinner when the animal had made an appearance, and undoubtedly noticed the bond between Eli and Concordia. She didn't doubt that Madame Durand was involved too: at the very least turning a blind eye to her husband's enterprise, if not actively helping.

How Pierce and Durand came to be partners in this scheme, and why Durand wanted the amulets so badly, Concordia didn't know. But she was certain Eli was *here*, and that was all she cared about at the moment.

She had to go in. Now. Since she couldn't break in, it would have to be the direct approach. Taking out her pad and pencil, she scribbled a quick note, tucked it back in her purse, and stepped forward to ring the front doorbell. She straightened her jacket and took a few deep breaths for courage.

A diminutive maid opened the door. "Yes?"

Concordia's acting skills left a lot to be desired, but she knew she could pass as worried and anxious, most certainly. "Would it be possible to see Madame?"

The maid started to close the door. "I'm sorry, miss, but she only does consultations by appointment."

"Wait—I am sure she'll see me," Concordia said quickly. "I am one of her associates from the college. It's quite urgent."

She held out her card, counting upon Madame's curiosity to overrule her common sense. "Please?"

"We-ell, I can't say as she's available... but I'll ask." The girl opened the door wider and ushered Concordia to a small parlor.

She was in, but that was the easy part. She still had to find Eli.

A few moments later Madame Durand came in. She wore a lounging robe of deep wine velvet with flowing sleeves. Concordia noticed the sleeves didn't quite hide several angry red scratches on her forearms. Madame's face was arranged in an expression of concern.

"Miss Wells? What is the matter?"

Concordia sighed and shook her head. "Thank you for seeing me like this, Madame. I have had a most unfortunate thing happen, and I was hoping for your help."

"Of course, *ma cherie*."

"I found an amulet left to me by my father; but now, it has been stolen."

"Oh, dear," Madame Durand said.

Concordia put her handkerchief to her nose and sniffed. "It was the last thing of my father's, and is of indescribable sentimental value. Perhaps, you can call upon your... spirit guide to help me find it? You were able to bring my father's spirit back to communicate with me before. I believe he *has* been trying to communicate with me. Could we try that?"

Madame Durand smiled. "Ah, it is not as easy as it seems. But we can try, eh? Fortunately, I am free for a little while, before I must go out for the evening."

"That is most kind of you," Concordia murmured.

"But I must prepare," Madame said, standing. "My husband will come in shortly to handle the final arrangements." And with that, she left the room.

Concordia was unsure what "final arrangements" Madame was referring to. Until Monsieur Durand walked in several minutes later. He bowed.

"Miss Wells, Madame is happy to be of service to all who seek her help," he said, "but we ask that her clients make a small donation…"

Ah.

"Naturally," Concordia said, opening her reticule. She pulled out a bill. "Will this suffice?"

"Indeed, yes," he said, holding out a small box for her to put it in. "If you will follow me, Madame is ready."

In what once looked to be the dining room, Madame sat, now with a full, blue satin cloak clasped at her neck. Heavy draperies on the windows plunged the room in darkness, only alleviated by flickering candles scattered about. The air was sharp and heavy with exotic incense. In the middle of the room was a large round table with another candle in the center. Madame was seated at the table, near the window.

Monsieur Durand seated Concordia and left, closing the door softly behind him.

"Let us begin," Madame intoned, in a somber voice. "Clear your mind of all distractions. Focus only on the candle, and nothing else."

Concordia complied, as Madame began to hum and sway.

"Since the dawn of time, man has sought answers from the dead," she chanted. "We ask of thee, spirits, to guide us poor mortal beings. Give us wisdom; give us sight." She paused, as if listening to something Concordia could not hear. "Meti, are you here?"

Concordia gave a little shriek as the table rocked so violently it knocked over the candle and snuffed it out. She picked it up, but Madame paid no heed. "Ah, my Meti, you are here. We need your help. Miss Wells has lost something from the tomb of your own lands. The tomb is lost to us, covered perhaps for all time. But it is the amulet she seeks, from her father."

Things were becoming clear to Concordia at the moment, too. Now she realized who Pierce's accomplice really was.

In a moment, a ghostly glow appeared between them, and Concordia felt a light tap upon her shoulder. That would be sufficient, on top of everything else. Time to stop this nonsense.

"Oh!" Concordia exclaimed, sliding to the floor in a faint.

When Concordia opened her eyes, she was laying upon the settee, Madame chafing her wrists. "What happened?" she asked weakly.

"You fainted," Madame said. "I am sorry; sometimes the spirits, they get a little out of control. I should have warned you."

"I feel so silly," Concordia said, a hand to her head.

"You should rest here a while," Madame said. "If you will excuse me? I have to dress for a dinner engagement. Monsieur Durand will check on you shortly, and see you out."

"Have you any smelling salts? I still feel a little woozy," Concordia said.

"Of course." Madame left the room.

As soon as the door closed, Concordia sprang into action. She pulled out her pre-written note.

Madame. Thank you for your hospitality. I feel better now, and decided to go home to rest. Yours, C.W.

Concordia hoped that Madame's smelling salts were where Concordia typically kept hers: in her bedroom. And that Monsieur Durand was nowhere nearby.

First, she scooted down the hall and pulled at the front door, leaving it open just a bit, as if she'd neglected to latch it securely behind her. Then, she peered down the back hallway. Which door led to the basement?

There it was. She hurried over, opened it quietly, and slipped inside, pulling it softly shut behind her.

It was as dark as pitch. She groped her way carefully down the steep stairs, holding onto the wall as she went. When she reached the bottom, she stifled an exclamation when something rubbed past her legs. She sighed in relief when she heard purring.

"I could have tripped over you, you wretched beast," she whispered to the Cat, continuing her groping search of the basement's dirt floor. Her eyes were adjusting now; she could make out lighter shades of gray amidst the black. She headed toward the weak light coming from the transom. If Eli was here, she knew he must be gagged and restrained; the Durands would have never allowed her inside otherwise.

"Eli, if you can hear me, tap the floor or something," Concordia said. She waited, her heart pounding in her throat.

Tap, tap, came faintly from the left corner. She felt her way toward the sound, nearly stumbling over the boy where he lay.

"Oh, Eli," she whispered. She pulled off the filthy rag they'd tied around his mouth, gave him a quick hug, then set to work on his bonds. There were a lot of knots.

The boy was a mess, his hair matted and encrusted with dirt, a bruise blooming on his cheek, tear-streaks mingling with the dirt on his face. He worked his lips and tongue around, trying to talk.

"I wish I had water, but we'll get you out of here soon," Concordia said. She bit off an angry exclamation as he winced at the rope burns on his wrists. The Durands had a lot to answer for.

Finally, she got his hands free. He shook them to get the circulation going, grimacing. "I'm awfully glad t-t-to see you, miss," he croaked. He hung his head. "I'm-I'm s-s-sorry for taking—"

"Sh-h-h, it's all right, Eli," Concordia soothed. "They captured your cat, hadn't they? Did they threaten to hurt him if you didn't follow their instructions?"

He nodded. She gave him another brief hug, then went to work on his ankle bonds. "Well, both of you are fine now. Let's get out of here." The final piece of rope came away. "Try to stand. It might hurt, at first."

Eli suppressed a gasp as Concordia helped him to his feet. "Ow," he muttered. But he kept taking halting steps, Concordia supporting him.

After a short time, he was walking more steadily. "I can do it, now," he said.

"Okay," Concordia said. "Let's go."

They heard heavy footsteps in the hall above, and the creak of the basement door. Eli quickly lay back down as Concordia loosely wrapped the rope around his wrists and draped the gag over his mouth. He curled up facing the wall, pretending to sleep.

Concordia grabbed the cat—who was surprisingly cooperative—and retreated to the farthest shadows. She hoped to heaven they were making just a quick check and wouldn't look too closely at the boy. She glanced over to where Eli lay and saw a small lump in the shadows.

Her heart sank. Her reticule. She'd set it down to untie him and had forgotten all about it.

Two sets of feet clattered down the steps.

"Let's make this quick, Jacques. I still have to dress before the party."

She noticed that Madame no longer spoke with an exotic European accent, but in the slightly clipped tone of a foreign-born British transplant. Concordia could see Jacques Durand's face, as he carried a light over to the boy. "He's sleeping. Why won't you let me just kill him?"

Madame Durand set a tray of food on a stack of boxes nearby. She looked at Eli. "He's just a child. All we have to do is get him out of the way temporarily. Then we'll be long gone."

"But we have been doing so well here, Isabelle. There are some very wealthy believers in this town."

"We discussed this already. It has been decided. We sail for England tomorrow. My healer in London will know what to do with the stones. Then I will make even more money. You'll see. There are many rich people in London. Far more than here."

Durand gave a resigned sigh and set down the lamp.

"I've drugged the food and the tea," Madame said. "That will keep him sleeping for several more hours; enough time for you to move him to a more secure place. Is it all arranged?"

Durand nodded.

"What's this!" Madame exclaimed, reaching down to wake the boy, and picking up Concordia's reticule. "And look, he's been untied!"

Eli scrambled and made a bolt for the door. Jacques reached out to grab him. Concordia stepped out of the shadows and, making a mental note to apologize to the beast later, threw the cat at the man's face. With a howling screech from cat or man or both, Durand grabbed at the hissing, clawing ball of fur, as Eli ran.

"Get Capshaw!" she yelled to Eli, as he sped up the stairs and out the door. Concordia was not so lucky. Madame flung herself at her and knocked her to the floor.

The world went black.

Chapter 32

God hath given you one face, and you make yourselves another.
                                                              III, i.

Eli ran two solid blocks, zig-zagging in and out of alleys, before his trembling legs finally gave out and he had to sit and rest. He slipped behind the grocer's and sat against the brick wall on an overturned crate. His chest hurt. It took a few minutes for his breathing to slow and his head to clear.

Get Capshaw, Miss Concordia had said.

Out of all the policemen he had met in his short life, Capshaw seemed the most agreeable. Or at least as agreeable as a policeman could be. He didn't scowl like the other coppers, or shake him by the back of his collar. He actually smiled sometimes. And, as Miss Concordia had pointed out, he had saved them on the balcony that day. *I would trust him with my life*, she had said. Maybe she was right.

But the last place Eli wanted to go was the police station. He knew there'd be too many uniforms to get through before anyone would believe him enough to let him talk to Capshaw. Most grown-ups didn't pay heed to boys and what they had to say. Except Miss Concordia. And Miss Sophia.

That gave him a better idea. Feeling a fresh spurt of energy, he walked to the corner, turned left, and broke into a run again.

Concordia was aware of light seeping through cracks. She fluttered her eyelids, and her vision came into focus. Her head was pounding. She felt something stiff and dried—blood?—

along the side of her face. She was also covered in dust from head to foot, as if she had rolled around an exceedingly dusty floor. She sneezed.

"She's awake," said a voice.

She tried to get up, but couldn't. Orienting herself, she saw that she was tied to a hard-backed chair in the middle of what looked to be the inside of an old, rusty railway car. She could see her breath in the cold air.

She looked around. The hated faces of the Durands had turned her way. Concordia was heathenishly gratified to see a number of deep red scratches on Jacques Durand's pale face.

"We're running out of time," Durand whined to his wife.

"Miss Wells and I need to have a little conversation first, my love," Madame said. She walked over to Concordia and shook her head in exasperation. "Miss Wells, you are a major inconvenience to me. First, you make me late for a very important dinner party given by the mayor and his wife, and now I will have to miss it altogether because you helped that wretched boy escape."

"What a pity," Concordia said, and got a stinging slap in return.

"You shall not address *me* in that way, if you want to live," Madame Durand said.

"Why pretend you have scruples?" Concordia said, licking at her cut lip. "You are already a fake. Your very *profession*, if I may use the term loosely, is full of tricks and flim-flammery. You have brutalized the sensibilities of a little boy, and then, once he had served your purpose, proceeded to bind him, hand and foot, in a dank cellar. Am I supposed to give you a medal because you hadn't worked up the nerve to kill him yet? You conspired to kill Colonel Adams by stealing the Adams' key and letting in *your father*. Oh, yes, I know that Red is your father," she added, seeing the look of astonishment on the medium's face.

Concordia had finally made the connection during the séance. When Madame, in addressing her "spirit guide," had said: *the tomb is lost to us, covered perhaps for all time*, Concordia had realized the extent of Madame's knowledge. The origin of the amulets had never been generally known. Except for Pierce, the one man still alive from the original expedition, only Concordia, Miss Phillips, Sophia, and the lieutenant had known the story of the tomb's collapse and its consequent obscurity.

Pierce must have related the story of the expedition to his daughter, no doubt greatly amended in his favor. Then he promised her the amulets in exchange for her help in exacting his revenge on Adams and getting the map from Concordia. He'd probably told her some hokum about the mysterious power of the amulets and she'd believed it. *The healer knows what to do with the stones*, Madame had told her husband. It was a fair assumption that the spirit medium expected the amulets to work some sort of magic.

Madame Durand was also the right age to be Pierce's daughter, something that Pierce himself had pointed out at Madame's first Spirit Club demonstration. *Madame Durand seems to be a charming young lady—not much older than yourself, Miss Wells.*

Randolph Wells' journal had made reference to Pierce's "pretty little daughter." Now that she looked for it, Concordia could see some resemblance. Something about the mouth and set of the jaw. Even the timbre of her voice, when stripped of the fake accent, was akin to Pierce's.

Madame seemed to have recovered from the shock of Concordia surmising so much. She smiled sweetly.

"Well, aren't you clever, my dear. Yes, I am his daughter. I'm proud of it. He is a great man. I would do anything for him. He certainly didn't deserve what happened to him. *Your* father"—she pointed an angry finger in Concordia's face—"is to blame. He was jealous of him, of his success, and did not want to share the fame. I know what *really* happened, how your father and the colonel conspired against him, sabotaged him, and finally left him, crippled and alone, to die."

Concordia could see that Madame had been told a significant variation of what was recounted in Randolph Wells' journal. Concordia wasn't confident that she had the entire story, either. They would never know.

"My mother left him after that," Madame continued. "She took me away with her. I never saw him again—not until a few months ago. We found each other quite by accident. The colonel's donation to your college drew my father here, to get the map to the tomb. I came in search of the amulets."

Yes, that made sense, Concordia thought. Madame Durand had become a fixture at Hartford Women's College shortly after Pierce had become dean. And the spirit medium had been such a frequent visitor at Sycamore House that President Langdon had mistaken Concordia for her when he saw a lady in the parlor.

Concordia should have realized the connection long ago. There was the time when Madame had reacted to Concordia's question: *Who is Red, and is he here?* at the planchette demonstration on Halloween, sending the board sailing off the table. Concordia could kick herself for not seeing it sooner.

"You wanted the amulets so badly because you believe they have some special power," Concordia said. "Are they worth a woman's life? Your father nearly killed Lady Principal Grant to get one of them."

"Pah! Miss Grant... that foolish old woman? The amulets are worth twenty of her kind. In the hands of a true healer, they will give me psychic abilities that you cannot imagine. They were already powerful enough to draw me to Hartford, and my father as well. The spirits brought us together."

"Does that 'togetherness' extend to murdering Colonel Adams?" Concordia asked, not attempting to keep the sarcasm from her tone.

"I was glad to help my father get his revenge," Madame said, unruffled. "It was easy enough. I had been there many times, consulting with Lydia Adams. I knew about the spare key. I had established the colonel's night-time routine. My father gave Adams a chance to live, but he refused to open the safe for us. He even tried to ring for help. My father had no choice but to shoot him. Unfortunately, that meant we had to search on our own for the amulet and the map."

"What made you think that Adams had the amulet once more?" Concordia asked.

"Jacques overheard you and Miss Phillips discussing the possibility after our first Spirit Club demonstration," Madame said.

Concordia remembered the flutter of curtains near the stage, which she'd assumed was a draft.

"The only problem was that after you killed the colonel," Concordia prompted, "you didn't have a chance to break into the safe. Someone interrupted you. The colonel's young daughter."

Madame shrugged. "Yes. Little Amelia came in. Jacques struck her before she had a chance to see anything, fortunately."

Concordia struggled to suppress another wave of anger that made her stomach churn. She must keep Madame Durand talking, hoping that Eli would get Capshaw and find her in time. *If* they could find her. She shivered. The cold was seeping through with full force now, inching up her feet and ankles. She couldn't feel her hands.

"Before making your escape, you *did* take two Egyptian antiquities that belonged to the colonel—the collar, and the fertility statuette, correct?" Concordia asked.

"My father recognized them as valuable, yes," Madame said. "He still has contacts abroad where they would fetch a good price."

"And the séance in the Adams house the night after the colonel was killed, where you staged my father's 'presence'— you were trying to goad me into looking for the map, weren't you?"

Madame smiled. "That, too, was my father's idea, after the colonel's study turned up nothing. Since Randolph Wells had done all of the research, he would have kept possession of the map. Father was sure that your father, being the scholar he was, would never have destroyed it, no matter how stubbornly he stayed away from Egyptology the rest of his life. When I saw the bracelet that he had left for you I made it my task to learn all about you and your relationship with your father. It was no great matter to find that out. Your mother, in our séance sessions, told me everything I needed to know. It was logical that your father's papers, including the map, had been hidden for only you to find."

Concordia shuddered at how closely she had been monitored all this time. "And Pierce had the audacity to encourage me to solve the colonel's murder"—which the man himself had committed, he must have enjoyed the irony of that—"and clear Sophia by searching for my father's papers. And I did find his papers. Very clever."

Madame scowled. "Although it ultimately got me the amulets, you have the map and my father is in jail. It does him no good. Once again, he is suffering at the hands of the Wells family." She took out a kerchief and stuffed it roughly in Concordia's mouth. Concordia coughed and struggled, trying to twist her head away, but it was no use. Jacques Durand clamped his hands upon her head as Madame secured the gag in place with another scarf, tying it tightly against the back of Concordia's neck.

"But I will have my revenge, now. You are correct. I don't have any scruples about killing you. And it won't be quick. No one will find you in this old rail yard. We'll be putting a stout lock on the outside when we leave, just in case." She crouched closer, looking into Concordia's widened eyes, watching her struggle against the ropes. "You will experience some of what *my* father went through, Miss Wells, after *yours* left him in the tomb to die. Immobilization, helplessness, fear, thirst. Instead of pitiless heat, you will feel numbing cold. An equitable exchange."

Jacques touched his wife on the arm. "We shouldn't stay any longer."

With one last contemptuous look from Madame, they left, taking the lamp with them. In the gloom, Concordia heard the door slide shut and, just as Madame had promised, the sound of a padlock being snapped into place.

Concordia fought her panic by listening for the Durands' carriage wheels crunching on the gravel. She waited until they were very faint. The last thing she wanted was the Durands lingering outside to thwart her escape. It was just a precaution, of course; Jacques Durand looked particularly eager to leave.

A flash of animal eyes, through one of the rusted-out gaps of the car, made her jump. She hoped it was too big to come through, whatever it was.

Concordia's mother had always complained about her "obstinate streak." Well, she was going to need it now, for she had no intention of sitting and waiting for the end to come. She was going to fight her *Eternal Reward* with everything she had.

Chapter 33

How, now, a rat?

III, iv.

Capshaw returned to the station. "Any messages?" he asked the desk clerk.

The man shook his head. "Not since I been here—oh, wait a minute—a young lady left you a note." The man rummaged around, finally producing a scrap of paper, marked *Urgent.*

Capshaw frowned over the note. He sighed when he recognized the handwriting. Miss Wells. A most trying young lady—he would never understand *college people*, especially when they were the female of the species. But she had good instincts, he had to give her that.

He read it through quickly. Hmm. The boy's absence *was* worrisome. Perhaps he should send a man out to the college and fetch Miss Wells.

"Who's here that can go to the ladies' college right quick?" he asked.

The desk clerk checked the roster. "Merrimack's kickin' around here somewhere, Lieutenant."

"Good. Send him over to the school to bring Miss Wells back to the station."

"Very good, sir." The man hesitated. "Oh, and one more thing about the young lady. Rodgers said she asked permission to see our crippled man."

Capshaw glared at the man. "And... did... she?" he said, his voice carefully even.

The clerk shifted from one foot to another, clearing his throat. "Um, yes, sir. He saw no harm in it, what with the prisoner bein' in a chair, and all. Besides, the orderly was right there and she weren't allowed to stay but a couple o' minutes."

Without another word, Capshaw turned on his heel and headed for the cell block wing.

Chapter 34

Tis bitter cold, and I am sick at heart.

I, i.

Concordia wasn't making any progress in getting out of her bonds. In fact, she was in a worse position now. In her attempt to test the strength of the chair, which seemed to give a little along the upright part, she'd instead succeeded in tipping herself sideways to the floor, sending a sharp pain along one of her already-aching shoulders. Please heaven she hadn't broken anything. Her hair had come down loose over her eyes, but she had no hands free to push it back. Only a combination of shaking her head and blowing at it got it to move. Not that it mattered much in terms of sight—the closed-up car was as black as pitch—but it tickled her nose and annoyed her. She'd had enough annoyances for one day, to say the least.

Long fingers of numbing air plucked at her ankles, neck and hands, slipping under clothing wherever they could. Her teeth chattered. She was *so* tired.

This was hopeless. Even if she got herself untied, how would she get out? She was locked in from outside, in an abandoned train yard. No one would hear her cries for help.

She lay still for a minute or two, willing herself to continue the struggle.

Then she heard scuttling noises, and a *squeak*.

Rats.

If ever Concordia wished for Eli's Cat, now was the time.

Eli pounded on the back door, then crouched with his hands to his knees, fighting to catch his breath. The cook opened the door, grumbling.

"Eli!" she exclaimed. "Why, what's happened to you!" She looked at him closely, noticing the dirty, disheveled hair, the pinched hollows of his cheeks, his raw wrists.

"I need to see Miss Sophia right away. Miss Concordia's in turrible trouble."

There was something stimulating to one's motivation, Concordia thought, now that rats were involved. If she *were* to die here, she was *not* going to be a trussed-up meal for the rats to feast upon.

Her right side was still pinned to the floor, so she tested the strength of the chair and the ropes on her left, sliding this way and that with her torso, feeling around with cold-stiffened fingers. If she was lucky, perhaps a section of the wood had splintered.

The wood felt intact, although one section wobbled a bit. Feeling around further, she discovered why: several screws had worked their way loose along the left side of the chair back. Perhaps they'd be rough enough to fray her ropes.

Twisting to the best position she could manage, she began rubbing, back and forth, giving a tug at the fibers whenever they caught. Her shoulders were throbbing in agony, but she kept at it. If she could only get her hands free...

Chapter 35

Foul deeds will arise,
Though all the earth o'erwhelm them, to men's eyes.

I, iii.

Capshaw came out of the prisoner's room, shaking with anger. Pierce had no regard for human decency and cared nothing about a vulnerable little boy. Capshaw had no leverage to use against him. The man had nothing more to lose.

His thoughts were interrupted by the clerk hurrying toward him. "This just came for you, sir," he huffed, catching his breath.

It was a message from Sophia. Capshaw took a quick look at the contents. "I'm going to the Adams' house. Call Merrimack back. Miss Wells is *not* at the college. Have all the men we can spare go straight over to the house of Jacques and Isabelle Durand. *If* they are still there, hold them." He passed over the slip of paper with the address. "I'll join you shortly." He ran outside to flag down a cab.

Capshaw leaned forward impatiently in his seat as the vehicle was hampered by the crush of evening traffic, made worse by the surge of Christmas season shoppers along the downtown blocks. At last, they pulled up to the Adams house. Capshaw jumped out and told the driver to wait.

As he took the front steps two at a time, he noticed the most mangy excuse for a feline squatted by the door.

The door opened before he could even ring the bell. Sophia and Eli were waiting for him. The cat slipped in before he could stop it, but he forgot about it when he saw the boy.

Capshaw's mouth tightened in a thin, angry line as he took in the sight of Eli, bruised and scratched, clothes torn and mussed, cheeks sunken, a blanket wrapped around his shoulders. But the boy's eyes lit up when he saw the cat.

"Where did *you* come from?" Eli said, looking down. The animal wrapped around his legs and purred vigorously. He picked it up and rubbed his face in its fur. "I'm glad that bad man didn't hurt you," he murmured.

"That beast is *yours?*" Capshaw asked.

Eli nodded.

"I suppose it's coming along, then," Capshaw said, grudgingly. "We don't have time to get you cleaned up, son. I have a cab waiting. You can tell me what happened as we ride."

Sophia touched Capshaw's sleeve. "Bring her back safe, Aaron. Please."

Capshaw covered her hand briefly in reassurance, then hurried back to the cab.

Now that they were away from the downtown section, the vehicle went at a brisk pace. Eli held onto the Cat more tightly during the bumps in the road.

"Tell me everything that happened at the Durands, and what you think they are going to do next," Capshaw said.

The boy told him the whole story, about how he'd worked for Madame in exchange for a place to sleep, because he wasn't allowed to stay at the college anymore. He recounted how he'd found the key in Madame's bedroom, when he was sent to look for her reading glasses, and recognized it as the Adams' house key. He didn't understand why it was there, but he slipped it in his pocket. Later, when Madame threatened to harm Cat if he didn't steal Miss Concordia's amulet, he left the key behind in Miss Concordia's bedroom, hoping she would understand what it meant.

"And what do *you* think it means, young man?" Capshaw asked.

"That Madame killed the colonel," Eli said promptly.

"Smart boy. She is at least involved. However," Capshaw said, "I can't find any previous association between Madame

Durand and Colonel Adams, save for the recent connection of the colonel's wife as Madame's client. But Pierce could not have done it alone from a wheelchair. Madame, along with her husband, obviously helped him. The *why* of it still escapes me."

"Then it must be because she's his daughter, sir," came the astonishing response.

Capshaw gave the boy a startled look. *Out of the mouths of babes oft times come gems.* "Madame Durand is Pierce's *daughter?*"

Eli nodded. "After I brought her back the amulet, they kept me in the basement"—he shuddered—"but I could hear them plain, talking about her father."

"It's a wonder that Miss Wells found you, although she should have come to me, and not rushed in alone," Capshaw said, mentally clucking at the heedless young lady. Miss Wells would inevitably take matters into her own hands and leave him scrambling to catch up and do his own job. *He* didn't try to teach book-learning to college girls; what made her think *she* could catch criminals? These people were ruthless. She wasn't prepared.

The cab slowed in front of the Durand house.

"Miss Concordia rescued me. She's in danger now because of it. We have to save her," Eli said softly.

The Durand house had the unmistakable look of abandonment: dark, shuttered, rubbish dropped upon the steps. Still, Capshaw and Eli went inside, and Capshaw did a quick walk-through of the building, paying close attention to the basement, crouching down and shining a powerful lantern along the dirt floor.

There was a small bit of blood, but not enough to signify a grievous wound. The dirt was quite trampled. A wide section of it rubbed in one direction, as if something large had been put down and then dragged up again.

As he stood and dusted his hands off on his trousers, he spotted a woman's reticule in a dark corner and picked it up. "Is this hers?"

Eli nodded and looked curiously at the area Capshaw had been examining. "What can you tell from *dirt?*"

Capshaw pointed to the smudges. "See here? Looks like she was rolled up in a rug of some sort. They may simply be trying to keep her from being found before they can make their escape. They knew you were going for help. There's hardly any blood. Miss Wells may be injured, but I'm fairly certain she was alive when they took her," he said grimly.

They went back outside.

"They'd need a conveyance," Capshaw mused aloud. "A fair number of belongings are gone. They had their own carriage, correct, son? Do you know what it looks like? Anything distinctive about it? I'm going to have my men comb the neighborhood for anyone who would have seen it and what direction it might be headed." He waved to a patrol wagon that had just pulled up, discharging uniformed men.

Eli gave Capshaw as good a description as he could remember.

Capshaw took a few quick notes, nodding. "Good. The scraped paint on the left door might help jog folks' memories." He turned and issued final instructions to the group before they broke up.

"Will they k-kill her?" Eli asked anxiously.

"Not if we can help it," Capshaw said.

Chapter 36

To be or not to be, that is the question.

III, i.

As exhausting as it was to saw at her ropes on a rusty old screw, at least it helped to keep her warm. Concordia could feel the fibers beginning to fray, which gave her an additional burst of energy. With each pass she made, the skin of her wrists was rubbed raw against the bonds, but she ignored it.

At last. One final tug, and her wrists were free. The relief to her screaming shoulders was immeasurable. She quickly pulled the kerchief from her mouth, coughing and spitting out the horrid sensation.

Still pinned to the floor she rested, wincing as the blood trickled back into her hands. When her fingers recovered more of their sensation, she felt around the ropes at her midsection for the knots. They were underneath her right side. She couldn't reach them.

Leaning away as much as she could, she slid her right arm under her and tried pushing away from the floor. After a few attempts, she finally got the chair upright. She gingerly rubbed both wrists.

Ropes remained around her ankles and her middle, tying her to the chair back. She couldn't lean forward far enough to reach her ankles, so she first worked on the knots around her midsection.

After what seemed an interminable, fumbling interval, she was able to pull the ropes away and lean over to work on her ankle bonds. Her hair fell in her eyes again. This time, it was *glorious* to be able to sweep it away from her face and pin it back.

The ropes around her ankles were a bit easier, or perhaps she had developed more skill. She felt a giddy excitement when the last of the bonds fell away. She was free!

She stood for the first time in hours, holding onto the chair for support. Her legs buckled and she winced as the circulation gradually returned to her feet. She took steps around the chair, still holding the back of it, until she felt confident that she could walk without falling on her face.

She looked around the railcar, her dark-adjusted eyes seeing lighter bits of gloom that peeked through the rusted-out walls.

Now what?

Eli and the Cat huddled under the lap robe inside the dark cab, as Capshaw and the other policemen knocked on doors along the row, making inquiries.

The animal slept soundly in Eli's lap. He stroked the Cat absently, taking comfort in its softness. Until he felt some hard, sticky bumps. "What's that you got stuck in your tail, there?" He looked closely in the dim light. Several black tarry clumps also adhered to the cat's haunches. Eli plucked one off. It stirred a memory.

The cab door opened and Capshaw stuck his head in. "We have a few leads. Neighbors saw the Durands' carriage turn up the block toward Woodland. They could be heading out of the city entirely. Did either of them ever mention relations in Boston, or parts north?"

Eli shook his head, holding out the piece of tarry gravel. "The cat's been near train tracks tonight. I got a mess o' this stuff in my hair once when I was sleeping in a rail yard. And the cat follows Miss Concordia around a lot."

Capshaw leaned in for a better look at the cat. "Possible. There's an abandoned branch of the old Reading Line not far from Woodland, near Keney Park. It's doubtful, though, that your cat could have gone all that way, and back, tonight."

"What if he'd jumped in the back of their carriage, without them noticing? He could've walked back from wherever they took Miss Concordia. He does look awful tuckered out."

"You've got a good head on those shoulders, young man," Capshaw said. He stepped back out of the cab. Eli heard him barking orders to his men. Then he quickly jumped in.

"Let's go!" he shouted to the driver.

After determining that the padlock was indeed securing the door from the outside, making it impossible for her to open it, Concordia started to grope her way carefully around the inner boundary of the box car. If the rats could come in and out, there had be to a few holes somewhere. Besides, there was that flash of eyes she'd seen, just after the Durands had left. Something from outside had peered through a crevice. Larger than a rat—a raccoon, perhaps?

The box car had deteriorated into unusable condition long ago, left to rust into obscurity. The weakest areas seemed to be near the floor. After a great deal of groping around, Concordia found one especially corroded section, where more light came through.

With only a passing care for her skirts—she was already filthy—Concordia positioned herself in front of the weak section of the wall and kicked, hard. She did it over and over again, resting at times to catch her breath.

With her stout boots she was making some progress, but the hole wasn't big enough yet to crawl through. She kept kicking.

Finally, she slipped off her petticoat. It was her second best one, too. She mercilessly tore it into strips, then wrapped them around her hands and fingers.

Lying flat on her stomach, she could just peer outside. The old-track gravel beds and rusted structures were bathed in bright moonlight. It was a cheering sight. She felt a resurgence of energy and worked on the gap, twisting, bending, and pushing at the broken pieces with her cloth-wrapped hands.

After what felt like an eternity, she judged that she had made a large enough opening. Concordia thrust her head and upper torso through, and paused to breathe in deep lungfuls of the open air. She was dangling three feet above the ground, going head first. Taking great care so she wouldn't land on her head, she started to push herself through the rest of the way.

And got stuck.

Drat!

It was at this inopportune moment that Concordia heard the sound of wheels popping on the gravel, getting closer. A wave of panic rushed over her. The Durands were coming back, after all. To kill her. She wriggled and squirmed harder, but to no avail. She was wedged tightly at the hips. She couldn't go forward, *or* backward.

It was enough to make a lady regret that second scone with an extra spoonful of clotted cream. If she were a bit thinner, she would have made it.

The sounds were getting closer still, and sounded louder than she would have expected. Concordia held her breath.

There were not one, but two vehicles—a cab and a larger wagon. They pulled to a stop, and uniformed men began rushing out of them, fanning out for a search. She recognized the tall, slightly stooped form of Lieutenant Capshaw, and Eli, with the Cat trotting at his heels.

Concordia, hardly able to catch her breath in her exhaustion and sheer relief, called to her rescuers as best as she could. "Over here! I'm here!"

Dangling half out of a railcar is not the most dignified position for a lady to find herself when a squad of policemen discover her.

Capshaw, hurrying over, looked sufficiently startled at the sight. "Eli, let her lean on you so she doesn't sag," he instructed. One man found a crowbar and, working carefully near Concordia's waist, soon had the corrugated tin side pulled away.

Two other policemen gently pulled her through and guided her to the ground.

Tears streaming down her face, Concordia sat on the ground, hugging Eli and the Cat, which had promptly jumped into her lap and was contentedly kneading her grimy skirts.

Capshaw crouched down next to Concordia and Eli. He ruffled the boy's hair. Eli smiled. "This young man would make a formidable detective one day, Miss Wells. Ten minutes' conversation with him caused the scales to fall from my eyes. We found you much quicker than we would have otherwise, I can assure you."

Concordia smiled her thanks to the boy, and held him close for a moment.

"Are you ready to tell me what happened here?" Capshaw asked.

She nodded.

When she'd finished, Capshaw shook his head. "We've had this conversation before, miss. You should never have gone in there alone."

"I tried to reach you, lieutenant, really I did. But I couldn't delay any longer. I was worried about what they might do to Eli."

Capshaw muttered to himself, "I'll never understand these modern women. Can't wait for anything. Have to plunge in..."

"What happens now?" Concordia asked, interrupting the familiar rant.

"We take you home," Capshaw said.

"What about catching the Durands?"

"We have a watch set out for them."

"They mentioned sailing for England. Will you be watching the ports as well?"

"'Sailing'?" Capshaw repeated. "Why is this the first I heard of it, Miss Wells?"

"Well, I thought I—didn't I tell you? Oh," Concordia said. "When they were talking, Madame Durand said that they would be sailing tomorrow for England. She has a 'healer' there, who

will use the amulets in some way. I'm sorry. I thought I said so."
She was very tired.

"There's a regular steamer packet that sails from Boston to
Liverpool," Capshaw mused aloud.

He stood and gestured to one of the patrolmen. "Run over
to the station; have them telegraph Hadley at Boston Harbor.
Tell him what's going on and give him the Durands' description
so he can put out an alert." He turned to Concordia and Eli. "It
looks like we won't be able to make the long detour to the
college, Miss Wells. We're going to have our hands full tonight.
I'll take you two back to the Adams' house, instead—it's on the
way. I know Miss Adams won't mind if you spend the night."

"Actually, there *is* someone at the Adams' house I want to
talk to, lieutenant," Concordia said.

Chapter 37

A little more than kin, a little less than kind.

I, ii.

The bath felt *wonderful*. The warmth eased her aching shoulders and back. Concordia soaked in it until the water started to cool. She hoped Eli was getting equally clean. The Adams' housekeeper had taken charge of the boy; she didn't look the type to tolerate any dirt.

As she dressed, she thought back to her conversation with Lydia Adams when she first got to the house. Concordia had insisted upon speaking with the widow before cleaning up or getting her wounds tended to.

"Mrs. Adams," Concordia began, as they sat in the parlor, "take a good look at me. Do you see my condition? I know Sophia has told you some of it, but let me tell you the rest. Your younger stepdaughter's well-being depends upon you accepting what has *really* happened."

Lydia Adams clasped her hands tightly together and sat rigidly in her chair, staring in disbelief. Concordia could see that the widow was taking in her disheveled appearance: her filthy and torn skirts, the rope burns on her wrists, her tangled hair, her bruised temple, her cut lip.

As concisely as possible, Concordia described Madame Durand's kidnapping of Eli, and then her own capture. She recounted Madame's gloating confession of her role in helping Pierce kill Colonel Adams.

Mrs. Adams put her face in her hands. "I believed in Madame," came the muffled response.

"I know. She has victimized a number of good people," Concordia said gently.

Concordia stood next to Lydia Adams and put a hand on her shoulder. "But you now have someone else to care for, so you cannot succumb to self-pity. Amelia needs you. Put an end to these commitment proceedings. We know now, without question, that Amelia had nothing to do with your husband's death. She was a victim herself, struck on the head by his killers. The rest has all been confusion and misunderstandings."

Mrs. Adams lifted her tear-streaked face to Concordia. "I don't know…how…to care for a young child."

"You will learn," Concordia said. "Sophia will help. You two are all she has in this world. Just love her."

This family had a lot of healing left to do, thanks to the people who had brought on all this grief: Pierce, Madame Durand, and Jacques Durand. At least Pierce wasn't going anywhere, but Concordia shuddered at the thought of the other two escaping.

After her bath, Concordia made herself as presentable as she could in one of Sophia's gowns, even though she had to hold up the hem to keep from tripping on it. She went in search of Eli, following the delectable scents of cream of leek soup and toasted bread. Wherever there was food, the boy was bound to be. Her own stomach was rumbling, too. When had she eaten last? She remembered a roll at breakfast, when she'd spoken to Miss Phillips.

Instead of Sophia waiting for her in the dining room, however, it was *David Bradley*, of all people. Concordia stopped, mouth open, at the sight of him ladling soup into a bowl that he then passed to her, as if it were the most natural thing in the world.

"David! What are you doing here?"

"Sophia sent word as soon as she knew you were safe. We've all been worried about you, Concordia. Especially me."

The man, indeed, looked strained, with deep shadows under his eyes, pale-edged lips, and furrowed lines along his forehead. Tears prickled the backs of Concordia's eyes. She'd felt so alone in that railcar. But she really hadn't been.

Sophia walked in.

"Where's Eli?" Concordia asked her.

"He's finished with his supper, and the doctor is seeing to his wounds now. You're next," Sophia added, gesturing to Concordia's wrists, "and heaven knows you need tending to, so eat up." She paused, as if to say something more.

"What is it?" Concordia asked.

Sophia smiled. "I don't know what you told Lydia, but thank you. She came to me a short while ago, wanting to set things right between the three of us. She's talking about treatment for Amelia, and our holiday plans together." She shook her head. "I would not have thought it possible a few weeks ago."

"Thank goodness," David said. "Maybe there's hope for the woman, after all."

Concordia smiled to herself, finished her soup, and had a second bowl. It was *very* good soup.

At last, she felt contentedly full, and ready for the doctor. Perhaps he could give her something for the dull throbbing in her temples. Then she was looking forward to bed.

The doorbell rang.

At this late hour?

"The doctor's in the study. You go on. I'll get it," Sophia said.

David, determined not to leave Concordia's side, followed her to the study.

It was profoundly altered from its use in the colonel's time, Concordia noted. Gone were the artifact collections, sword displays, and military awards cases. In their place were shelves of well-thumbed books. The heavy oak desk had been replaced by a lighter one of teak, with gracefully-turned spindle legs; the windows now sported airy sheers instead of the dark burgundy

274 / K.B. Owen

velvet drapes. Sophia had a hand in the transformation, no doubt.

She looked over to the fire. Eli was curled up asleep on the settee.

"Miss Wells?"

The doctor who had attended Amelia just after the colonel's death—was it only this past September?—gave a little bow.

"How is he?" she asked anxiously, looking over at the boy again. He looked so vulnerable, laying there: pale and pinched around the hollows of his cheeks, the sweep of his dark lashes deepening the bruise under one eye. But he slept easily, his breathing even. "Will he be all right?"

"Right as rain, given a week or so," the doctor said. "The injuries are superficial. But I feel sorry for what the poor lad went through." He shook his head. "Sturdy fellow."

"The light is better over here," the man added, pointing to the lamp. "Shall we take a look?"

The doctor was still applying ointment and bandages to tender spots when Sophia came in with Lieutenant Capshaw. The policeman looked subdued. Concordia felt a lurch of disappointment in the pit of her stomach.

"It's bad news, isn't it?" she said.

"Not entirely," Capshaw answered. He passed a weary hand across his red hair, making it stand on end. "Jacques Durand has been taken into custody...." He paused.

"But not Madame," Concordia finished.

He shook his head.

"The harbor police can get nothing from Durand. He refuses to even speak," Capshaw continued. "I'm going up there to question him myself and bring him back."

"I'd be happy to accompany you, sir," David said.

But it would take too long to retrieve Jacques Durand, Concordia thought. Isabelle Durand could be anywhere by then. Had the couple decided to flee separately to better avoid capture, or did Madame have something else in mind?

Concordia began to get a glimmer of a very bold plan by Isabelle Durand. The woman who would do anything for her beloved father. The woman who would do anything for her beloved father.

She pulled away from the doctor's ministrations and stood. "Lieutenant, do you still have Pierce in custody? I think we'll want to make sure."

Chapter 38

Angels and ministers of grace, defend us!

I, iv

Capshaw left David and Sophia back at the Adams' house, but took Concordia with him, so she could explain the logic that led to this astonishing line of thought. Who would be daring enough—and foolish enough—to risk capture by freeing a crippled man in police custody? And a woman who was herself wanted by the authorities, at that.

During the short drive to the police station, Concordia explained what she had come to understand about Madame Durand's all-consuming devotion to her father, and her sense of invincibility. It didn't seem like enough of a reason, Concordia acknowledged, but something else—something she had overlooked and couldn't quite remember now—was telling her it was possible.

Capshaw gave her skeptical look. "I suppose it wouldn't hurt to make sure."

As they pulled up to the station, every lamp was blazing, and several uniformed officers had congregated outside.

Concordia bit her lip nervously. She'd hoped she was wrong about Madame's intentions. Then she remembered. Another woman had visited Pierce in jail today. The sergeant had made reference to a "lady visitor, quite pretty," when Concordia had asked about Pierce. Had it been Madame Durand?

The spirit medium was certainly a beauty, with a piquant face, lustrous black hair, and clear blue eyes, although that loveliness now struck Concordia as cold and monstrous.

Frailty, thy name is woman.

Capshaw jumped out before the cab had come to a complete stop. "What happened?" he called out.

Concordia shamelessly stuck out her head and listened.

A nearby sergeant snapped to attention. "A woman, sir. Dressed as a hospital aide, showed us her authorization to check on the cell conditions and care of the crippled prisoner. It looked genuine and she was just a petite little thing. Seemed harmless—" the man shook his head. "Well, she walloped the orderly over the head when his back was turned, tied and gagged him and locked him in before she escaped with the prisoner. We only discovered the orderly a few minutes ago. We were just coming to get you. I'm sorry, sir."

Capshaw made a low grumbling sound in his throat. "Is the orderly alive?"

"Yes, sir, thankfully, though he'll have a nasty headache."

"He'll have more than a headache when *I'm* done with him," Capshaw said, grimly, "and I will deal with *you* later, sergeant. What woman would be out in the middle of the night on such an errand? Think, man!"

The man cleared his throat and looked down at his shoes.

"So she arrived about an hour ago?" Capshaw asked. "In what sort of conveyance?"

The man referred to his notes. "It was a private vehicle. The driver got pushed out by Pierce about a mile away after they left here. The fellow's just walked back to report it." The policeman pulled forward a small man from the cluster of people. The driver certainly looked the worse for wear: clothes muddy, forehead scratched, one eye swollen shut.

Still, Concordia knew him right away. *Oh, no.*

"Isaac!" she cried. Her mother's driver.

Capshaw looked at her, then the driver, and groaned. "You *know* this man? Do you mean to tell me...?"

"Yes," Concordia said. "It looks as if *my mother* has helped them escape."

Chapter 39

The lady doth protest too much, methinks.

III, ii

A very anxious Mrs. Wells answered the door when they rang. She opened it herself, but her face fell when she saw Concordia and Capshaw. "Oh. I wasn't expecting you. I thought you might be—Isaac!" she cried, getting her first glimpse of her battered driver, standing behind them. "What's happened? Is Madame injured?"

The driver snorted in derision, but Capshaw held up a hand. "May we come in?"

"Oh, yes—of course." She ushered them into the parlor, where a newly-stoked fire was burning brightly.

She rang for the housekeeper as they sat. "What on earth is going on? Concordia... can you explain this?"

"Mother, did you lend Madame Durand your carriage?" Concordia asked.

"Yes...was there an accident?" she asked anxiously.

"N'aught hardly," the driver retorted. "Tha' devil-woman an' her da in the charr attack'd me. Threw me out o' the carriage an' kept goin'."

Mrs. Wells put her hand to her mouth in horror. "*Isabelle* did this? Who is this man he's talking about?"

"Her father," Concordia said bluntly. "*Red.* And she just broke him out of prison."

Her mother's eyes grew wide with shock.

The housekeeper walked in at that moment, a robe hastily wrapped around her, hair in a long gray braid over her shoulder.

"Mrs. Houston," Concordia said, "can you take Isaac to the kitchen and tend to him? He's had a difficult evening."

The housekeeper looked over at Mrs. Wells, who nodded mutely.

"Now, Mrs. Wells," Capshaw said, when the two had left, "I want you to tell me everything Madame Durand said—what she needed the carriage for, where she was going. *Everything.*"

"Well, she looked distraught," Mrs. Wells began. "I'd never seen her that way before. Her demeanor is always so calm and controlled. I was quite concerned. She said that her aunt had become grievously ill and she needed to go to her immediately. However, their own carriage was in need of repair and would not withstand an out-of-town trip."

"Did she say *where* her aunt resided?" Capshaw interrupted.

"No, but I had the impression it was south of here," she said vaguely.

Concordia, who understood her mother's nuances of expression, raised an eyebrow. Was she still trying to protect Madame Durand?

"Continue," Capshaw said, scribbling notes in a quick hand.

"For a generous sum, my driver was willing to go with her. Madame assured me that he would only be gone for a few days, and she would send him back with the carriage as soon as she reached her aunt."

"Why were you waiting up?" Concordia asked. "Did you expect her to change her mind and return?"

"I don't know; she was acting strangely, and seemed angry and preoccupied. I didn't understand why her husband was not with her, and she wouldn't explain. I wondered if I should contact Monsieur Durand myself. I was worried and couldn't sleep."

Mrs. Wells turned to Concordia, eyes pleading. "Surely there is some mistake. How could she have done this? How could she be Red's daughter? How did Red, an associate of your father's from two decades ago, come to be in prison, *here?*"

"Red is actually Augustus Pierce, the former dean of our college," Concordia explained. "Do you remember the man in the wheelchair, the night you attended Madame's demonstration at the college? That man. He was arrested for attacking Lady Principal Grant, and *me*, and he probably murdered Colonel Adams, too."

Mrs. Wells' mouth formed a silent 'o.'

"You hadn't read about the arrest of Dean Pierce in the papers?" Capshaw asked.

"Why, yes, but there was no mention of Colonel Adams or Concordia. I was under the impression it was an isolated incident brought on by an unstable invalid. I had no idea." Mrs. Wells looked at her daughter. "Are you all right? Why didn't you tell me?"

"I'm fine. I didn't wish the incident to be a topic of conversation between you and Madame Durand," Concordia said acidly. "She seems to know a great deal of our personal affairs."

Mrs. Wells flushed, but said nothing.

"You had never met Red, when Papa was alive?" Concordia asked.

Mrs. Wells looked down at her hands. "Once. But that was more than twenty years ago. It is a time I wish to forget."

"Well, you have no choice," Concordia said, more harshly than she'd intended.

She stood up and walked over to her mother, leaning close. She pulled away the collar of her gown, revealing the faded bruises from Pierce's attempt to strangle her. "*Red* did this when he tried to get Papa's map of the tomb from me." Then she pushed up her sleeves to show her bandages and cuts. "*This* is what your beloved Madame Durand did to me when she tied me up and left me to die in an abandoned railway car tonight. That was after I had freed a little boy she'd kept prisoner and terrorized, all to get the amulet from that long-lost tomb. Do you see? We cannot forget, because Papa's past is here with us, *now*."

Mrs. Wells' lips had gone white, and she looked ready to faint.

"Enough, Concordia," Capshaw said, with a warning gesture. "Get your mother a glass of water."

Concordia took several deep breaths to regain her composure. The depth of her anger threatened to overwhelm her. Her knees buckled, and she grasped the chair for support.

Capshaw eased her into the chair, then grabbed the pitcher and poured water for them both.

"Now," he said, when both women were calmer, "no one here is to blame for these incidents." He gave Concordia a hard look.

Concordia, chastened, moved to sit beside her mother. She patted her hand consolingly. "I'm sorry, Mother. It truly is not your fault. But you cannot protect Madame Durand any longer."

Mrs. Wells, still trembling, nodded silently.

"We are dealing with desperate people, Mrs. Wells," Capshaw said. "They must not be permitted to escape. Do you know where Madame was heading?"

"She didn't tell me," Mrs. Wells protested.

"We know that," Concordia said, "but surely, after all of the time you've spent with her, she has told you some things about herself? I remember at the Thanksgiving dinner that the two of you seemed very close. You'd become more than a client to her, and more like a friend. What can you surmise, based upon what you know?"

Mrs. Wells stared at the fire. Concordia and Capshaw waited.

"I remember her speaking of a mentor, in New York," Mrs. Wells said finally, sitting up straighter. "Yes, an elderly lady… Mrs. Washbourne."

"Any idea *where* in New York?" Capshaw said, leaning forward eagerly.

Mrs. Wells frowned in concentration. "Well, she said they had formed a Greenwich Clairvoyant Society among their group. Could that be the locale, Lieutenant?"

"Mrs. Washbourne, in Greenwich," Capshaw repeated. "That should be enough." He stood, as did the ladies. "Thank you."

"Concordia, stay here with me tonight," her mother said softly, clasping Concordia's hands. "We have a great deal to say to one another."

Concordia felt the prickling of tears behind her eyes. "Yes, we do." She looked pleadingly at Capshaw. "Get them, Lieutenant—*please.*"

Capshaw left, closing the parlor door discreetly behind him as mother and daughter hugged and cried together.

Chapter 40

There's a divinity that shapes our ends.

V, ii

Week 14, Instructor Calendar
December 1896

The campus was a festive place, as the girls put on their Christmas revels and choruses, visited each other with gifts and tokens, and attended the rounds of class teas and chapel services. In the generous spirit of the season, the girls had made and signed a get-well card for the former lady principal before Miss Grant and Mr. Harrison had left Hartford for good.

In a few days, when the students went home for winter recess, the college would be cleared of the bustle and noise. But Concordia knew she would miss the chaos.

The exhibit was recovering nicely. Miss Phillips reveled in the school's additional acquisitions from Colonel Adams' collection, recently donated by his widow.

Eli and the Cat were installed at the newly-renovated Settlement House, while the mice population tentatively ventured back to Willow Cottage.

"Ugh," Ruby said, after disposing of yet another rodent that had braved the kitchen, "I miss that boy's kitty. Maybe we should get one of our own?"

Concordia didn't answer.

The doorbell rang. "I'll get it," Concordia said. She opened the door to Lieutenant Capshaw.

"Come in!"

He stamped the snow off his boots and removed his cap before Concordia led him into the parlor.

"You have news?" she asked.

"Madame Durand has been captured at last. She led us a merry chase through the boroughs of New York, but we worked with the local men and were finally able to close in on her. She's now in our custody."

"What about Pierce?"

Capshaw hesitated, unsure how to tell her about that final stand-off with Pierce and Madame Durand. He had witnessed it all: the barricaded house, the threats, the entreaties, the breaking down of the door, the raving look of a desperate man, and the shot that had ended it.

"He died during capture," he merely said.

Concordia took a moment to absorb this. She didn't know how she felt about that. Regret? Relief?

"I see," she finally said.

"I wanted to let you know before you read it in the papers," Capshaw said. "Mr. Rosen has an exclusive article about the entire chase and capture that will be published tomorrow."

"You gave him exclusive access?" Concordia said incredulously. She would have thought the police wouldn't want a nosy reporter anywhere near the scene.

Capshaw nodded. "He was actually quite helpful to us. As I think you know, he's been researching a story about spirit mediums. He followed Madame Durand for months—even before she relocated to Hartford. He saved us invaluable time finding her associates in New York."

How ironic that the man Concordia had once thought might be Red would be instrumental in the capture of the real one. She felt a little silly for suspecting him in the first place.

"What will happen now to Madame Durand? And her husband?" she asked.

"We've already turned over Jacques Durand to the French authorities. They had several outstanding warrants on him, and they were eager to get him back. A cold-blooded killer, they called him. As for Madame... she's blaming her actions on the evil influence of her father and making quite a show of it. She probably won't hang, but she'll be giving séances to her jail-mates for the rest of her life."

At least she'll have an audience, Concordia thought. That's probably what she wants the most.

"How is your mother? I imagine this has been difficult for her, too," Capshaw said.

"She's much better," Concordia said. After Capshaw had left to resume the chase that night, Concordia and her mother had talked until dawn. They had not spoken of Madame Durand. Instead, they had talked of Papa, and Mary; of Mother's grief and loneliness, and the loss of the father that Concordia had long imagined as all-too-perfect. It had been a frank discussion, with no recriminations. It had cleared the air between them, allowed them to reminisce, and even to laugh a little. She smiled, remembering.

"How is that young man, Eli?" Capshaw asked. "He's a sharp one, that boy. I'd like to recruit him to the force now. I'm not sure we would have found you without him."

"Actually, he was impressed by his experiences with you, too," Concordia said. "He says he wants to be a policeman now. And, after finding out that policemen need to read and write, he is much more motivated to attend to his studies. Sophia says he's making remarkable progress."

Capshaw nodded.

"I hear that Amelia is also doing well," Concordia added.

"Yes—at last, she is able to recount at least *part* of her story," Capshaw said. "There aren't any surprises in it—close to what we thought, in fact. She said that she was sneaking some of Mrs. Lewis's shortbread from the pantry when she heard a noise coming from her father's study. She remembers opening the door, and then everything went black. She awoke beside her father's body sometime later. She was covered in blood. She doesn't remember anything after that, but we can surmise the rest based on Miss Adams' account. The doctor thinks the shock, compounded by the blow to the head, was responsible for her reaction. He feels confident she should fully recover. Needless to say, it's a great relief to Miss Adams."

"Speaking of Sophia," Concordia said, "I understand that you two have been spending a great deal of time together lately." She grinned.

Capshaw blushed to the roots of his red hair.

Ah, so there *was* a budding romance between Sophia and the lieutenant. Concordia couldn't think of a nicer man for her friend. Although born and bred to a higher social status than the policeman, Sophia cared not a jot for convention. Her life in the settlement house was a testament to that. Concordia knew the differences in their backgrounds wouldn't be an impediment should they come to love each other. Time would tell whether it blossomed into that.

"Miss Adams was wondering the same about you and Mr. Bradley. I noticed he seemed quite attentive the night of your rescue," Capshaw said dryly.

Concordia laughed and threw up her hands in a gesture of surrender. Although David planned to return to Boston for the spring semester, she *would* be seeing more of him at Christmas. Lydia Adams had invited Concordia and her mother to celebrate the holiday with her and Sophia and Amelia at the Adams' country house in the Berkshires, and invited David and Eli (and the Cat, of course) to come along, too. Concordia strongly suspected some matchmaking was going on between her mother and Mrs. Adams, but the anticipation of the visit brought a glow to her cheeks nonetheless.

"Oh, I have something for you," Capshaw said, digging into his pocket. He pulled out two familiar black oval stones. Concordia had not seen them both together before.

"Madame still had them in her possession. I offered Mrs. Adams the one that belonged to her husband, but she doesn't want anything to do with it. She asked that I give them both to you."

"Thank you," Concordia said, holding them in her lap.

She stared at them for a while, silent. She didn't want them either.

Capshaw stood. "I need to be going." He cleared his throat awkwardly. "Miss Wells, I appreciate... all of your help. Have a Merry Christmas," he added.

"And to you as well, Lieutenant," Concordia answered with a smile.

He tipped the brim of his cap, and left.

She checked her watch. Goodness! Time for the staff party at DeLacey House. It was the final celebration at the college before the winter recess.

She had an idea.

Quickly, she ran into the parlor and scrounged among the litter of tissue paper and ribbons. She hesitated, holding the amulets up to the light for one last look. Yes, this was the right thing to do. They had never been hers. She wrapped them securely in bright green paper topped with a gold bow. She affixed a small tag: *To Miss Phillips... From Santa.*

That should do it. She perched the package atop the other wrapped gifts, and shrugged on her coat. Balancing the stack in her arms, she stepped out into the light dusting of snow.

THE END

Afterword

It's a great time to be a historical author, with the wealth of digitized historical material available on the world wide web. For anyone interested in the background research that went into the writing of this book, I've shared some wonderful primary and secondary sources on my website, **kbowenmysteries.com**. I'd love to see you there.

I hope you enjoyed the novel. Should you feel so inclined, please consider leaving a review on Amazon or your favorite book venue. Word of mouth is of invaluable help to fiction authors. Thank you!

Ready for the next Concordia Wells mystery?

Coming in 2014:

Unseemly Ambition

A murder... a missing boy... a secret society's bold and deadly plot...

It is 1898, and Professor Concordia Wells has come to expect the hectic routine of classes, clubs, teas, and the inevitable student pranks at the women's college. If only she could avoid the cantankerous dean, Randolph Maynard, who has learned about her past experiences as a "lady sleuth." To Concordia's dismay, he scrutinizes her every move for evidence of unseemly conduct.

The dean will certainly scowl over the lady professor's behavior when a disastrous turn of events affects those she loves. First, a mysterious woman claims that Concordia's young friend, the eleven-year-old Eli, is her long-lost child. Soon after, they find the woman murdered and the boy gone. Lieutenant Capshaw is given the case, only to be abruptly replaced by a junior associate. An innocuous reassignment, or something more?

Concordia calls upon a former ally, Penelope Hamilton, for help. As they search for the child and untangle the mystery of his mother's death, Concordia realizes that not even her own colleagues are above suspicion. Not knowing whom at the school to trust as she attempts to side-step Dean Maynard's continual scrutiny, she must tread carefully. Far more is at risk than the loved ones she seeks to protect, and there is no turning back.

CPSIA information can be obtained
at www.ICGtesting.com
Printed in the USA
LVOW13s2254270318
571425LV00010B/174/P